House of Illusions

Pippa J. Frost

House of Illusions

PROLOGUE

BARE TREES CAST EERIE SHADOWS ACROSS THE bedchamber I shared with my sixteen-year-old brother, Orell. Hidden in the cocoon of furs draping the bunk under the xhardness. I imagined the flash of his cool blue eyes. "And it'd be best if you spoke no further."

Fear thickened my throat at the deadly bite in his last words.

"You're a fool, Timo Fürst. You underestimate them. Heed my words: you'll come to regret this." Tears clotted Mutter's voice when she said, "Have you considered the children and the danger you put them in?"

I jumped at the sound of a fist hitting the table. Orell winced and released a string of curses. The pain in my head throbbed.

"Piera, your concerns involve tending the household and nothing more," Vater said.

"And my children," Mutter said with helpless urgency.

I held my breath, too afraid to breathe, and waited for the outcome of Mutter's unwillingness to withdraw.

"Your vater spoiled you," Vater said. "You know nothing of hardship."

"And you, my dear husband, are about to know a kind of hardship you've never experienced before." Mutter's tone was calmer; weariness echoed in her voice. "I must go check on the children. We will worry Valentina. She had another one of her headaches today. They grow worse each year, and the doctor can't understand what causes them. I wish you'd let me take her to the healer. Perhaps—"

Feet shuffled and glass shattered. "You stay away from her. Do you hear me?"

"Let go. You're hurting me," Mutter said.

"Why must you test my patience?"

"Did you ever love me? Or was Papa's wealth what appealed to you?" she asked. "You have squandered my dowry, and with your recent tomfoolery we stand to lose this farm. You gambled away our home in the village. Papa purchased this cottage and land for the children— for their future."

"I won't listen to any more from you. I have animals to feed," Vater said. Footsteps stomped across the dirt floor then a door squeaked open and slammed, sending a gust of wind and a powdering of snow scurrying under the gap between the floor and our chamber door.

Moments later Mutter opened our door, and I lowered the furs. She stood on the threshold, lantern in hand, a vision in a blue velvet frock; the last of the luxuries she had brought with her from Italy. Nonno had been a wealthy man, and my mutter—Piera Francesco—was his only child. The times I'd met him, he'd exuded the same kindness as Mutter. His robust and infectious laugh would jiggle his rotund stomach and long, frosted beard. I remembered how he'd bend and scoop me into his arms before sinking into a rocker. He'd give me a peppermint stick and tell me grand stories of my mutter as a little girl. Tucked in his arms, I observed how joyful tears had dampened Mutter's dark eyes. Her smile had shone the brightest on his visits.

"Hello, my darlings." Mutter mustered a cheerful greeting as she swept into the room and set the lantern down on the night table.

Orell had swung his legs over the side of the bed and sat up upon her entry. "Why must you argue with Vater. Can't you see you anger him?" His tone was sharp and accusatory.

"I'm sorry, my love." She stroked my brother's wheat-blond curls. "You need not worry about Vater and me." The light from the lantern gilded her beautiful face as she pressed her lips to his forehead. He cringed at her touch and pulled away. Pain reflected on Mutter's face, but she remained silent and stepped back.

Orell was becoming more like Vater each year. He lacked empathy and showed no concern for Mutter or me. I feared him as much as I did Vater, perhaps more. Sometimes I wondered if Mutter did too, as I'd catch her observing Orell when no one was looking and a great sadness would wash over her. But whenever I grew angry over Vater's mistreatment of her, she'd say, "Hush now, my Valentina. You mustn't judge Vater and Orell too harshly."

Mutter's dainty hand brushed Orell's shoulder. "Rest, son. Everything will be better in the morning."

His eyes narrowed, but the long day spent splitting wood had wearied him, and without a reply he lay back on his cot and turned his body away from us.

Mutter moved to my bed and lowered herself onto the edge, her gown flouncing about her. I reached out and touched the soft fabric. Mutter gently touched my shoulder and pressed me back against the bed linens. "How is your head?" she asked.

"The same as most days. Do you think the healer could help me?"

"I don't know." Her eyes drifted for a moment, as though stolen by troubling thoughts.

"Mutter," I said, "why don't you write to Nonno and ask for his help if we have no coins?"

Her fingers traced my face. "It's not only coins that trouble me. And those matters, Nonno can't help me with."

"What does Vater plan to do?" I searched her face.

"You mustn't worry. Everything will be fine." She could not conceal the worry in her eyes. Leaning close, she cupped my face in her hands and kissed each of my cheeks. "The mountains have eyes. You must remember this, Valentina."

Confused by her statement, I said, "I will, Mutter."

She straightened and smiled. "When you marry, make certain your prince is truly a prince."

I bobbed my head in agreement. "Only a prince."

CHAPTER 1

Schläfrigz—Valentina

YEARS HAVE PASSED SINCE MY PARENTS' disappearance. For weeks the villagers had helped my brother search. Torches lit the forest surrounding our homestead like thousands of fireflies until eventually they flickered and faded as people returned to their lives.

Although the hunt for my parents had ended, whisperings and far-fetched stories of their vanishment filled the marketplace and the taverns. Villagers blamed the woman who'd lived by the healing springs for their disappearance. Accusing her of witchery, they burned her at the stake. Helpless to stop it, I'd stood in the blood-hungry mob as the flames took form. Orell stood beside me, pumping his fist in the air. "Burn," he'd screamed, his eyes fierce with rapture.

Excruciating pain had ripped through my head and I'd feared it was another headache, but it was different, more severe. The pounding of my heart reverberated in my ears, and the crowd seemed to fade. I'd tried to call to Orell, but my lips wouldn't move. I had become trapped in my body as though asleep. Vater had been right: evil had been at work with the healer.

Later, when the animals of the forest started disappearing, legends spread that a creature believed to dwell in a cave in the mountains was responsible. Some said the healer, transformed, had returned to seek revenge on the villagers. My parents had scarcely been gone two years when I heard the blind storyteller, circled by eager, dirty-faced street urchins in the market square, tell a tale of their death. *"Limb by limb, the beast feasted on them, using the woman's delicate fingers to clean its teeth,"* he'd said.

As time went on poverty had swept through our canton, and with hunting scarce the poor scrounged to find whatever food sources we could while the rich grew fatter. However, my fight for survival was governed by the darkness burrowing deep in my brother's soul. Each day I yearned for the one security I'd had in life, but Mutter was gone, and with each passing year my hope of her return dimmed.

Winter had swallowed up the valley and my family's farm, in the foothills of the Alps, sat tucked in the embrace of the mountains. Today the barn lay nearly empty of livestock. Animals that hadn't escaped through the dilapidated fence in the north pasture Orell had sold, then squandered the money to sustain his lust and greed. Trips to the village turned into days spent at brothels and taverns. When the ladies of the night and drink didn't occupy his time, he and his friends had taken up robbing wealthy travelers along the roads. The maintenance of the homestead fell on me. My attempts at repairing the fences and cottage were endless, and it all seemed for naught. Our home was crumbling around us. And, as usual, the responsibility of selling our goods and securing enough coin to eat for another week weighed heavily on my shoulders.

The bite of early morning's chill burned through the holes in my threadbare woolen mittens as I harnessed the mare to the wagon for my journey into the village. I glanced at the cottage, and indignation at my brother simmered. He and his friends lay splayed on the table and the floor in front of the hearth. Keeping watch on my chamber door and their drunken snores had robbed me of sleep.

A flash of movement near the tree line twitched the mare's ears. Over the back of the horse I got a clear view of them watching me, as they often did. They never came closer and always observed me from afar. I found comfort in the whisperings and scurrying feet of the earthmen. Mountain earthmen lived high in the Alps while the mine-dwelling earthmen inhabited the lower regions. Herds of chamois had come down to the lower slopes for the winter to feed on the sprouts of conifers and broadleaved trees, bringing with them their herders—the mountain men. My dearest and oldest friend, Flicker, was a mine-dweller, but his spirit was too big to be harnessed underground. I could often find him mingling with the villagers and carrying on, if not creating a spectacle of himself. He possessed the ability to shed radiance on the bleakest days.

Pulling my furs tighter around me, I climbed into the wagon and cast a glance at the tree line. Lifting a hand, I waved, and the little men darted for cover. I smiled to myself and flicked the reins, and the horse plodded off toward the village.

I drove the wagon along the road, the towering trees on either side standing stark and naked against the bright canvas of Old Man Winter. As I neared the fork in the road I caught sight of a convoy of enclosed carriages turning down the tunnel-like lane, darkened by the tree canopy that led to the abandoned estate of Lord Winslow. The home had stood empty for years after he and his daughters had returned to their estate in England. Had they returned?

I shivered as I remembered accompanying Flicker into the dark, serpentine drive leading to the secluded mansion. The home had sat in decrepitude, entangled in a veil of vines, windows protected only by the wrought iron bars over broken windowpanes. The front doors hung crooked on their hinges, open to the environment. Leaves had blanketed the floors, and back when animals filled the forest they'd roamed freely through the home. It would take months to make the house habitable, if not years.

I urged my gaunt mare on toward town. Two crates containing cheese, ointments, and oils I'd concocted clattered in the wagon's bed. Choices at our family's stall would be limited, and I worried that villagers would overlook the goods and pass by. The supplies I used to make my salves was depleted, and our livestock required food. I'd rationed out the provisions for Orell and myself for as long as I could, but surpassing the magnitude of worries was his threat to sell the cottage. The necessity to earn had become ever more grueling.

CHAPTER 2

Kingdom of Himmelart—Mountain Dwarves

PRINCE SIXTUS KISSED THE SERVANT GIRL'S AMPLE breasts before trailing his mouth up to her full lips. Her moans of pleasure made him smile. He'd become skilled in winning the maidens of the kingdom, much to his vater's dismay. A passionate toss in the hay appealed to his manly desires more than tedious negotiations in the Great Hall. The endless bickering between the tribes of Alps earthmen and the demands of the peasants would dull anyone's senses.

Behind him, someone cleared their throat. "Your Highness, your vater wishes to speak with you."

Sixtus leaned back on his knees and adjusted his trousers. The girl beneath him scrambled to cover herself. The prince smirked and gave her a wink before rising to his feet.

Turning, he eyed his vater's manservant. "What is it my vater wants?"

"He did not say, Your Highness." The servant kept his head bowed.

"Come now, Lio, we both know that isn't the truth. I'm sure he wishes to bore me with princely matters."

The kitchen girl, tying the laces on her bodice, hurried past them. Sixtus leaned forward and smacked her buttocks. She giggled, gripped the sides of her skirt, and raced across the courtyard to the kitchen. At the doorway she swung around to look back at him, pulling her lip between her teeth before smiling bashfully and disappearing inside.

Sixtus brushed the hay from his clothing. His dashing good looks had assured his choice of the most beautiful of women, but when his urge was great a scullion wench would do. "Come, let us see what His Grace wants." He gestured for the servant to lead the way.

His expression masking any astonishment at Sixtus's lack of respect, the manservant turned on his heel and exited the stables.

Sixtus stepped out into the courtyard and peered up at the turquoise dome of ice sheltering the mountain kingdom from any outsiders who would dare enter the mountains uninvited. Below it, glimmering bronze roof tiles reflected the illumination from giant glass spheres ignited by dwarf magic up to the curtain aloft, and he shielded his eyes from its brilliance. The muttering and bustling of palace servants filled the yard. A stable boy led the prince's white horse toward the blacksmith's shop. To his right, two servant girls eyed him as they beat a silk Kashan rug with brooms to displace the dust. He gave them a half bow. They paused in their task, and lashes swept down over rosy cheeks. But it was the scent of the fat sizzling on a pig roasting over an open fire that wet the prince's mouth and captured his attention. A hunger more considerable than the warmth of a woman tugged at him, but his king beckoned so he strode after Lio into the palace.

They threaded through gleaming corridors crusted with luminous pink rock crystals toward the golden double doors of the Great Hall, their surfaces etched with the script King Jörg had written after he agreed to peace between mountain dwarves and humans. Two armed guards clad in brass armor over the blue-and-gold garb of the king's army stood on either side, staring straight ahead like the snowy marble owls perched on each corner of the curtain wall. There Sixtus and Lio paused at the sound of the king's outrage.

"We will stop this once and for all. If my son is to govern all of Himmelart, he must start carrying himself as a prince and not the debaucher he has become. With the recent developments in the human village, he should be concerned with more pressing matters."

Lio opened one door and motioned Sixtus forward. "My prince."

Sixtus's mouth set as he pushed past the manservant and marched into the room.

His vater, clothed in a robe of scarlet and gold, stood

behind a grand table embedded with gems mined by the earthmen of the Schattenberg kingdom. The knights gathered around him straightened at the prince's approach, and all eyes turned to him.

"There you are." Annoyance pinched the king's face. "Leave us." He gestured at his men with a hand gleaming with jeweled rings. Looks of pity crossed the faces of some, and displeasure appeared on the faces of others.

Sixtus squared his shoulders. He wouldn't subject himself to their disapproval, nor that of his vater. It was hardly his fault that he had inherited more beauty than most earthmen. If his vater was looking for a more suitable heir to sit upon his throne, he should have sired another son with one of his four wives. Instead, only girls had sprung from his loins.

As the men filed out, Sixtus preoccupied himself with studying the vibrant colors cast in elongated patterns across the floor from the stained glass windows. Inspired by those found in the Catholic churches in the canton, his vater had had artisans replicate their beauty in his Great Hall. Between them, shield-shaped alcoves in the walls housed statues of his ancestors. As a boy he'd found the figures fascinating, and he'd basked in his vater's prideful stories about his predecessors.

"I have summoned you here today because I have a secret mission I'm assigning to you and General Crispian."

"What is this mission?" Sixtus asked, his interest piqued. He'd rather be out on the road seeking the next adventure than be confined to the castle. The open air on his face and the responsibilities of castle life at his back was where he found the most contentment.

"Patience, son. Let us first discuss the reasoning for this mission."

Sixtus bowed at the waist. "As you say, Your Grace."

"There is unrest and resentment in King Gian's kingdom. The people cry of the continuing disappearances of earthmen, which is of grave concern. The elders of Schattenberg have come to me about this matter, and another that has caused stirrings amidst their tribesmen."

"What is the concern you speak of?" Sixtus folded his arms across his chest.

"We're a peaceful people, but the thirst for power has always driven my cousin. Gian has dabbled in necromancy. This is not only a threat to the tribes that claim these mountains, but to all of existence," the king said. "His elders revealed that he has been on the hunt for the Zwilling power."

Sixtus dropped his arms to hang at his side. "But, we—"

"I know, but he can never know about the woman. The elders didn't say what Gian intends to do with the twin power. But if he were to learn that it survives here in these mountains, I fear no earthmen would be safe until he obtained it. Its whereabouts must remain hidden or he will stop at nothing, no matter who is in his way."

"He wouldn't harm his own tribesmen," Sixtus said with conviction.

"You are a fool. You idolize a monster, a man capable of unleashing destruction upon us all. He would plunge his sword through your heart, remove it, and walk over your dead body without a second thought." The king's lip curled in disgust before he folded his arms over a belly so rotund it threatened to topple his diminutive frame. It shadowed his tiny feet, hidden within oversize shoes.

Sometimes the prince wondered if his vater's gorging at feasts and evening meals was a way to conceal the feature he hated most about himself. *You have the feet of a woman.* He recalled hearing King Gian's jab at his cousin when Sixtus was but a small lad. The hatred between the cousins had gone on for decades. The prince and the grotesque king, marred with scars of the battlefield, shared a dislike for the humans. King Gian hadn't inherited the prince's rakish looks nor Jörg's jovial demeanor, but he feared nothing.

"You worry too much. If Gian seeks the Zwilling, you have the Träger tucked away where no one will ever find her."

"The carrier of the power?" The king gritted his teeth at Sixtus's response. "Think, Sixtus. It isn't the only way he can raise the Zwilling."

Sixtus frowned. "You speak of the Träger's offspring?"

"Yes. If my suspicions are right, they hold the purity and the soul-eater elements of the power."

"And if he possesses the Reinheit and the Seelenfresser, he won't need the Träger; he can still attempt to raise the Zwilling."

The king nodded. "And that is where you and the general will come in. Today you are to journey to the village."

The prince raised an eyebrow and started to protest, but the king lifted a hand to silence him. "You've no freedom to protest," his vater said. "It is an order."

"But, Vater, humans?" Disgust coated his words. "I despise the earth the weaklings trample. I won't endure their insufferable company."

"Humans and dwarves have coexisted for years. If you're to take over my throne, you will learn to put aside your bruised pride and carry yourself as the Prince of Himmelart."

Sixtus didn't hold the same love for the humans as his vater. Despite the rumors that he'd been born from the womb of a human, who had been too fragile to survive his birth, Sixtus had another reason besides human weakness for his contempt. *Never again will I be made a mockery of; never again will I fall for their trickery.* His thoughts raced back to the human who'd caught him in her web of seduction. *We'd been two long years on the battlefields,* he reminded himself, remembering the song that had risen above the rattling of shields and armor and the hoofbeats of his army's mounts.

The lull of her voice had summoned him to the banks of the healing springs, where a squirrel hung, roasting above a small fire. But it was the creature next to the fire that lured his steps and his heart.

A young woman sat on a fallen log beside the fire, her crimson mane lying in billowy mounds on either side of her. Captivating green eyes lifted as he walked toward her.

Raising a gloved hand the prince halted his men's advance, not wanting to scare the woman.

"You and your men look weary." She gestured with a slender hand for him to join her on the log.

He handed the reins of his horse to his squire. "We return from the battlefield."

"What battle do you fight?" As she bent forward to rotate the spit the fire gilded the creamy flesh of her cleavage, drawing the prince's eyes. Sitting in the company of a woman delighted him, especially one whose appeal tightened his chest and aroused a yearning in him.

"Our brethren in the north," he said.

"Brethren?" Her inquisitive gaze held his. "Why would your king march on your kinsmen?"

"They sought to overturn our kingdom."

She retrieved an apple from a satchel at her feet. Her bare feet were dainty, and her slender ankles were embellished with woven twigs and flowers. "Men are such peculiar creatures. They look to control and master another." She wiped the apple on the bodice of her light blue dress. "Tell me, stranger, what do you seek to possess?"

As if she had enticed the words from him he whispered, voice thick with desire, "You."

She tilted her head, and an alluring smile pulled at her full pink lips. "Ah, I see, your desire is that of many men. A desire only a woman can fulfill." She sank her teeth into the apple and made a sound that heightened his need to feel the warmth of a woman's body against his. "You and your men must be thirsty. Let me quench the thirst." She trailed her fingers along his thigh, and his breathing caught.

She rose and disappeared into the dark of the night, only to return with several skins of mead slung over her shoulders. She ambled across the grass to the tree line, where his men waited. A roar of enthusiasm rose as the bewitching goddess laughed and wove gracefully amongst them, intent on tempting his small army.

Returning to the prince's side, she offered the skin she had reserved. "Drink up, my prince." She held the skin to his lips, and he drained the contents as the moans from his army reached his ears. The woman's eyes hardened, and a smile of satisfaction spread across her face. "Women are not beings created to fill your needs or those of your army, Prince Sixtus."

The pain ignited in his gut, and he sprang to his feet as her drug took effect. "You will pay for this…" Then darkness overtook him.

The king's booming voice snapped him back. "Don't think I won't replace you with someone more suitable to sit upon my throne."

Bitterness swelled within Sixtus's belly, and he laughed. "Who, Vater? One of your daughters?" His mockery resounded. The king's admiration for and desire to live in harmony with the humans while aiding them in whatever way possible revolted him. "You'd become the laughingstock of all the tribes. Not to mention the king of Schattenberg. What would he say? You know he has coveted your throne for years."

"Have you not heard anything I said?" The king's ruddy cheeks deepened to a royal shade of purple. "Gian is a detriment to us all. That bungler will never have my throne. He isn't worthy of it." He puffed out his chest. "Nor does he hold enough wisdom to rule a kingdom."

"Yet he does." Sixtus strolled casually around the room, regarding his vater's prized artifacts—bounty collected from the kingdoms of his enemies. He recalled the years when his vater was known as a great conqueror. When peasants and noblemen alike chanted his name and wished him longevity and prosperity. Mutters held out their babies to be kissed by the king whispered to be a god. But he was no god. Seasons had changed him, and the warrior was no more. In his place stood an enfeebled man, a shadow of his former self. He and the elders spoke of peace and unity when the prince longed to return to the days of old.

He paused in front of a golden tiger with bared ivory teeth and flaming ruby eyes. The beast peered down from its perch on a bronze tree limb. The king had the statue placed to remind him of his sins against the living. A spoil of war returned home in the early days of his reign from a kingdom he and his army had invaded. Greed and his thirst for blood had been his guide, and he refused to become that man again.

"Enough of your chatter. You will prove you're worthy of my throne by going to the village and taking care of a delicate matter."

"What sort of matter?" Sixtus twisted the ring on his index finger, engraved with the royal crest.

"You will see soon enough. My steward will inform you of what's to be done. Now, I must be going."

"Going to the tower again?" Sixtus heaved a deep sigh, weary of the argument that had stewed between vater and son for far too long. For years King Jörg had climbed the stairs extending into the heavens to visit the woman in her confinement. "The Träger grows stronger each day. Do you think it's wise to have trained her?"

"I have not heard of this magic in hundreds of years. It's believed the humans are incapable of controlling such power."

Sixtus threw his hands in the air. "Because they're weak vessels incapable of owning such wizardry."

His vater disregarded the hatred boiling inside Sixtus. "But the light struggles to defeat the darkness. I'd think it impossible for her. It's remarkable," he said.

"The question you forget to ask yourself is how she came to hold the power of the Zwilling. Surely a human with such vitality is a menace to us all, a threat that should be done away with, and swiftly. Do you not recall how, injured and near death, she broke through our barrier walls? Has she put a spell on you?"

"You read too much into our time together, son."

"How long do you think you can constrain your prisoner? She may take her own freedom and use her powers as she deems necessary, and then may the gods help us when the Teufel himself vents his wrath."

"The demon's wrath is not to be taken lightly." The king slammed the table with his fist. "Go now!" His order clapped like the skies before a storm, and he clutched at his chest as if in pain.

The prince jumped at his vater's sudden outburst. "Forgive me, Your Grace. You must calm yourself. The healer said you can't be getting upset. It's not good for your condition."

His vater struck his chest with a fist. "My heart is stronger than a hundred earthmen—" He broke into a coughing fit.

"It will be as you say, Your Grace." Not wanting to agitate him further, Sixtus bowed and dismissed himself. *Fool*, he muttered under his breath, and strode from the Great Hall. A human with the power of the Zwilling would bring death to them all.

CHAPTER 3

Valentina

RMS WEIGHTED WITH A CRATE, I ENTERED THE bustling market square. The light wind snapped the vivid fabrics canopying the open-aired trader stalls. Street merchants and customers—earthmen, villagers, and travelers—crowded the courtyard. Stalls and trader carts stretched across the yard, stocked with gems, spindles, honey mead, exquisite silk brocade, and some of the finest cheese found in the canton.

I wandered past a gantry of decadent chocolate molded by the town's own Italian chocolatier and moaned, imagining the creamy sweetness melting over my tongue. The scent of freshly baked bread and pastries wafted from the baker's shop, located a street over from the square, and the cavern in my stomach rumbled.

A barrel-chested earthman stood bickering with

the butcher over the price of a whole pig. "Why, you're a thief!" He glowered up at the man.

The butcher wiped his bloodied hands on his crimson-stained apron. "That is the price, dwarf. Do you want it or not?"

"I'd rather starve than deal with the likes of you." The earthman spat at the man's feet before storming off.

The butcher cursed. His eyes fell on me, and the scowl on his ruddy face deepened. "Where's that scoundrel brother of yours?"

"He is busy with our cow. I'm afraid she's fallen ill." I didn't want to add to the townies' distaste for my brother. Although my vater had been born and raised in the village, they'd never liked him. Instead, it was my mutter—the foreigner—who'd won the hearts of the villagers. When Vater had permitted it, she'd devoted her time to helping those in need and gained their respect. Many still grieved her loss.

"He owes me. He gave me his word he'd attend the market today and clear up his debts. But I've yet to see him or the riffraff he keeps company with."

"I can account for my brother and nothing more," I said. "When I see him, I will tell him you were looking for him."

Orell's debts were many, and I feared what would befall us as people grew tired of his excuses. It was only a matter of time before they came looking to collect.

"Very well. I wish you prosperity today." The tightness in his round face eased.

I adjusted the crate in my arms. "Thank you, Signor Zesiger, and to you."

"You're a good girl, Valentina. It is a shame you're left at the mercy of that goat brother of yours."

"I offer apologies for my brother." I wished him a good day and promptly made my departure, threading between carts and stalls until I came to my family's hut. I set the crate down and rubbed the ache in my arms before returning to the wagon.

I climbed into the wagon bed and pulled the last crate to the edge before jumping down. As my feet touched the ground, a cheery voice chirped behind me, "That looks a wee bit heavy for a lady."

Grinning, I pivoted to find Flicker, his face returning my delight in our meeting. His mischievous dark eyes twinkled, and his ever-rosy cheeks flushed rosier with the nip of the mid-morning breeze.

Balling my hands at my waist, I bestowed upon him a feigned look of disapproval. "You know I could have clobbered you for sneaking up on me."

Extending his hands, he said with a snort, "I'm small, but I'm mighty. That's something you human folk forget." He strode up to me and huffed and grunted and with some effort lifted the crate. Stubbornness oozed from every inch of his three-foot frame. Scarlet-faced, he said, "Best get those wee feet of yours moving if you don't want this crate upended." He staggered off toward the market square.

I laughed and hurried after him. "What brings you to the village today?"

"My uncle has come to the market to trade. With his son's passing, he required a helping hand."

"Yet you have time to seek me out?" I said.

"I saw you were struggling, and as expected, Orell's nowhere to be found. Up to his usual antics, I assume?"

"Yes, it's as you suspect." Flicker was the one person I'd always been honest with; it was a promise we'd made as children.

"It's time you considered marriage."

"I have. And when I find a man of quality, I will. Until then, I'll make do on my own."

"Ludicrous," he scoffed. "Your cheekbones stick out more each time I see you. And the gray circles under those brilliant blues of yours make you appear sickly." He set the crate down on the ground inside the hut.

I unloaded the contents and arranged them on the stand for customers to view. Flicker removed the cheese and displayed it on the opposite end of the counter. "Slim pickings today," he said with a grim expression.

My shoulders slumped as he voiced the worries that had plagued me on the journey to town.

He touched my arm, and I lowered my gaze to look at him. Genuine solicitude shone in his eyes. "I wish I could help you more. But my trips to the valley become fewer with the demands at home. And the little I earn working in the mines scarcely takes care of Mutter and my siblings."

My throat tightened. "Please don't worry on my account."

He cast a look around before grabbing my hand. "Here, take this." He forced something into the wool of my mitten.

I looked at the burnished ruby I now held and gasped, quickly closing my fingers to conceal the gem. "Are you crazy?" I said through clenched teeth, my voice low. "Where did you get this from?"

"Where do you think?"

"I can't take it. I won't see you punished for me." I held out my closed hand for him to take the ruby. He folded his arms across his chest and refused to relieve me of a crime I wanted no part of. Come what may, I'd never disgrace myself as my brother had done.

He inched closer, his dark eyes pleading with me. "I won't see you starve."

"Everyone knows to steal from the dwarves means trouble for the villagers. We live in peace, and I won't risk people's lives."

"It's not stealing if a dwarf gave it to you," he said.

My mouth unhinged. "But you stole it from the mines. The villagers made a treaty with the earthmen to stay away from the mountains in exchange for peace. Rumors travel of the kingdom of Schattenberg and King Gian's ruthlessness toward any human who'd dare enter the mountains. No man, woman, or child is foolish enough to break the treaty. Besides, stealing is stealing, no matter whom you take from, despite your rationalizations to make it acceptable."

His jaw set. "One little gem? No one will miss it."

"Flicker, your stubbornness outweighs your reason."

"Me!" He poked himself in the chest with a finger.

"Think of your family."

"I am. I feel it's my responsibility to help—"

A cough rattled, and we spun to find two dwarves waiting in front of the stand. One, a notably handsome, dark-haired man with eyes as black as a raven's feather, unapologetically stared. Beside him, his ginger-haired companion stood quietly observing.

"Are we interrupting something of importance?" the dark-haired earthman said.

Flicker and I pulled our heads apart and I dropped my hands to my sides, my fingers gripping the gem.

The dwarf's unnerving gaze roved over me. My heart pounded. Had he come to retrieve the ruby? The sudden urge to kick Flicker under the stand mounted.

"Nice. Very nice. Don't you agree?" he said more to himself than to his mate. "Though she could use a bit of fattening up. I do prefer my women with some substance."

I disregarded his lewd statement, but a deep, throaty growl came from Flicker, and I hurried to distract them. "My friend and I were simply discussing a missing crate I must have left at home."

"Is that so?" He eyed Flicker, who widened his stance and gave the man a callous stare.

"What's it to you, peasant?" Flicker jutted his chin at the brash earthman.

The dwarf's eyes narrowed. "Watch who you are calling—" He stopped in mid-sentence when his companion elbowed him. Regaining his composure, he glanced at the salves and oils before directing his attention back to me. "I've heard whisperings of healing ointments made by a farm girl, and I've come to purchase some for my woman."

The earthman possessed a godlike beauty, and he appeared entirely aware of it. I got the inkling it would take a confident woman to fall for a man like him. "What ailment does your woman have, mister?" I asked.

"A broken heart," his mate said behind a staged cough.

Ignoring him, the other man said, "She can't sleep, as she has contracted a cough that keeps her up at night."

"I have just the treatment." I tucked the hidden jewel into the pocket of my skirt before picking up a tin of the ointment made of lemon, pine, and myrtle oils. "Tell her to apply a smidgen of this to her chest and back at night. It should ease the cough and help her sleep."

"Very well." He reached into his cloak and retrieved a coin and held it out. I removed my mitten and offered an open palm while holding out the tin in the other. He placed the coin in my palm, his fingers lingering as his index traced a callus on my hand. "Farm girl indeed. As beautiful as a maiden, but with the hands of a galley maid."

I withdrew my hand, seizing the first treasured coin of the day. I caught sight of a gold pendant that glimmered in the sun as he adjusted his weatherworn cloak. A poor man's attire did not conceal the cavalier earthman who was hardly a peasant. Why had he come dressed as one?

Without so much as a "good day," he turned and glided into the crowd as if floating on air.

"I wish you well." The ginger fellow graciously bowed his head before turning to catch up with his friend.

"Pompous ass!" Flicker's remark was intended for the cocky fellow. "His head is puffed up with more arrogance than anyone should possess. I ought to have landed him nose-first in horse dung."

CHAPTER 4

ORNING DISSOLVED INTO AFTERNOON. FLICKER had grudgingly taken the ruby and departed in search of his uncle. Patrons paused at my stall for a quick glance before carrying on. My one customer had been the earthman, whom I blamed for casting an unpleasant aura over the day. The constant dickering and calling out to patrons had left me parched and weary. Tears of frustration welled in my eyes as a woman I had almost persuaded to purchase a wedge of cheese turned up her nose, gathered her children, and continued down the line of peddlers.

Turning to hide my disheartenment from onlookers, I raised trembling fingers to wipe away the tears and lowered myself onto an upturned crate, keeping my back to the crowd. My mind spun with the burdensome responsibilities of our homestead. The animals could not go another day without food. I'd given the last of the hay to the mare so that she could make the journey to town. Our dairy cow's milk had dried up months ago, after Orell had sold her calf and the bull to bide his time with his debtors. In the spring, our goat had kidded two kids, but her milk never came in and I had no choice but to give the kids to a moneygrubbing farmer for an absurdly low price. In recent weeks the hens had stopped producing eggs, and I'd found one dead that morning.

"What captures your mind, little one?" a husky voice asked, pulling me from my fretting.

I froze. My heart raced. Could it be? *Nisse.* I stood and whirled to face him. "You're back!"

Before me, cloaked in furs and leather, stood the master watchmaker's son, his tawny, shoulder-length hair fastened back with a black ribbon at the nape of his neck. He gracefully bowed at the waist, and a grin parted his lips. "Well, if it isn't the beautiful Valentina. Oh, how you've grown." He stood, holding the reins of his horse. The animal happily munched off a nearby stand, much to the disadvantage of the merchant with his back turned. Nisse was a childhood friend of my brother's. I was ten when their friendship ended, and although he had never told me why, I assumed Orell was to blame.

The day I'd fled the market square in tears after hearing the blind man's tale, Nisse had seized me as I raced by him in the alley. And within his arms, I'd found comfort as he stroked my hair and dried my tears. *"There, there, little one,"* he had whispered as one would to a little sister. *"It can't be that bad, can it?"* I had clung to him and unleashed my grief at the loss of my parents and the horrors of the blind man's fictions.

As I recalled that day, my cheeks warmed, and involuntarily, my hand slipped to my throat. How I'd wanted to remain in his arms forever. To bathe in the safety his presence had provided. To grasp a few stolen moments in which I mattered. All feelings I hadn't felt since my mutter disappeared. Such desires somehow seemed trivial now, as the need to survive exceeded the whims of a young girl.

After that day, I came to see Nisse as something more. I'd daydreamed on trips to town of running into him. Sometimes I'd watch him through the large window of his vater's shop as he dealt with customers. On one of those occasions, he'd caught me, and before I could duck out of sight, he waved. Then came the day when I learned he'd left on a crusade with other men from the village. Brokenhearted, I'd spent the days that followed weeping, until anger replaced the melancholy. It had been years since I'd seen him, and I was no longer that love-struck young girl.

Today a full beard masked his face, giving him a more rugged, outdoorsy appearance. Time had etched lines around his eyes and forehead, but the ever-present gentleness in his kind eyes endured. "It's been far too long," he said, looking me over with concern.

"Could you use some ointment or oils? Maybe some cheese?" I unwrapped the cotton cloth to reveal a wedge. My gaze fastened to the exposed flesh peeking through the open laces of his cream cotton shirt.

He reached out as if to inspect the cheese, but his hand encased mine. My heart pounded as I elevated my gaze. "Is your brother not taking care of his responsibilities?"

"I do not rely on my brother to care for me. I've become capable—"

"Well, I'll be. Nisse!" Flicker's sudden appearance drew our attention as he circled the stand to join me.

"Ah, Flicker, my good man." A broad smile spread across Nisse's face and settled the storm rumbling in his gray eyes. He bent forward and thrust out a hand, which Flicker gripped between both of his and shook vigorously.

"When did you get back?" Flicker asked, withdrawing his hands and planting them at his waist.

"Just rode in. The men headed to the tavern. I was on my way to see my vater until a familiar face stood out against many." He winked at me.

"He'll be pleased to see you." I clasped my hands in front of me, then quickly tucked them in the folds of my skirt when his gaze settled on the holes in my mittens.

The tenderness of moments ago returned to his eyes. "He's written to me over the years, telling me how you've come by the shop to visit with him. Says it helped keep the loneliness at bay. I hope he hasn't bored you too much with stories of his homeland."

"On the contrary, he too has helped fill the loneliness." Through the years his vater had given me coins and food—which Orell had stubbornly returned and spat in his face, saying we didn't need handouts.

"Vater is a noble man, and he has always cared for your mutter."

I winced at the mention of her.

"I didn't think. Please forgive me." He stepped forward.

"No need to fret," I said. "Some say I should have moved past the pain by now, but the unknown still troubles me."

Nisse looked around as two women came to stand a few feet away, eavesdropping on our conversation. He reached into his furs and withdrew a few coins. "This should take care of the rest of your goods." He leaned close and whispered, "You can close the shop early and join me for a stroll." His voice rose. "Maybe where one might speak without stretched necks." He intentionally emphasized the last words, and nudged his head at the women.

"No, you mustn't," I said. Everything in me screamed to take the coins and hold them tight, but pride swelled within me. I didn't want Nisse to think of me as Orell's little sister. A child. No, I wouldn't become indebted to him. My stomach grumbled its protest.

Flicker waved a hand in dismissal. "I'll have the goods delivered to your vater's shop."

"Better yet, have the goods handed out to the poor," Nisse said.

"Struck it lucky while you were away, I see." Flicker eyed the coins he pressed into my hand.

"Fortune did not shine on me. I'm happy to be home and in a charitable mood, is all."

"I'll see the goods are handled accordingly." Flicker gave me an eager shove forward. "Well, go on then, off with you."

Caught off guard, I tumbled forward and gripped the table to steady myself. Shielding my face from Nisse's view I narrowed my eyes at Flicker, who offered me a debonair smile before broadcasting loudly, "Well, what are you waiting for? You mustn't keep the weary traveler waiting."

Nisse laughed.

Behind him, one woman coughed. They tucked their heads together and whispered.

"*Gossiping is poison*," Mutter had always said.

Nisse swung to address the women. "You ladies had best be on your way. The lady has sold out."

The women shook their heads in disapproval. "She's hardly a lady, with her torn clothes and dirty face," the plumper one of the pair said, her eyes roving over me.

Heat surged over my flesh, but I wouldn't allow the women's judgment to affect me. Jutting my chin in the air, I said in a silky voice, "Ladies, may your day be rich and joyous." I curtsied, showing the poise of the affluent before rising to give them a brilliant smile.

A smirk skipped across Nisse's face, and behind me, Flicker chuckled.

"Away with you, before you find my boot up your arse." Flicker thrust a fist in the air.

The women gasped, then muttered between themselves before taking their leave. A trail of "Tsk-tsk" echoed after them.

"Don't pay them any mind. They ain't nothing but old crows. Ain't that right, Nisse." Flicker's jovial mood returned.

Nisse shook his head. "And Miss Brandenberger wonders why Vater never accepted her efforts to court him."

I exited the stall with the desire to evade any more naysayers. "Maybe you'll tell me about your adventures." I forced a smile as I strolled past him.

Not waiting for him to catch up, I wove through the crowds until I reached the main street, which lay vacant and peaceful compared to the clamor of the market, now a murmur in the background. The clip-clop of Nisse's mount pulled my awareness to him, and I slowed my footsteps until he caught up. I mumbled an apology and fell into step with him.

"Such eagerness to flee," he said. "You need not concern yourself with such tasteless chatter."

"I've grown used to pity in people's eyes as much as I've become accustomed to the disgust. Orell does not differ from what Vater was. I remember as a child how people would look at Vater with disdain and offer Mutter the same look they give me."

His jaw tensed. "Orell's a fool. He should act the man of the house and take care of you. You look thin."

"So I keep hearing," I said, giving the skirt of my gray woolen dress a shake to release the dirt and snow collecting from the cobblestones.

"Maybe it's time you consider marriage—"

I stopped, and he followed suit. I looked him square in the eye. "What is it with Flicker and you?"

"What?"

"Trying to marry me off," I said.

"It's just that by your age, most girls are married."

"I have yet to find the right suitor." I reflected on the words of my mutter. *"Make sure your prince is truly a prince,"* she'd said.

"An arrangement of marriage would suit. No?" Seriousness lifted his right brow, marred by a scar placed there by Orell. When they'd been roughly thirteen, the boys had returned from the forest and Orell stormed into the cottage and slammed the door. In my bedchamber, I had jumped at the sound, dropping the doll my mutter had purchased for my eighth birthday weeks prior. I looked out the window and saw Nisse standing in the yard, stunned, with blood streaming down his face. He'd then turned, mounted his horse, and whipping his reins side to side, he rode out, leaving a trail of dust in his wake.

I continued on down the street. "Like Mutter and Vater's marriage? No. I won't make the same error in choosing a husband."

"Surely you don't still think a prince is in your future. All the magic that dwells in the mountains can't bring you a prince, unless you would consider a dwarf prince. Ah, that's it—you're waiting on Flicker to request your hand in marriage."

I sputtered and glared at him. "You spew such

foolishness. Though Flicker's as fine a man as any, he's my friend and nothing more. And not an ounce of royal blood runs through his veins, or have you forgotten?"

He laughed. "Why, Valentina, I do believe you have grown up since I left. No longer a girl but a woman with more spirit than maybe one husband can control."

"Do you wish to control your woman?" I asked with honest interest.

"What? Of course not. I'm not your brother, nor your vater. Vater always said your mutter was too good for the likes of Timo Fürst. And it's no secret that Orell bears some of his vater's traits."

My steps weighted, I said, "I'm afraid he's far worse."

"Does he hurt you?" His voice was deep, controlled.

"Sometimes."

His hands tightened on the reins. "The day of reckoning is coming for Orell."

I shivered. I didn't want harm to come to my brother, but I imagined what life would be like without him. Would I miss him any more than I did Vater? The disquieting answer charged me with guilt. "You speak what has troubled me; I too fear his day of judgment draws near." That likelihood hung heavy in the air.

We soon said our goodbyes. Nisse left with a promise to come by the farm. I returned to the wagon, and an eerie sensation that I was being watched made me look around. A sudden gust of wind pushed tendrils of hair over my face, and I lifted a hand to smooth them back into place. Debris shuffled around my feet, and a piece of parchment caught flight and pinned itself to the front of my frock. Retrieving it, I scanned the words inscribed:

Help Wanted

Clean and tend a household. Board and salary included.

All interested parties are to inquire at Chateau Winslow.

The Winslow family had returned! After all these years. Curiosity pricked at me. Why had they returned? A chill from the frigid breeze chased up and down my spine. Again I scoured my surroundings. Finding nothing out of the ordinary, I attributed my paranoia to the overwhelming stress of the day. I tucked the parchment inside my mitten, boarded the wagon, and set off for home.

CHAPTER 5

THE MOUNTAIN HARE FED ON THE VEGETATION poking through the fresh blanket of snow, unaware of the predator that held him within their sights. I withdrew an arrow from the leather quiver and nocked it to the bow I'd made of mulberry wood and animal tendon. Steady of hand, I gripped the handle, took aim, and released. The whoosh of the arrow whizzing through the air was followed by a thunk as it found its mark. The hare dropped, nerves jerking its body, and then its movement ceased. I moved in and sank to my knees, whispering gratitude to the creature for giving its life so that Orell and I might eat. I grabbed the animal's legs and secured it to the tether at my waist. The muttering of the earthmen who had followed me on the morning hunt reached my ears.

"Steady hand, that one." A light chuckle. "I bet she'd outshoot even you."

"Don't be so sure, my friend. I was an excellent marksman straight from the womb."

I hid my smile behind my long, dark tresses. They were always there, watching and waiting, but for what I did not know. I thought of them as my guardians.

"I see you haven't lost your touch," a husky voice said behind me. I leaped to my feet, retrieved an arrow from the quiver, and took aim all before I realized who had crept up on me.

"Woo! Hold on!" Nisse stood with his hands in the air.

"What are you doing? I almost shot you." I swallowed my heart.

He rolled back his shoulders, looking self-satisfied. "My time wasn't wasted teaching you. Your marksmanship is remarkable."

"See, even he agrees," the dwarf whispered to his companion.

I snuck a look at Nisse but he hadn't noticed, and no reply came from the other earthman.

"Clean through the heart. A quick and painless death." Nisse lifted the hare dangling from my belt.

His praise sent a wave of warmth through me. "I'm a quick study."

"Then that makes me a good teacher." A smug grin creased his face. His eyes gleamed blue against the backdrop of crystalline snow-covered branches and fallen brushwood.

"I suppose it would." I laughed, and the forest echoed my merriment. "What are you doing out here?"

He tapped the bow and quiver strapped to his shoulder. "I stopped by your homestead to see if you'd join me on a hunt. Finding you absent, I noticed fresh tracks in the snow and followed you here."

"Has Orell returned?"

Hardness crept into his eyes. "I saw no sign of him. Lucky for him."

"He's been gone for a few days, and it leaves me to wonder what he is up to."

He studied me. "Surely you don't long for his return."

"The cottage seems almost peaceful when he's gone," I said with more honesty than I should reveal, but somehow Nisse had always put me at ease.

"Let's not let Orell steal the joy of the day." An ebullient smile broke over his face. "Let's find meat for your table."

"I'm capable—"

"I know. You're capable of taking care of yourself. I can see that," he said. "Tell me, Valentina, is it so absurd for people who care about you to want to help?"

Care? My heart skipped a beat. "I appreciate your consideration," I said.

"You always were stubborn, even as a young girl."

"Stubbornness keeps me alive." I poked him in the chest with the bow and walked past him.

"There is truth in that, but it may be to your detriment, too." I heard his footsteps breaking through the snow behind me.

"Have you come to school me?" I turned to look at

him. He didn't stop until he was almost on top of me. Out of the corner of my eye, I saw the earthmen dart to find cover behind a cluster of young saplings. Nisse's closeness put their presence far from my mind as he stood regarding me in a way I'd never seen him do before.

His expression sober, he said, "There's no child to school."

Goose pimples rose on my flesh as I searched his eyes for meaning. Did he see the woman I'd become? "If you intend to join me for the rest of the hunt, I suggest you try to keep up." I pulled myself from his enchantment and trudged on.

His chuckle lifted, and I smiled at the delightful sound.

It was late afternoon by the time we sat down on a ridge to eat the bündnerfleisch, cheese, and bread he'd brought. Hunger knocked at my ribs, but I forced myself to savor each bite of the dried meat. Besides the hare and the squirrel on my tether, we had spotted no other signs of life.

"I remember when these woods were filled with life." Nisse jutted his chin at the meadow below.

"Something has changed. It started after my parents disappeared. I found blood trails but no carcasses. Then seasons passed, and spring after spring, no new life was seen. With no signs of reproduction and the older animals being hunted for food, one comes to wonder if there's truth in the villagers' chatter."

"So you give heed to the tales?" he asked.

"I recall a few years back when a hunter rode into the village, claiming to have seen the beast. He was terrified, and to this day, Signor Agosti refuses to enter these woodlands." I remembered Signor Agosti's face: eyes wide, sweat pearling his brow, teeth chattering from the shaking of his body as he recounted his story. "Animal life is disappearing. I haven't seen a red deer in years, and sightings of brown bears and ibexes are rare."

"Vater wrote of his concerns and it's the reason I've returned. Maybe it's time we followed the others heading to North America to seek work. I saw an advertisement of steamship passage that will take people across the Atlantic from Le Havre."

My stomach clenched. "You would leave?"

"What choice do families have? There's no work, the hunting grounds are barren, and I have Vater to think of. Business is slow, and with his condition the doctor says a warmer climate may help."

The thought of never seeing him again carved a vast ache inside of me. "But the condition the council offers is enough reason to stay." I'd heard talk of the emigration subsidy offered by the council, hoping to end the economic recession that had plagued our country for years. If a person took the subsidy, they agreed to never return to Europe, and if they returned, they had to reimburse the subsidy with added annual interest calculated from the day it was awarded.

He twisted to look at me. "Do I sense you wouldn't be pleased if we left?"

"No." I glanced down at the bread in my cold fingers. "What I mean to say is, you'd be missed. A friendly face is always welcome. Your vater has been good to me." *Coward,* I rebuked myself. *Say you'd miss him too.*

"We should go before our bodies turn to frozen statues on this ridge." He stood and offered a hand to me. I took it, and he pulled me up. Our chests met, and we stood unmoving, my hand, small and insignificant, in his. He pressed our hands to his chest, then lifted his other and captured the side of my face with his palm. His thumb stroked my jaw, then slowly he lowered his face and kissed my cheek. Before he lifted his head to search my face with his eyes, a charming smile touched his lips. "Let us go, little one."

CHAPTER 6

WEEKS HAD PASSED SINCE THE DAY IN THE FOREST. I removed the iron pot of bündner gerstensuppe from the fireplace and placed it in the center of the small plank table. Pressing my palms on the table, I stared down into the steaming pot of meatless soup. My stomach rumbled and burned with hunger, but no meat would ease our need that night. I considered sneaking a spoonful before Orell returned home, but the pounding of horses' hooves drew me to the window. Drunken laughter and singing pierced the quiet of the night and sent a tremor scurrying through me.

Orell sat on a horse behind Helias, the son of a wealthy factory owner. Helias's vater had never been particularly fond of his son's choice in friends. And though I assumed other girls would consider Helias an excellent catch, even husband-worthy, I did not. He was an ogre to the highest degree, and I believed that was what forged Orell's and his friendship.

Orell's usual companions, Maël and Lorik, arrived in a flatbed wagon. The lewd stares and vulgarity I had endured at the hands of these men knotted my stomach. I moved away from the window and picked up the blade lying on the table and tucked it into the pocket of my apron. I removed bowls from the shelf over the fireplace, the shaking of my hands making them rattle, and arranged them on the table for our guests. Inwardly I rebuked Orell for bringing his friends when we had scarcely enough to feed ourselves.

The door swung open, and I pulled my shawl tighter against the bite of winter that swept through the cottage. Light poured over the hearthstone and cast the men's silhouettes across the floor like dancing puppets. I tried to calm my mounting anxiety.

"Aren't you a lovely sight on this winter night?" Helias pushed by the men and strode into the room. Cloaked in exquisitely woven wool-silk garments, his dark hair trimmed and his face clean-shaven, he carried himself with unyielding pride. Unlike Orell, Helias could handle his liquor, but its effect gleamed in his wandering eyes.

I turned and busied myself with gathering utensils. "Sit," I said in the sternest tone I could muster.

Arms grabbed me around the waist, and I screeched and whirled around. I stood facing Helias, who pressed me tight against his chest. I looked over his shoulder at Orell, imploring him with my eyes for help.

"Valentina may be beautiful, but she's a bore," Orell said with a dismissive wave. "Always a do-gooder and responsible. Much too boring for a man of your taste."

Helias's gaze lingered on my mouth, his desire evident in the way his breath caught. "A man requires a woman with all the qualities you possess. Women of the night will bring a man all the excitement he needs for the moment. But they don't know the first thing about managing a home." He stroked my cheek with the backs of his fingers. "So delicate, yet strong," he said with a groan. "You will be pleased to know, my sweet, that I've offered your brother a handsome dowry for your hand in marriage."

"Shouldn't Orell be paying you the dowry?" Maël interjected in his high-pitched voice, then crowed with laughter, neck bobbing, like a rooster.

"He has nothing to give," Lorik thundered, jiggling with merriment.

Orell scowled at him and slapped him on the back of the head. "You about rattled my teeth down my throat," Lorik whined.

"Ain't got much left to lose," Orell said.

"I will have Valentina, and Orell will ensure she does as she's told," Helias said.

"I will not marry you, or any of you lot!" I pounded his chest with my fist and fought to escape his hold—which only intensified Helias's lust. The men yelped, finding pleasure in my struggle. Again I looked to Orell, who stood with arms folded across his chest, reveling in his friends' taunting.

Helias tossed me at Lorik, who caught me and grasped two handfuls of my backside before sending me into the arms of Maël.

"Let me have a go at her." Maël licked his lips, smelling of sweat and alcohol, and lowered his head to sniff deeply at my throat. Fear paralyzed my limbs. A gleam of ecstasy surfaced in his beady eyes as he lifted his gaze to meet mine.

"Give her here." Helias's tone dripped with agitation as he quickly grew bored with the game of cat and mouse.

"Don't go getting all up in arms. She's fair game." Maël twirled me out of his arms and shoved me forward. Helias snatched me possessively in his grip, leaving me gasping for air. He forced wet kisses on my cheeks, lips, and neck.

No, stop, my mind screamed. I remembered the blade in the pocket of my apron and tried to free my arm to retrieve it, but Orell had become jaded with the lack of attention from his friends.

"All right. Enough!" His bellow startled us all.

Pain ricocheted in my skull, and my hand froze on the concealed weapon.

"Let us eat," Orell said with impatience. Dropping into a chair at the table, he gestured to the men. "Sit."

Lorik gulped as Maël closed his gaping mouth, and both hurried to comply.

Helias leaned close, undeterred by Orell's demands, and whispered in my ear, "You will be mine." He stepped back with a smirk, his dark eyes confident, then pivoted and took a seat on the opposite end of the table from my brother.

I was shaken to my core. I couldn't do this anymore.

The piece of parchment hidden under the straw mattress in my bedroom stroked my memory. *What if…?* I chewed on the inside of my mouth, not daring to look at my brother.

"Woman, must we wait all night?" Orell smacked his palm on the table.

Silently, I walked to his side and ladled soup into his bowl.

He moved the contents around with his spoon. "What is this slop?"

"There's no meat," I said. I was too scared to antagonize him, though everything within me wanted to smash his face into the hot broth.

"Did you not make coin at the market?"

"A little, but I had to buy feed for the animals."

"You foolish wench!" He struck me across the face.

Dropping the ladle, I bit down hard to keep from crying out and lifted a hand to cradle my cheek.

"We will dine on goat tomorrow. Now go. Feed my friends and apologize for the pitiful meal you serve."

I bristled as I moved around the table, filling each bowl as instructed.

Soon the men's conversation turned to the recent robberies. Helias's vater would be outraged to hear of his son's transgressions. The Rechisteiner family had more than enough money to satisfy Helias's greatest desires. But the rogue in him couldn't be satisfied with any amount of his vater's wealth.

As he ate each mouthful, his eyes followed me. After

a few moments, he said, "Orell, I do not wish to wait." The seriousness in his tone stopped the conversation, and all eyes turned to him. "You'll see that she's delivered to my household in the morning."

My hand froze in midair, and the pounding in my chest intensified as the men gawked at Helias.

"But, your vater?" Orell sputtered, sending bits of soup across the table. "He won't approve of such a lowly marriage. I do not seek to be the recipient of his vengeance."

"You let me handle him. I will have your sister and end the games she plays with me."

"What games? I've done nothing to gain your attention," I said, tears constricting my throat.

Helias's eyes glittered with an unnerving desire. "The sashay of your hips and your coquettish, downcast eyes aren't your ploy to be taken? Come now, Valentina. We've all witnessed your desire to be mounted."

"No! It isn't true." Tears tattered my voice at his vulgarity. I looked at my brother. "Orell, please, you must remove these men from our home. For my honor, you must—"

"Silence!" Orell lifted a hand. "I grow tired of your whining, sister."

A quiet fell over the room.

"What's your offer?" Helias had captured Orell's full attention. Greed flashed in my brother's eyes.

Helias rolled back his broad shoulders and rested a hand on his thigh. "Five horses, three cows, and a small chest of gold should be fitting for a woman of your sister's beauty."

"That's hardly suitable," Orell said. "She's my only sister and I've no more to wager."

"It will take me months to fatten her up. A heap of bones will hardly keep a man's bed warm on these dreary winter nights. I will not give you an ounce more," Helias said.

Orell lowered his gaze to search for an answer in the bottom of his wooden bowl. I stood, pleading for him to look at me, but he did not. He regarded Helias with a hard stare. "Very well. I seek to be rid of her. I will deliver her to your estate by noon."

Helias grinned. "I'm glad to see you've come to your senses. Go get the drink from the wagon," he said to Lorik. "This arrangement requires a celebration."

Lorik scraped back his chair and sprang to his feet like a dog obeying his master. He disappeared outside and returned moments later with a keg of ale balanced on his shoulder.

Orell rose and strode around the table and thrust an open hand toward Helias. "Let us drink, brother."

CHAPTER 7

THE MEN'S INEBRIATED GAIETY CARRIED ON long after I'd escaped to my room. Fully clothed, I lay under the covers on my bed with my eyes pinned to the door, too afraid to sleep. Like an animal in heat, Helias's lust had evolved with each of our encounters, and I'd wondered how long I could evade him. But that was out of my hands now. Orell had seen to it. Offering me up as a wife to satisfy his greed, as if I were only property. I touched the tenderness on my cheekbone, and relentless tears cascaded from my eyes to sink into the burlap cloth of my mattress. Forced into a loveless marriage to Helias…I'd die first!

When the men's snores eventually rose and a chill crept throughout the cottage, I threw back the covers and retrieved my cape. I wrapped it around my shoulders and tied the ribbons before slipping my feet into fur moccasins. Then I removed the slip of parchment and a red ribbon that had belonged to my mutter from under my mattress, gently rubbing the strip of fabric between two fingers and kissing it before putting on my mittens, tucking the last piece of my mutter within the warmth of my hand and the wool. I folded the paper and placed it in the leather pocketbook strapped to my chest.

Lifting the hood of my cape, I crept to the door and gripped the handle. I slowly pulled it open, halting when the hinges squeaked loudly and someone stirred in the main room. I peered anxiously through the narrow gap and my heart jumped into my throat when one man sat up and mumbled something inaudible. I pressed myself against the chamber wall, listening for footsteps. When none came, I peeked into the main room and saw the man again splayed out on the floor. I couldn't risk waiting any longer. Treading lightly across the floor, I moved to the outer door and reached for the handle.

My hand rested there as I took one last look around the cottage, gathering the memories of my mutter and searing them into my mind. A sob swelled in my throat, but the dark, bulky form of Orell slumped over the table, his back to the low fire, squelched such emotion. There had been a time in my early childhood when I'd been enthused by everything my brother did. I'd loved him then. But the day in the meadow when he'd bound me to a tree and forced me to watch him torture an injured fawn had opened my eyes to what lay within him. When I told Mutter what I'd witnessed she'd tried to punish him, but he'd overpowered her. That was the first time I saw fear of

Orell register in her eyes. Naively I'd thought it was after that day that we'd come to loathe each other, but now, at two and twenty, I understood that he'd hated me since the first day I drew breath.

In the faint glow of the fire, his hair gleamed like threads of gold. He was all I had left in the world. With that knowledge I opened the door wide enough to squeeze through and slipped out, closing it silently behind me.

Overhead the master of the night, a luminous globe of light, stood proudly with an army of knights adorned in twinkling armor stretching across the dark velvet sky. I'd count on their radiance to guide me. The need to be free of Orell pumped fiercely in my chest as I raced toward the barn with the moonlight chasing my back.

Inside, I lit the lantern and hurried to bridle and saddle the horse. I swung onto the mare's back, but as I was about to take off the cow let out a deep, pitiful bellow. I glanced at the open doors, feeling the need to escape as a palpable thing. I looked over my shoulder at the cow and grappled with the decision for a moment before dismounting and moving the horse over to the wagon. With the threat of Orell and his friends waking spurring me on, I hastily readied the wagon and hung a lantern on the lamppost.

I entered the cow's stall, looped a rope around her neck, and dug my heels in to pull and urge her out. After securing the cow to the back of the wagon, I returned for the goat and put her on the floor of the driver's seat, then went back for the hens. I raced around the pen, cringing at the flurry of clucking that threatened to rouse the men from their slumber. I had to leave, and leave now. Snatching one hen at a time, I pushed them into a wire cage, lunging for the last elusive hen and catching her by the legs. She squawked and flapped her wings in sheer panic. "It's for the best, Luzey, you'll see," I whispered, wrestling the ornery hen into the cage.

What if the Winslows didn't hire me? And in the off chance they did, how would I persuade them to take me and all these animals? *"You're weak. Just like her."* Orell's ridicule repeated in my head. But what truly makes one weak?

I had nothing to lose by leaving our homestead and I was too scared to remain. I climbed into the wagon and drove out of the barn, not stopping to bar the doors. When Orell woke he'd know I was gone and come looking, and by then I hoped to have vanished just as *they* had. I clung to the hope that he'd think the fate of our parents had also become mine.

CHAPTER 8

THE LANTERN HOOKED ON THE LAMPPOST SWUNG wildly as the wheels hit frozen ruts in the road. My breath appeared as wispy clouds that dissipated into the black night as I adjusted to the bewitching music of the forest. An owl perched on the crooked limb of a mountain oak tree, its head bobbing rhythmically side to side, mesmerizing me until the mare snorted and elevated her head as if startled, snapping my awareness back to the road.

I squinted ahead to the ridgeline. My blood ran cold. Multiple sets of yellow eyes observed us from the bank, stirring with impatience. I heard the wolf pack's low whines, and I fought the urge to slap the reins and speed toward Chateau Winslow. That would only send the pack charging toward us. Keeping my eyes trained on the ridge, I mumbled a prayer to whatever ethereal was listening.

Minutes that seemed like hours passed. Then the tension knotting my insides grew into sheer fright as, with a burst of excited yipping, the pack charged. They glided effortlessly over the snow, as if their paws never touched the ground. I whipped the reins and shouted a command at the mare, and she broke into a full gallop, all too aware of the danger closing in on us. The goat lost its balance and was propelled forward; I jammed my heel into the footboard and caught the rope to keep the animal from tumbling over the side.

The fork in the road was a hundred yards ahead. I checked over my shoulder. They were gaining on us. The cow was in an all-out panic, the whites of her eyes showing as she bawled in protest.

The wagon almost toppled over as I guided the mare down the lane leading to the old Winslow estate. I shrieked in terror but regained control, tears blinding my vision. I imagined the hot breath of the beasts on the nape of my neck; at any moment, I'd feel the bite of their fangs.

I didn't see the rock jutting out of the ground until it was too late. The wheel struck it, and I was launched over the side as the wagon flipped over. I hit the ground hard, every bone in my body jolting with excruciating pain. The panicked horse charged down the lane, dragging the cart and cow behind her. Brightness engulfed the thicket next to me as the lantern ignited it.

I clambered to my feet and looked back toward the wolves. They had stopped several feet away, their eyes locked on me. One edged forward but immediately leaped back, whining. Why weren't they advancing? I was right here, vulnerable, and on foot.

I wasn't staying around to find out. I turned and limped on, my body screaming in protest. I stumbled over an obstacle in my path but stayed upright. Looking down I saw the goat lying in an awkward position, its neck broken. I bit down on my lip to keep from crying out. I couldn't stop. My only chance was to continue, and hope the goat's body would distract the wolves. I hastened my steps.

I heard the hens—those that had survived—clucking frantically. I couldn't see the cage, and I wouldn't risk stopping to search. I glanced over my shoulder, listening for any sound from the wolves. Nothing.

When a bend in the lane concealed me, I again picked up my pace. I came across the cow, her rope tangled in the branches of a thicket when, I assumed, she'd tried to leave the road and escape into the forest. Not sensing the wolves, I went to her and fumbled to free the rope in the dim light from the moon. The task seemed impossible, but then the rope came free and I gave her a slap on the backside; she took off down the lane.

When the mansion finally came into view, a tremor coursed through me. The estate sat eerie and somber against the backdrop of the night. The main doors had been repaired and now stood upright and closed. Lanterns on each side of the doors flickered and cast elongated shadows over the overgrown front gardens. I fought the urge to flee—*flee to where? Back toward the salivating wolf pack? Or to the cottage where Orell decided my fate and sold me to a swine of a man?* Summoning my courage, I trudged through the maze of short shrubs to the grand marble stairs rising to the double doors.

On the landing, I lifted the brass lion door knocker and struck twice before stepping back and pulling my cape closer to keep out the chill. My heart thumped faster as I started to second guess my decision. What if whatever waited behind the doors was far worse than what I'd left behind? The howls of the wolves interrupted my thoughts, and I rushed at the door and struck again and again. Pounding with my fist, I looked past the shelter of my hood and down the lane. "Please, help me. Let me in!"

"I'm coming!" a woman called. The door swung open.

I bolted inside, pushed the human form out of the way, and slammed the door shut. I pressed my body against it and slid to the floor, where I drew my knees to my chest.

"What in heaven's name are you running from, lass?"

"Wolves," I whispered, my voice barely discernible. I looked up into the face of the woman towering above me. She stared back at me through wire-framed spectacles that rested on the tip of her nose. Red curls peppered with silver poked out from under her nightcap. Was she real, or a ghost playing dress-up in Lady Winslow's nightclothes? People from the village had spread tales of the haunted chateau. Rumors that the spirit of the Winslows' first-born—dropped from the balcony by the deranged healer months after its birth—roamed the estate's grounds and corridors. Lady Winslow had birthed twin daughters a few years later, but never fully recovered from the loss of their first child. She fell into a deep depression that slowly stole her mind. Desperate to save his wife, Lord Winslow had sent her home to her family in France. Soon after, he received word she'd taken her own life. Heartbroken, he took his infant daughters and returned to England.

"What are you doing out at this time of night?" the woman asked. Her caterpillar-shaped eyebrows flattened.

My words turned to icicles in my throat. "I-I…"

She waved her long fingers. "You can speak later. Best get you warmed up."

"But I don't know if—"

"Don't sit there blabbering, lass. Up with you." She bent and hauled me up with remarkable strength.

I looked past her to the dimly lit corridor, and a shiver rushed through me. "I'm mistaken." I turned to the door.

"Oh no ya don't." Her fingers dug into my flesh. "You aren't going anywhere." She spun me around and I stood pressed against the door, her very solid grip holding me captive. She tried to smile, but her face didn't seem like she smiled often. Still, the softness in her eyes gave me pause. "Don't be frightened, lass. I will not harm ya. Perhaps a cup of tea will thaw the ice in your bones." She released me.

I swallowed hard and nodded, thinking of a dungeon or labyrinth beneath the stone floor where she'd confine me for the rest of my days.

"Follow me," she said abruptly, then turned and strode down the corridor, none too graceful on her feet.

I crept by the shadowed walnut staircase in the empty foyer and down the darkened corridor. The light from web-encased wall sconces reflected on dusty portraits of what I assumed were the Winslow's relatives. They hung over peeling and discolored wallpaper.

The woman stopped at a doorway at the back of the home and turned back to me. "Hurry now; I haven't got all night."

I hurried to catch up, but she had already disappeared inside. At the threshold I peered into the room, which appeared to be the kitchen. The warmth of a fire burning in the brick fireplace drew me into the room. I removed my mittens and held my hands out to warm them. A candelabra burned low in the center of a long wooden table scrubbed clean after the evening meal. The scent of boiled cabbage, spices, and stewed beef lingered.

She removed an iron kettle from the fireplace and set it down on the table before walking to a shelf to retrieve a teacup. From jars she gathered an assortment of herbs and placed them inside cheesecloth, which she tied into a pouch with twine. "Come, take a seat." She gestured at the bench on the side of the table closest to the fire.

I sat down. "I've come to inquire about the job posting," I said as she put the steeping tea on the table in front of me.

"You might have wanted to wait for morning. It isn't safe for a lass to be out alone at night, what with the beasts out there."

Beasts and humans alike, I thought bitterly, cringing

at the memory of Orell's friends. "I really need this job. I'd hoped to be the first in line to inquire." I swaddled the cup with cold hands.

"Desperate, are ya?" Her calloused fingers lifted my chin. "Let me take a gander at ya." Her brow puckered. "Got yourself some cuts and bruises. It looks like your journey hasn't been an easy one."

"My wagon hit something on the carriage trail, and it threw me," I hurried to say.

"Ahh, yes, there's a boulder Lord Winslow has scheduled to be removed." She released my chin. "It appears you have broken nothing."

"A little skinned up is all."

"Ya look knackered and half-starved to boot," she said. "You could stand a nibble or two. I will fix you something to eat. You can stay the night and speak to his lordship in the morning."

"Thank you, Frau…"

"Mrs. Potts is the name."

"Can you tell me more about the posting? What task is his lordship looking to have done?"

"You must take it up with him in the morning. I'll give you lodging for the night. First, you eat. But know that if you're not awarded the job, you must find shelter elsewhere." She waited for me to acknowledge her.

"Yes." I wriggled under her stare.

She prepared me a plate of cold stewed beef and cabbage, proving I hadn't lost all my senses. I used my fingers and scarfed down a hunk of meat while grabbing for another.

"You'd best slow down, lass. Ain't no critters going to take your food." She lowered herself down on a chair.

I continued at a pace more pleasing to her while satisfying the distress swirling in my stomach.

When I finished Mrs. Potts lifted the candelabra and exited the kitchen, turning immediately to a narrow set of stairs designed for the house staff. We climbed in silence to the second floor and walked down several corridors until we reached the far wing of the house. She paused outside a closed door. "We were unprepared for guests, so this will have to do." She opened the door and strode in to set the candelabra down on a stand by the bed.

The cold and dusty chamber contained a bed without a mattress, a night table, a wardrobe, and nothing more.

"This should suit for the night. I'll bring you extra blankets. I'm afraid we can't start a fire in this room, as the chimney needs repair." She strode to the wardrobe and removed a piece of clothing. "Here, you can wear this night shift."

"Who does the gown belong to?" I asked. It was clear no one had slept in the chamber in years. In the dim light from the candelabra, I noticed two sets of footprints in the dust: Mrs. Potts's and mine.

"Lady Winslow," she said. "She won't be needing them, so you're welcome to it."

Lord Winslow's dead wife? I reached for the garment to mask my knowledge of the rumors.

She picked up the candelabra and walked from the room.

I stood in the middle of the moon-drenched chamber, contemplating if I should slip out the back door and be gone before the household awoke. Imaginary fingers tickled my back, and I dropped the dead woman's night shift and glanced about the room for any sign of movement. Finding nothing, I climbed onto the bed and huddled in the far corner of the bed frame. Sleep had to have found me soon after, because when Mrs. Potts returned with blankets I never woke and remained in that position until morning.

CHAPTER 9

THE NEXT MORNING I'D BARELY OPENED MY EYES before a knock sounded on the door, and before I could respond the door swung open. A lively girl of maybe five and twenty entered the room with a pail of steaming water, and a white cloth draped over her arm.

"Mrs. Potts sent me up to assist you," she said. "My name is Yara." Without waiting for a response, she waved her hand for me to follow. I climbed off the bed and hurried after her down the hallway to another room. Two grooms entered after us, carrying a copper basin I'd only seen in shop windows. I believed the rich referred to them as bathing tubs.

"Put it there, by the fire." Yara nodded toward the fireplace. When the grooms were gone, she poured the bucket into the tub. She was a fleshy girl with straw-colored hair and a friendly face. "Are you from the village?"

"No."

"The forest?"

"I'm not from these parts." I glanced from her to the boat-shaped hunk of metal. "What do you intend to do with that?"

Her brow puckered. "You've never seen a bathing tub before?"

"I've never used one." My voice sounded scratchy with the dryness gripping my throat.

Her eyes remained fixed on me, as though trying to read me. "It works the same as a river, except there's a lot less water. The rich find it quite convenient, but the ones that have to do all the carrying and boiling of the water, we think differently."

I stood like a post as a cold sweat broke out on my back. "How does one keep from drowning?"

Her dark eyes narrowed. "It won't be filled. You add just enough water to get you cleaned up."

The grooms arrived and emptied their pails before leaving and returning three more times. After they left, Yara closed the door and swung back to me. "Let's get you cleaned up, shall we?"

"I can manage on my own." I crossed my arms over my chest, letting her know I wasn't about to be bathed like a child or the ladies and lords she was accustomed to.

She was having none of it. Her hands pulled at my dress, her freckle-dusted face determined. "Come now; you ain't got nothing I haven't seen before. If you're to meet his lordship, you need to be presentable. And from what Mrs. Potts said, you're desperately in need of a job."

Had I groveled that much? Yes, I suppose I had. Hesitantly, I unfastened the cape and let it fall to the floor. My arms dropped to my sides. She bent and pulled the hem of my threadbare gray dress up and over my head. I used my arms to hide my nakedness, but she never blinked; it was as if she had lost all sense of modesty. I guess bodies would become uninteresting to a chambermaid. Perhaps it was like a midwife or a physician, who'd sworn an oath to care for the sick no matter the circumstance.

The thought didn't stop the heat from warming my cheeks as she said, "Off with the boots and stockings."

Maybe you should have had me do that first, I grumbled inwardly. With as much modesty as I could muster, I kicked off my boots and wiggled out of my stockings. With my clothes and boots lying in a dirty heap on the floor, I looked at her. She stood staring at the birthmark staining my hip.

"Does something trouble you?" I asked.

She pulled from her trance and pointed at the tub. "In you go. Don't stall."

I dipped my toes in the water and quickly jerked them back.

"It's a little hot at first, but it'll cool down all too soon," she said.

I placed one foot in the tub and then the other. Slowly, I lowered myself down, gritting my teeth as the heat of the water touched the gashes from my fall the night before.

Yara walked to the solitary piece of furniture in the room, a stand under the window, whose dusty green drapes had been pulled open to let in the morning sun. She lifted a silver tray of oils and soap and set it on the floor by the tub. Lifting one of the glass bottles, she poured a few drops into the water, and the scent of jasmine wafted through the room. Next she retrieved a bar of soap and held it out to me. As I took the soap and began to scrub my body, my aching muscles relaxed, soothed by the warmth of the water.

Yara scooped water from the tub into a pitcher. I eyed her suspiciously, but never had time to process what she intended to do with the water before she poured it over my head. I shrieked and dropped the soap. Coughing and sputtering, I grabbed at the sides of the tub, fighting to climb out. "No, no," I gasped. Water splashed everywhere.

I tumbled out, hitting the floor hard. Scrambling to my feet, I skated across the floor, slipping and sliding into the corner, where I crouched, my mind vaulting back to the day at the river.

"What happened?" Concern etched Yara's voice as she approached me.

"Stay away from me!" I scurried closer to the wall. Uncontrollable sobs burst from my throat, racking my body.

She held up her hands in defeat and inched backward. I rested my head against the wall.

Orell tried to drown me—

Shortly after my parents' disappearance the water

beckoned, promising refreshment on an unusually hot summer day. Blocked from my brother's view, I let my dress fall to the ground and raced into the river. I sank into the cool depths and let the water take me, then surfaced to float on my back, peering up at the white patterns stretching across the bluest of skies. Closing my eyes, I allowed all my stress and worry to subside.

Then hands grabbed me by the shoulders, and I opened my eyes to find Orell, fully dressed, holding onto me, his eyes strange and unseeing. He forced me under, his hands steady and unyielding.

"No," I gasped between gulps of air and water. I clawed at him. Why? My mind tried to make sense of what was going on. I gurgled water, and my lungs burned. I couldn't breathe. His form above me eclipsed the sun and blue sky as the water pulled me down.

My fingers relaxed. I drifted down and down to the rocky bottom below. Peace encompassed me.

Then, I saw her. Mutter. Her sweeping robe moved like the fluttering wings of a moth as she looked into the horizon. When she twisted so I could look upon her face, I saw her rage. "No, it isn't your time," she said.

I reached out, wanting to touch her, wanting to feel the safety of her embrace.

"Fight, Valentina. You must fight." I heard panic in her voice.

But I don't want to, I tried to say.

"Fight!" Her cry became weaker, and then she was fading.

My fingers outstretched, I struggled to reach her. *Come back. Please come back.* A sob caught in my chest.

Muffled voices rose, seeming far away, as if they came from another world. Something slammed into me, and the water splashed around me as a struggle took place. I couldn't make out what was happening. I fought to open my eyes, but I couldn't. Hands grabbed at me and dragged me to the bank; I was too weak to resist them. Someone placed their head to my chest, and a mouth touched mine. Hands pushed on my chest, faster and faster, as though in a panic. I realized they were trying to save me. *Orell.* My heart sang. He had made a mistake. He hadn't meant to harm me.

I coughed and sputtered and rolled onto my side.

"That's right, breathe," a man said, the voice unfamiliar.

I fought to see his face, but the fogginess in my brain blurred my vision.

"Will she be all right?" another said.

"Murderous bastard nearly killed her. He was wise in having us watch the girl." The other's voice was laced with concern.

He? My mind raced. I sank back against the earth as I realized what had happened. Orell hadn't regretted his attempt to kill me. Hollow sobs formed deep in my chest, and my hands gripped fistfuls of earth. Rage and hurt rushed through me, and over and over, I struck at the ground.

Sometime later, I sat up and looked around. I was alone in the forest with no sign of the men or of Orell.

"You're safe. No one will harm you." Yara's soothing voice pulled me back. She was kneeling beside me, her fingers brushing the damp hair from my eyes. "You needn't worry. This Orell you speak of isn't here."

Had I said my brother's name aloud? He could never know I was here. He would have started searching for me by now. *The wagon tracks!* They would lead him straight to me. In my attempt to escape the wolves, I hadn't covered our trail. "I must go."

"You're scared out of your skin. You aren't going anywhere. Do you need the position here or not?" she asked.

I became aware of my nakedness. "Yes."

Kindness gleamed in her eyes. "If you stand a chance at nabbing this job, we must make you look presentable. And I'd suggest you don't go like this," she said with a laugh.

I laughed softly. "I suppose not."

"I know what it's like to be alone and scared, and something tells me you could use a friend." She rested a hand on my shoulder, and I allowed her to help me to my feet. "We can do this differently. You finish bathing, and then we will wash your hair. All right?"

I nodded and wiped away the tears. What choice did I have? I had to trust her.

CHAPTER 10

BATHED AND DRESSED IN A BLUE WOOLEN DRESS, I allowed Yara to brush my hair before pulling it back into a plait and securing it with a ribbon.

Downstairs we found Mrs. Potts on her knees, scrubbing the floors in the foyer. She used the back of her hand to wipe away the sweat trickling down her forehead and pooling inside her spectacles. "Never thought I'd see myself scampering around like a house lass," she said to herself.

Yara cleared her throat and alerted Mrs. Potts to our presence. She jumped and almost upended her pail of scrub water.

"You mustn't sneak up on people." Mrs. Potts pushed to her feet and strode toward us, her gait wide and grace-less. She stared openly at me. "Well, you look a spot better than you did when you wandered in here yesterday eve."

I forced a smile. "Thanks for giving me shelter."

"Aye." She wiped her rather large hands on her apron. "Let's not keep him waiting. I've been informed the line outside is growing."

I frowned.

"You didn't think you'd be the only one to inquire, did you? People started arriving shortly after the sun came up." She turned on her heel and sauntered down the corridor.

I glanced at Yara, who offered me an encouraging smile. I hurried to catch up with Mrs. Potts. She led me to a room at the front of the mansion to the left of the foyer. In the daylight, the eeriness of the home seemed to fade, and it appeared as an old home in desperate need of repairs. Servants and workers bustled everywhere. A mason grouted loose flagstones while two men teetering on ladders removed broken windowpanes. Others tinkered at gas chandeliers and scraped away worn wallpaper. A maid opened the door and shooed a hare out with a broom.

"It appears the forest critters have made a home of the place in the family's absence. We're finding them in every cranny," Mrs. Potts said with disgust. "They've made a fine mess of the furniture and trimmings."

I wiped sweaty palms on the sides of my dress and listened to the chatter of the applicants waiting outside. I gazed out the window at a line of women's lined winter bonnets and men's felt caps. The need to impress the earl became ever more pressing. "Am I the first of the day?" I asked.

"Aye. I'd advise you to not squander the opportunity." Mrs. Potts pressed her lips together and rapped on the heavy mahogany door.

"Come in," a stern male voice said.

Mrs. Potts's mouth twisted with annoyance, and I wondered why she seemed suddenly agitated. Taking a deep breath, she mumbled a few words I didn't catch and opened the door. "Lord Winslow, this is the first applicant of the day," she said tartly. I peeked at her, even more mystified by her behavior.

Standing at the window with his hands clasped behind his back was a broad-shouldered, dark-haired man. He didn't turn when we entered but continued to gaze over the grounds. "Mrs. Potts, you may leave us," he said.

The door closed with a soft click behind me and I swallowed the nerves constricting my throat. I was alone with him.

"Mrs. Potts informed me that you showed up after the house retired last night."

"My apologies, but—"

"What do they call you?" He tilted his head as if cocking his ear for my reply.

"Valentina, my lord."

"You sound young. Are you sure you're capable of minding children?" he asked.

"Children?"

He swung around, and alluring dark blue eyes roved over me. He stared with no restraint, and I squirmed under his gaze. His lordship was dapper and handsome, but the grimace on his face warned me to advance with caution. "Yes, children. Am I to believe you were unaware of the position you were inquiring about?"

"A housemaid is what the advertisement stated."

He cranked his neck side to side and cursed. "Take a seat."

I seated myself in the chair in front of his desk and folded my hands in my lap.

He moved to the desk, but before lowering himself into the leather-bound chair, he adjusted his black tailored suit and smoothed back his hair, using a polished statue as a looking glass. Once seated, he leaned forward and rested his elbows on the desk. "Where do you come from?"

"From the north." I squirmed mentally at the lie.

"How did you hear of the position?"

"I was passing through town when your advertisement found me." At least the last part was truthful.

I Iis brow arched. "Found you?"

"It was blowing around on the ground."

He looked away, his hands clenched on the desk, then relaxed as his focus returned to me. "This morning, I awoke and saw the oddest sight from my window. Do you care to know what it was?" An uncanny coldness surrounded him.

I wondered if all he had suffered had caused his lack of emotions. "If you choose to share."

"There was a horse with an upturned wagon still attached, eating the hay by the south stables," he said. "Does the horse belong to you?"

I swallowed hard. "On the road, a pack of wolves

tried to overtake us. I tried to outrun them, and they were gaining on us, until the strangest thing happened. We turned down the lane and they stopped. One started to advance, but then he withdrew and whined as if injured."

His brow knitted. "Yes, quite odd, indeed. That would explain why Mrs. Potts told me you arrived badly shaken and scraped." He sat, unsmiling. "The stable master also informed me he found a cow and a hen or two roaming about the grounds. Am I to assume they also belong to you?"

I avoided his intense stare, and the clawed foot of his desk seized my gaze. "Yes."

He leaned back, drumming his fingers on the desk. "Did you bring the whole bloody stables with you? Or am I to think you're a thief?"

My head swung up, and my hands clenched into fists in the folds of my dress. "I am no thief. I may be many things, but that I am not. It was a matter of life or death. If I were to leave the animals behind, their fate would be death. Influenza took my vater. With no other family around, I couldn't make payments on the farm, and the bank came to collect our debt. Left without a home, I had to seek work elsewhere."

"And the animals? Surely you could have fetched a coin or two for them."

"I suppose I may have, but overcome with grief, I wasn't capable of logic. I was passing through town when I saw your job posting. I do hope you will consider me for the position."

"Do tell me, what has Mrs. Potts told you about the position here?"

"She didn't. But the ad mentioned housekeeping," I said with surprising clarity. "And I've done my fair share of housekeeping and farming."

"There isn't much to you. Don't suppose you'd last a day in the work yard," he mused as if considering the idea. "I didn't expect to arrive to find the place in such disarray. My time will be occupied in getting this estate in order. The children would need to be kept in line and out of my way." He leaned forward. "Do you like children, Valentina?"

"I haven't been around many," I said. Again, his brow rose. Suddenly aware of my blunder, I rushed on. "Well, what I mean to say is…I like children." Or at least I believed I did.

"And you have no bastards of your own that will turn up in the coming weeks if I were to hire you?"

My mouth unhinged, then snapped shut. "I assure you there is no cause for concern."

"I have two children. Twin daughters. They're ten and a bit to handle. I've had trouble keeping a governess. The last one stayed one week before she packed her bags and returned to France."

What was wrong with the children?

He waited for me to digest the information, and when I sat unwavering, he continued. "I would require you to bathe them, ready them for bed, and accompany us on outings. Most days, they're with their tutor, Mr. Evans.

During such times, you would perform the household duties Mrs. Potts lays out for you. If you're chosen, you will receive room and board and a small salary. However, the state of the animals and your gaunt appearance make me wonder if you're capable of caring for anything that draws breath."

"Please, I beg you, give me a chance. I'm an honest and hard worker." I hated stooping to begging, but desperation pushed me to it.

"Very well. I have a full afternoon of candidates. Until I have spoken to all the applicants, you will take a seat in the parlor and wait. And I will let you know my decision."

"I thank you." I rose.

He grumbled and waved a hand in dismissal.

I turned and took my leave. Outside, I wandered down the hall, looking in each room until I located what appeared to be a parlor and took a seat on an embroidered burgundy settee to wait. Glancing around the room, I reflected on what life would have been like as a lady from an aristocratic family. Mutter hadn't been a lady with a title, but she had come from a prosperous family. She'd told me stories of their servants, and the luxurious belongings she'd had. I wondered if her chambermaid was like Yara. I'd asked her once why Nonno had approved her marriage to Vater. Weary and void of emotions, she'd said, *"Because the one truth your vater speaks is that Nonno spoiled me. I was sickly as a child, and as his only child he gave me all my heart desired."*

"I did it, Mutter. I'm finally rid of him," I whispered.

Voices filled the corridor, but time ticked by and no one had come to wait in the parlor with me. "Excuse me," I said to a tall, slender man walking by.

"Yes, miss?" He ducked to step through the doorway, and I marveled at how his bald head shone like polished silverware. "Can I help you?" He straightened to his full height.

"Is this the parlor? Lord Winslow told me—"

"No, miss. This is the music room. The room you're looking for is down the corridor. The second room on the right."

I bounced to my feet, hurried past him, and mumbled a thank-you over my shoulder.

At the doorway, I paused and peeked into the room, hoping no one would recognize me, or me them. Spotting no one familiar, I walked into the room and took a seat on a chair in the corner.

The man I'd spoken to in the hallway returned and called out a name, and as hours passed, the room began to empty. When only a woman and I remained, he called my name. "Lord Winslow wishes to see you. Come with me," he said.

Nerves twisted my stomach as I walked to his side. What if this was it? What if he didn't award me the position? Where would I go?

"Go on in; he's expecting you." The steward opened the door and gestured me in.

Cautiously I entered the room and stood in front of his desk.

He sat writing on a piece of parchment. He never looked up. "I've made my decision."

Hurried footsteps and the giggles of children echoed in the corridor, and he stiffened. There came a soft rap on the door. "Come in." His mouth set in a firm line.

"Papa." A blonde girl raced across the room, excitement dancing in her bright blue eyes.

Lord Winslow put his hand up to stop her. "Zuna, you mustn't run."

She halted and stood several feet away from his desk. Tears brimmed in her eyes, but she curtsied and said, "Yes, Papa."

"This is Lady Zuna and Lady Farrah." He nodded at the somber, auburn-haired child standing beside her sister. "My daughters." He spoke the word as though it pained him. "Children, I'd like you to meet Miss…" He regarded me. "I'm afraid I didn't get your full name."

"Wolf," I said.

"Miss Wolf will be your new caregiver."

Farrah jutted her nose upward. "If you must find someone to care for us, maybe you should take a wife." She spoke with more opinion than was appropriate for a child.

Lord Winslow rose, strode around the desk, and perched on its edge. He clasped his wrist with a hand and rested it on his thigh. "Do not test me today, Farrah. I've no time for your fussing."

Zuna looked at her sister. "Remember, Mrs. Potts said no puss face."

Farrah let out a huff. "Well, there's no reason for her to be sleeping in our room. You may consider us children, but we don't require a nursemaid." The child conducted herself as though she was years beyond her age.

I wriggled in my chair.

"She will have her own room across the hall." Lord Winslow used his index finger and thumb to rub the bridge of his nose.

"Don't worry, Miss Wolf, our room's not as nice as we're used to either. But Papa's working hard to have the rooms repaired." Zuna came to stand beside me, her small hand resting on my arm. "We'll all feel at home very soon."

"Let's hope." I smiled at her.

Lord Winslow cleared his throat, and the girls' gaze turned to him. "You are dismissed. Return to your studies."

After they'd left, he said, "I expect you to join us for dinner this evening."

"Me?" I squeaked.

His eyes gleamed dark and dangerous. "Are there any other persons in this room?"

I wondered about his daughter's disdain for him, and Mrs. Potts's behavior. After all, he was an absolute delight, I thought sardonically. Should I be suspicious of him? Maybe I'd been wrong in thinking I'd find refuge in his household.

"I will do as you request, my lord."

"Good. Now I've work to attend to. Find Mrs. Potts. She'll inform you of your duties."

I curtsied. "Thank you."

I turned to leave but halted when he called out, "Consider yourself on trial."

I swung back around. "Trial?"

"I can't trust just anyone to watch my children, now can I?"

But you don't even like them, I wanted to say. His presence was like a cold breeze in the dead of winter, yet there was something alluring about his lordship. A woman would be blind not to notice. My pulse raced, not because of his dark charm, but the emotionless way he regarded me.

After he dismissed me, I walked down the hall to find Mrs. Potts. My thoughts dwelt on Lord Winslow. What was it about his daughters that triggered such contempt in him? Perhaps the pain of losing his wife and child still haunted him. I understood such emptiness.

CHAPTER 11

"The rest of the afternoon, you're to help in the stable yard," Mrs. Potts said when I found her in the kitchen. She made notes in a ledger as she strolled about the room. "No, no, you daft girl." She stopped in front of a young scullery maid. "If you expect the quiche to have any flavor at all, you must add more herbs and onion."

"Yes, Mrs. Potts." She reached for some dried herbs in a woven grass basket resting on the table.

"You." Mrs. Potts chased after a male servant who strode toward the larder with a sack of flour slung over his shoulder. The threads that sealed the burlap sack together had come undone, and a slow, steady white path flowed behind him.

I hurried after her. "But I thought—"

Mrs. Potts held up a hand to silence me. "Stop, you damn fool!" she said to the servant. "Can't ya see you're making a mess of the place?" She whirled to gesture at the mess as a hare hopped through the powder. She gasped, then shouted, "Someone, get that hare!" The kitchen staff jumped, and the buttons on the bodice of her dress looked almost ready to pop.

Scullions scurried after the animal.

"Not all of you, you imbeciles. Two will do. The rest of you, back to your stations. Lunch is to be served within the hour." She turned back to the servant. "You, clean up this mess." She looked at me. "What was it we were talking about?"

"The yards," I said.

"I will show you the way." She swiftly exited the kitchen while scratching something down in the ledger.

I picked up my pace. "But I thought the house and children were to be my responsibilities."

She came to a sudden stop, and I plowed into the back of her. I gasped and mumbled an apology, but she brushed me off as though I hadn't spoken. Her mouth set in a tight line. "His lordship gave the orders. Do you think it wise to question his wishes when you've scarcely been hired?"

I swallowed back panic. "No, on the contrary. I was curious, is all."

"Curiosity will get you nowhere here. You should stick to what you're told and don't pry into matters that don't concern you. Understood?" The warning in her gaze discouraged all further inquiries.

I inclined my head. "Yes, Mrs. Potts."

She walked on, then stopped at a door I'd seen servants coming and going from throughout the morning. "You go down to the stables and ask for Enzo. He's the stable master. He'll inform you of your duties." She lifted a gray woolen coat hanging on a hook. "You'd best put this on."

I wiggled into the coat.

"Well, off with you then," she said curtly.

Stepping outside, I lifted the collar of the coat to keep out the cold and went in search of the stable master. In the stables, a stable boy directed me to a man of small stature with gray-speckled muttonchops who was standing on an upside-down crate to brush a beautiful sable horse.

Behind me, a horse nickered, and I swerved to find my mare craning her neck toward me. Stray bits of hay hung from her mouth. I smiled and moved in to rub her snout. "Hello, old girl." She nudged me on the shoulder. "I see you're well cared for." Resting my forehead against her muzzle, I inhaled, finding comfort in her presence.

"Found her and a few others roaming the grounds this morning," a man said. I turned to find the stable master eyeing me from his post on the crate. "The coachman said he found a broken crate, a dead goat, and some scorched brush that must have choked out before it could take over the forest."

I left the mare and walked back to him.

He jumped off the crate and craned his neck to look up at me. "I'm to show you what's expected of you." Wiping his hands on his leather apron, he sauntered out of the stables and led me to a pile of wood around the back of a small stone outbuilding. "You're to restock each room in the house with wood." He pointed at the mountain of pungent hay and animal waste mucked out from stalls. "This waste is to be loaded on the cart to be hauled away. When you have a full cart you can find Rafael, and he'll haul it away. He's a stout lad. You can't miss him. He lost an arm in an accident when he was just a wee lad." He looked me over, sympathy shining in his amber eyes. "Ain't so sure you're up to the task. A bit small, you are, but I ain't one to question the master. You've got a full day ahead, so I'll let you get to it." He left.

I stood for a moment, feeling overwhelmed and fighting back tears. Then I forced them back and set myself to the task. I filled my arms with wood and turned to head into the house, and caught sight of the earthmen spying on me from behind one of the outbuildings. They pressed themselves back against the building and out of sight.

It was early evening by the time I finished carrying the wood inside. My legs burned from several trips up the stairs, and my arms dangled like hunks of meat hung to dry. As I shoved my shovel into the pile of animal waste I looked up at the mansion, and inside I jumped. From the window of his study, a solemn Lord Winslow stood observing me. When our gazes met he let the curtain fall into place, and for the first time I understood why I'd been assigned to the yards. He was testing me.

CHAPTER 12

THE SUN HAD SET WHEN MRS. POTTS WALKED into the stable yards. "What are you still doing out here?" Her eyes roved over me as if wondering how I still stood. "The children need tending."

"I've not finished this task." I shoveled another scoop of manure onto the cart. Exhaustion had set in hours ago, but I was determined to prove to his lordship that I'd take on any challenge he sent my way. I wouldn't go back. I couldn't. As I hoisted another shovelful onto the wagon, my foot skidded in the dung splattered in the yard, and before I could catch myself, I landed on my rear. Tears of frustration and defeat flowed freely down my cheeks.

"Come now, lass, up you go." Mrs. Potts bent over and thrust out a hand. "Don't let him see you cry or give him the satisfaction of your defeat," she said. Compassion softened her gaze as she helped me to my feet. "You've run out of light. Yara has drawn your bath. I'll arrange for a chambermaid to tend to the children's needs. You're to join the family for the evening meal, and you can't show up at his lordship's table smelling like the stable yards." Her nose twitched. "Let's go get you cleaned up, shall we?" She turned and marched toward the mansion.

I considered her position at the estate and concluded Lord Winslow had chosen wisely in selecting her as the head housekeeper. She gave orders and the staff jumped to obey, not out of fear, but respect. Regardless of her take-charge demeanor, I decided there was something likable about the strange woman.

Inside, we climbed the servants' stairs to the second floor and wove through the corridors until we reached a room in the west wing. "This will be your room." She opened the door and stood back to allow me entrance.

I stood on the threshold and marveled at the beauty of the chamber. Floor-length cream tulle curtains framed two large windows embellished with black wrought iron. Matching fabric hung from the pelmet over the rosewood four-poster bed, which was adorned with swan motif linens in various shades of cream, blue, and rose. A copper bathing tub sat in front of a crackling fire that enveloped the room in luminous warmth. Although I'd never been in the homes of the rich, I assumed a chamber of such grandeur wasn't fitting for a servant.

Mrs. Potts pushed past me into the room.

"The room is one his lordship would offer his guest, not a servant. Am I not to sleep with the others in the servant quarters?" I asked.

"Aye, this is true. But you're to be near the children. This is the only chamber besides his lordship and the children's in this wing." She opened the doors of the armoire that stood in a shadowed corner of the room.

"His private quarters are in this wing?" My voice hitched. The thought of his closeness unsettled me.

"Aye, that's what I said," Mrs. Potts replied.

I frowned at her back as she buried her head inside the armoire. Surely folks from Ireland weren't also a bore like his lordship. Although I had met no one from England before, I wondered if they all were born without a personality. Did one not smile there? Perhaps it was a dismal place. In all my years, I'd never been past the village limits, and I'd often daydream of Nisse and what adventures he was having abroad. Then I'd consider what life would have been like if I'd left with Nonno when he'd come some years after my parents' disappearance. The money he sent, my brother had intercepted, and although I'd never seen it, I always knew when it had come because Orell would return home with a new cloak and ale to last the week, or go missing for days on end.

Mrs. Potts walked into the light with a gown made of emerald green, blue, and gold. She held it up for my inspection. The gown's bustle mimicked a peacock's tail. My mouth dropped open in awe.

"A gown fit for the ladies and duchesses of England." She laid it out on the bed before returning to the wardrobe to fetch gold satin shoes adorned with gems that sparkled in the fire's radiance. "These should suit. I will send Yara up to assist you," Mrs. Potts said.

"I don't understand."

"What, lass?" Impatience pinched the corners of her mouth.

"Why am I to wear a dress and shoes fashioned for high society? Surely a clean wool frock will do."

"Because his lordship insisted that you not arrive too plain for his liking. Now no more questions." She spun on her heel and marched to the door.

After she left, I crossed the room and ran a hand over the fabric of the dress and lifted the shoes to inspect them. Were they also belongings of the late Lady Winslow? I considered what she may have been like. Had she had Zuna's gentle nature or Farrah's beautiful auburn tresses? Had her marriage to Lord Winslow been one of love or circumstance? I looked around the chamber and lamented the unbearable tragedy they'd suffered.

I moved away from the bed and discarded my clothing before stepping cautiously into the washing tub. My body sang as the water soothed my aching muscles, and I leaned my head back and closed my eyes, reflecting on the day. My thoughts turned to Lord Winslow. I'd endure his company and satisfy my hollow stomach, as the stew and bread served at lunchtime hadn't curbed my hunger.

A soft knock on the door made me open my eyes.

"Miss Wolf? It's me, Yara."

"Come in." I sank deeper into the murky water, hoping to conceal myself.

The door opened, and Yara's pleasant face peeked around its edge. "Good evenin', how are you faring?"

"Fine."

She stepped into the room, and carefully crossed to me. "I ain't looking to have a recurrence of this morning. We will do this your way."

"I concur," I said with a small smile, and glided the oatmeal and honey soap bar over my legs. "Two baths in one day, I've never been so clean."

"More baths than a lady takes. But after a day in the stable yards, you need one." She lifted a pitcher, and I knew what was coming next. "You ready?" Her hand halted in midair.

Needles prickled my flesh as I watched water drip from the spout, but I gulped back the anxiety gathering in my throat and nodded.

"All right, you just lean back, and we will make this as painless as possible." With gentle swiftness, she poured the water over my hair, taking care not to let it trickle over my face. My fingers gripped the tub and my chest pounded, but when Yara's voice rose in song I tuned in to the nostalgic sound of her voice as she softly sang the "Kühreihen," a song sung by farmers and cattlemen as they herded their cattle in for milking. Vater had been tone-deaf, but as he'd belted it from the fields Mutter had hummed it from the cottage. Now, tears flowed, masked by the water trickling down my cheeks as Yara rubbed the rosemary-infused castile soap through my hair.

When both my hair and body were clean, Yara held out a silk bathing cloak, and I stepped out of the tub and wrapped the luxurious cloth around myself.

"How long have you been employed by the Winslow household?" I asked.

She crossed to the vanity, and with her back to me, she said, "Most of my years. Why do you ask?" Tension stiffened her body.

"Curiosity, I suppose. The earl seems a bit disgruntled and not the friendly sort."

"Cantankerous knobhead, you mean," she said under her breath. Did all in Lord Winslow's household have the same distaste for their master? "He's a bit of a hard one." She adjusted trinkets that didn't need fixing on the vanity. "He's become as dry as a glass of his best port," she said, swinging to face me.

I arched a brow. She grinned. "Me and my man sneak down to the cellar and nab us a taste from time to time." She shrugged before her face tightened. "When Lady Risette died, it broke his heart. He used to be quite cheerful and charismatic, but life left him with decisions he wasn't equipped to deal with."

"Caring for the children?" I said.

"No one chooses to lose a loved one." She gathered the bottom of the gown and held it out to me.

"I suppose not." I stepped into the dark swell of fabric and poked my head through the neck hole of the gown. "I lost my parents."

"They died on ya, did they?" Sympathy reflected in her eyes. "My mum died with consumption when I was the ripe age of eight. I found a job as a cinder girl and have worked as a servant since." She pulled out the brown velvet-upholstered bench in front of the vanity and waved me forward.

"A servant? All your life?" I lowered myself onto the bench, then stood and arranged the flounces of fabric before seating myself again. I wondered why the affluent had to dress themselves in endless layers of fabric.

"It ain't all bad," she said. "At least I got a place to lay my head at night and two square meals. Ain't as inviting as the dishes that line his lordship's table, but better than the scraps my mum and I could conjure up. Looks like you haven't had a much better go at it yourself."

"It's all I've ever known."

"You ever want more in life?" she asked.

"Doesn't everyone?"

"I guess we do." Silence fell between us for a few moments before she said, "If you could ask for just one thing, what would it be?"

My mutter, the ache in me cried. "To go to bed without being hungry," I said.

"Is that all? There must be something more." She screwed up her face and lifted the silver brush engraved with a rose. She pulled it through my hair, stealing a glance or two at me through the looking glass.

"Someday, I hope to marry," I said.

"I don't think that will ever be part of my future." Her expression grew sad.

"Why not? Didn't you say you had a lover?"

"That I do, but he isn't available."

"What do you mean?" I asked.

"You see…" Her pale skin flushed, and her gaze fastened on a lock of hair she'd pulled the brush through. "He is married."

"Married!" I gasped. The memory of a woman's discarded petticoats on the ground and the moans and Vater's bare buttocks inside the Romany's wagon hauled at my heart. My anguish over his infidelities pained me as though they were yesterday. At a tender age, I came to understand that the first man in my life would never be my protector or my hero. Wasn't it every child's birthright to have parents who loved and protected them? Perhaps, but life was no fairy tale. Vater's perfidious behaviors had fueled arguments between Mutter and him. I had often wondered if Mutter's pride had kept her from divorcing him and returning to the comforts of Nonno's home.

"I didn't know he was married, or I would have given him the boot. It was only after I'd fallen for the bloke that he told me he had a wife and three children." I opened my mouth to speak, but she hadn't spoken her piece and continued with, "I know that doesn't make it right, but I've loved no one in this life but my mum. It was always just her and me, making our way in this empty world. Some days I miss her so much it hurts." Her voice quavered.

Yara's longing bled from her dark eyes, and I wanted to grab her hands and say, Me too. I yearned to tell her my story, the truth that had brought me here. That I was a farm girl who had lived a stone's toss away. A woman who was given against her will, I might add, to the son of one of the richest men in the canton. No amount of hunger would have me racing to Helias's home or his bed.

Tears dropped onto Yara's cheeks.

"Do not cry." I took her hands in mine and squeezed them earnestly. "We all have our wrongs in this life."

She snorted and used the back of her hand to wipe her nose. "You? I don't believe it. You seem to be so innocent…perhaps a wee bit naive."

"I assure you, I am not innocent."

"All right then, name it," she said.

I looked at her in confusion.

"The one thing you've done in this life that would make me believe you behave like anything less than a Sister escaped from the convent."

"Secrets are that for a reason," I said.

"Do you like chocolate?"

I studied her, puzzled. "Sometimes, when I was small, Mutter would treat me to a piece when we'd travel to the village."

"I will make you a deal. If you tell me your secret, I will meet you in the pavilion after the house has settled, and I will share my stash of chocolate."

"Where did you get it from?"

"Why, the kitchen of course."

"Aren't you afraid of Mrs. Potts catching you stealing?" I said.

Her eyes twinkled. "She'd have to catch me. My years of being a pickpocket in the slums have made me swift and undetectable."

I couldn't hide my displeasure at taking things that didn't belong to you.

She crossed her arms over her full bosom. "See, there ya go being all self-righteous. Ain't you ever taken anything that didn't belong to ya before?"

"No." I worried about her judgment.

"I knew it. You're too good for the likes of me. Ain't done a thing wrong in your life."

My desire for her to like me and to secure a friend at my new home pushed me to reveal something I'd kept a secret. "When I was eleven," I started slowly, "I spied on my brother's friend while he bathed in the river."

Her hand flew to her mouth before she dropped it and gasped with glee. "You didn't! Well, I'll be. Maybe you ain't so innocent after all. Did he catch you?"

I thought of Nisse's smooth flesh tanned by the sun. "No."

"Did you like what you saw?"

Heat rolled over my face, and I dropped my gaze.

She jabbed me with an elbow. "Out with it. Ain't no use holding back now."

"No," I said. "I-I mean…yes. Well, I never looked."

"But you just said you watched."

"I did, but when he rose, I looked away."

"And missed the best part?" Her mouth gaped. "They're coming for you."

Panic seized my chest. "Who?"

"The Sisters!" she said a little too loudly, and looked through the looking glass at the door as though expecting Mrs. Potts to come charging in and deliver the news.

I gawked at her in confusion.

She balled a hand on her ample hip. "You've escaped the convent, I'm certain of it."

Oh. I breathed a sigh of relief and expelled a nervous laugh. "I'm not from the church."

"Then why didn't you look?" Her brow puckered, then her eyes widened. "You liked this boy and were too embarrassed to look."

I lowered my eyes from her intrusive stare. That... and I wanted to respect him like I hoped one day he would me.

"That's it, isn't it," she said with a giggle.

"Yes."

CHAPTER 13

The shoes pinched my feet, and the fabric of the gown irritated my skin as I descended the spiral staircase. The merry chatter of children and the clanking of dishes drew me to a room near the front of the home, its light spilling into the hallway. From the doorway, I looked at the family seated at a table large enough to seat ten to twelve people. Servants dressed in black and white bustled around the table, adding dishes. A man Mrs. Potts had informed me was the butler stood at Lord Winslow's shoulder.

Knots formed in my gut at the thought of enduring his lordship's company, but the grumbling in my stomach pulled me into the room. Lord Winslow glanced in my direction. His tight expression relaxed and his mouth parted as he looked me over. My breath caught. The suspicion that I'd donned another of his wife's garments appeared to be true. The children were too young to remember their mutter, but had the gown stirred troubling memories for their vater?

He quickly recovered and assumed his usual distant demeanor. "Miss Wolf, it is kind of you to finally join us. I dislike being kept waiting. Please ensure you stay on schedule."

"Yes, my lord." I curtsied and crossed to the chair the butler pulled out. Mentally, I chastised Yara and myself for getting caught up in girly chatter. How had we lost track of time? Then I recalled never being given a time for when I was to join the family. Had Mrs. Potts and Yara set me up for failure from the beginning? Did they conspire with Lord Winslow?

"I hope you find your chamber suitable." Lord Winslow's voice pulled me from my fretting.

"Yes, it's lovely." I folded my hands in my lap and rolled back my shoulders, mirroring his stiff posture. I settled in for a meal that promised to be laborious.

Seated between her vater and me, Zuna looked charming and grown up in a mauve taffeta gown. She practically bounced in her seat as she eyed the food. "May we please eat, Papa?" She pulled her eyes from the dishes to address him. She appeared to be a healthy child, and I doubted she'd missed a meal in her ten years.

"Yes, child, eat," he said.

I winced at his interaction with the girl, but she paid him no mind. Permission granted, his daughters filled their plates as I sat, twisting my hands in my lap. My taste buds danced with yearning as the delectable scents made my mouth water.

"Did the afternoon in the yards not grant you an appetite?" Lord Winslow studied me.

"Yes," I said.

"Then do not dally—eat." He nodded at the food.

Without further hesitation, I forked a piece of braised pheasant and placed it on my plate before moving on to the next dish.

"You look like a real lady," Zuna said between mouthfuls.

I smiled at the endearing child. "Thank you, Lady Zuna."

"Doesn't she, Papa?" She boldly turned her attention to her vater. Silence followed her question. "Papa." Zuna grabbed his hand, resting on the table.

He jumped and quickly withdrew his hand as though her touch had scalded him. "Scrubbing away the layers of filth and a proper meal will put color in anyone's cheeks."

It would take an amiable woman with a lot of patience to put up with his lordship. I couldn't imagine life married to him would be anything but an absolute bore. I inserted my fork into the pheasant on my plate and placed the meat in my mouth, grateful to use a full mouth as an excuse not to engage with him further.

Overhead, a gas chandelier flickered and drew my attention, the beauty of the crystals glimmering off the wall and ceiling quickly mesmerizing me. It reminded me of the miniature crystal horse the Romany woman had given to Vater to ensure my silence. And it had, but it didn't stop Mutter from finding out about Vater's treacherous ways. I'd taken the trinket and crushed it with a rock until only a powdery substance remained.

Tears of guilt and shame had racked my small frame as I thought of the pain on Mutter's face when she had come upon him with a dairymaid in town. We'd gone to purchase flour and eggs to make gnocchi, her favorite dish as a child. Instilling a bit of her culture in Orell and me had been vital to her. She'd often said, "*You must always know where you come from.*" When we had returned home that day, I raced inside to my room and removed the toy concealed inside a lace handkerchief of Mutter's before fleeing to the forest to destroy Vater's and my secret.

"What is it about the chandelier that brings you such pain?" Lord Winslow asked.

"It's nothing, my lord." I forged a soft smile. "It's exquisite. We never had the luxury of pretty things."

"Tell me, Miss Wolf," he said. "If I'm to believe you're a poor farm girl, how do you come to speak like a girl from an aristocratic family?"

"My mutter was every bit the lady without a title. Her vater raised her with the luxuries your daughters have, and she too had a caregiver, and the best education Nonno's money could buy."

"Papa says our mum came from France," Farrah said. "She was lovely, people say."

"I'm sure she was. And it appears her daughters take after her," I replied, trying to find common ground with the girl.

"You're wrong." Her gaze challenged me. "I take after

our mum, but Zuna doesn't." Lord Winslow cleared his throat, and the child ceased her chatter. She moved her food around on her plate, her expression blank.

"The girls wish to visit the dressmaker to purchase some new gowns," he said. "If you're to accompany my children to social events and into town, I expect you to look presentable. You're to purchase a small wardrobe for yourself. My steward will inform you of your allotted allowance."

I couldn't recall the last time I'd had a new dress.

"I don't wish to be reminded of what I've lost," he said.

I gulped. "Pardon me?"

"You need clothing of your own. My wife's clothing will hardly do."

"I'm sorry, my lord. I didn't wish to wear the clothing, but—"

"There is no reason to explain, I'm aware of the circumstances." He raised a hand to silence me.

I pressed my lips together and lowered my head.

He raised a wine glass and took a large swig before he said, "A trip to the village should take care of everything."

CHAPTER 14

A FEW DAYS LATER, AND THE MORNING I ACCOMPANIED Yara and the children to town, the clouds had settled on the earth and crept across the grounds, shrouding the estate in a veil of white. As I stepped outside on the landing, the light mist cascading from the heavens danced on the tendrils of hair escaping the bonnet Yara had found for me in an old trunk in the attic. At the bottom of the stairs, a raven landed on the stone lion statue guarding the front entry and cocked its head before releasing a shrill caw.

Lord Winslow stepped from the hazy shadows at the foot of the steps, and the bird took flight. The pattering in my heart sped up as he stood gazing at me with an unreadable expression, only breaking his study when a black enclosed carriage circled the front drive and came to a stop at the carriage stone. The driver perched atop the private buggy wore a black silk top hat and a uniform of navy velvet trimmed with gold, matching the footman's attire.

"Let us go," Yara said as the footman jumped down and hurried to open the door. The girls bounded down the steps and greeted their vater before walking to the carriage.

He and Yara exchanged a few words I didn't catch before she quickened her step to catch up to the children. His lordship swung back to look at me. "Valentina." His tone was businesslike and cool.

"My lord." I inclined my head.

"I trust that you will manage the children with Yara's help. I would accompany you, but I have other affairs to attend to."

"As expected, my lord. No need to worry, we will manage," I said with more confidence than I felt.

"Let us hope." His intense stare revealed no signs of displeasure or satisfaction.

My eyes fastened to the lapel of his charcoal frock coat. Did a heart pump inside him, or was there only a dark cavern? I'd come to understand that, like Farrah, he thirsted for a challenge, and I was no stranger to it.

"I trust my steward gave you the funds to take care of the expenses," he said.

I held up my wrist, where Yara's drab drawstring purse dangled.

A muscle twitched near his left eye, though he made no remark. I sensed he opposed the condition of the purse. He swept his hand toward the open carriage. "Do not let me delay your journey."

He walked me to the buggy and offered a hand to

help me embark. I settled on the seat next to Zuna, who looked up at me with adoring eyes. Since my arrival at the estate, when the child wasn't busy with her studies, she'd turn up at every corner and accompany me as I carried out my chores. Her happy chatter had become endearing, but Lady Farrah appeared to resent the attention the child doted on me.

"You girls are to remember that Miss Wolf is in charge. You will obey and listen to her as you would me. Understood?"

"Yes, Papa," Zuna said with a vigorous bob of her head.

Farrah glared at her but held her tongue in her vater's presence. She fixed a smile on him. "We will be on our best behavior."

"Good." He stepped back and signaled for the footman to close the door.

The fog had lifted by the time our carriage halted outside the dressmaker's shop. All morning my nerves had hummed with building anxiety at the chance of someone recognizing me and reporting back to Orell or Helias. Yara and Farrah had watched with curiosity as I repeatedly leaned forward and pulled back the curtain to look outside before settling back in my seat.

When we entered the shop, I breathed a sigh of relief to find it empty except for a clerk stationed behind the counter. He glanced up and offered us a greeting before going back to tallying his ledgers.

A middle-aged woman with skin that the sun had

seldom touched entered the shop from a back room. Though her arms overflowed with bolts of various fabrics, she walked confidently toward us. "Good day," she said. "What can I help you with?" She placed the bolts of fabric on the counter.

"We require some new dresses for the children," I said.

"And for Miss Wolf." Yara looked the woman straight in the eye. Her years in the slums had given her spunk and a confidence I envied.

"Certainly. I am Fräulein Schmidt. And who may you lovely ladies be?" She clasped her hands and fixed a radiant smile on the children.

"We hail from the house of Lord Winslow." Farrah arched back her small shoulders. Yara grabbed the child's arm to silence her, but she pulled herself free.

"Lord Winslow? I wasn't aware he had returned." The woman's brow wrinkled as she glanced from Yara to me.

"Well, we—" I said.

"We just arrived," Yara interjected. I glanced at her as the fib rolled effortlessly from her tongue. It had been days since I'd arrived at the chateau, and weeks since I'd seen a convoy of carriages turning down the lane to the estate. Had she lost track of time?

"And where are you staying?"

"You ask a lot of questions, fräulein." Farrah narrowed her eyes at the woman as she untied the ribbons of her bonnet and removed it.

"Why, I..." Taken aback by the child's frankness,

Fräulein Schmidt pressed her hand against the hollow of her ivory throat. "My apologies."

"No, it is we who ask your forgiveness," I said before addressing Farrah. "Please mind your manners." I cringed when she mumbled an unapologetic apology, and I bestowed on the woman a winning smile. "What Lady Farrah means to say is that his lordship was informed of the quality of work you offer your clients and ordered that your shop be our first stop of the day."

Though my intention to charm the dressmaker had been flawlessly executed, I sensed from her dead silence that she wasn't easily wooed. Yara gave me a weighted stare, and I shrugged. I had to try.

When Fräulein Schmidt spoke, it was as if nothing had happened. "I'd be happy to assist you in any way I can." She stepped aside and gestured at the seemingly endless stands of fabric.

I moved to stroke a bolt of yellow silk on a table next to me. She followed behind me. "This one arrived yesterday. One of our finest families was in here just yesterday and purchased this fabric for a gown for their daughter. With Lady Farrah's hair color, it would look stunning."

I roamed through the aisles and stopped at some tightly woven brown wool. "I think this would do."

"Are you daft?" Farrah said from behind me. "We aren't servants, and we aren't about to blend in with them. I knew he was wrong in hiring you. Why, you're about as dull as the last governess."

"Farrah." Zuna pulled on her sister's sleeve.

"Lady Farrah," Yara said, "please allow Miss Wolf to speak."

"I will not." She stomped her foot. "She doesn't have a lick of sense. What drab fabric will you pick next?"

"Maybe it wouldn't be too awful," Zuna said, trying to defuse the situation.

Farrah turned her sass on her sister. "I won't be caught wearing either." She marched to a bolt of light green muslin. "This is the color that looks best on me. It brings out my eyes. I will have a gown made of this." She removed her glove and stroked the material between two fingers.

The dressmaker's mouth had unhinged, and she looked from me to the child. I gave her a nod, and she went to assist the impossible girl.

"You mustn't let the child speak for you in such a manner," Yara said in my ear.

"What am I to do? She has a mind of her own."

"You must remind her you're the governess, and she's the child." Annoyance at the child flickered in her eyes.

"Very well," I said before stepping in to rein in Farrah's control of the shop.

The next hour passed without further episodes from the child, and after fittings for new frocks, petticoats, and other undergarments were taken, we left the shop.

"On to the hatter's." Zuna skipped up beside me and slipped her hand in mine. We strolled the boardwalk and paused in front of the window displays of bonnets varying from simple to extravagant, embellished with feathers, ribbons, and silk flowers.

A familiar voice pulled my attention to a peddler's cart down the way. *Flicker!* My heart leaped with happiness. "Yara, can you take Lady Farrah and Lady Zuna inside? I've forgotten something at the dressmaker's shop. I'll be quick."

Yara tilted her head and studied me, but said, "Come, let us go inside." She placed her hands on the girls' shoulders and turned to open the door of the hatter's shop.

I hurried down the boardwalk. Footsteps echoed behind me, and before I knew what was happening, a hand covered my mouth while another circled my waist and pulled me into the shadows between the cathedral and the post office. My screams for Flicker were muffled by the gloved hand, and I struggled to get free. I dug my heels into the ground, trying to find leverage against my attacker.

"Valentina! It's me, Nisse."

Nisse?

"Promise me you will stay calm, and I'll let you go." His breath was warm against my ear. I bobbed my head. He released his hold and guided me deeper into the alley and out of view of passersby.

"What's wrong with you?" I beat my fist on his chest. "You frightened me. I thought you were Orell or one of his friends." I adjusted Lady Winslow's bonnet, which now sat lopsided on my head.

"You're safe." His hands held my shoulders as he inspected me as he had the day I fell out of the tree while spying on him and Orell. "The demon didn't take you."

He planted a kiss on my forehead and crushed me to his chest. His heart thundered against my ear.

"No, I left of my own free will," I said into his chest. I breathed in the familiar scent of leather and pine.

He held me at arm's length. "Orell's friends came into town some weeks back. They were naked and wrapped in blankets and furs, claiming the beast had made off with you and your brother. They said it invaded your home and ravaged the place, leaving them stripped of clothing. After tying them to the cottage rafters, it left them to the mercy of winter. Helias said the creature took the livestock."

Beast? If such a creature existed, I doubted it would leave them without clothes and alive. "Orell? He wasn't with them?" I asked.

"No."

"In their drunken state, perhaps hallucinations took over their minds," I said.

Nisse shook his head. "No, it scared them. You could see it in their eyes."

The thought of Helias and the others shivering naked and humiliated before the villagers brought a smile to my lips, and I didn't feel a lick sorry for it. They deserved that and much more.

"Here I am in the flesh." I thrust my hands at the heavens. "No beast carried me off. I left of my own accord. But you mustn't tell Orell, because I'm not going back. I assure you my brother is fine, and it is a story he and his friends concocted to explain my disappearance."

"It seems like something the coward would do," he said. "But why, after all this time, did you leave?"

I tilted my face so he could see the fading yellow bruise marking my cheekbone.

He gripped my chin in his hand and lifted my face. "He did this to you?"

"Yes." I pulled my chin away.

His jaw set. "I'll beat the bastard myself! He'd better not show his face around here."

"Orell agreed to marry me off to Helias for a price. Auctioned me off like one would a heifer. He will not give me in marriage to any man. When I marry, it will be to a man of my choosing. So, after they passed out from drink, I took what remained of the livestock and left. Don't trouble yourself with defending my honor with my brother. I'm free of him now. I took a position as a servant and caregiver in Lord Winslow's household."

His brow puckered. "Winslow? He's been gone for years."

"He has returned," I said.

"And is living where?"

"Where do you suppose?" I rested a hand on my hip. "At his estate, of course."

"But the place isn't livable. No one has lived there for years."

"Well, I assure you he and his daughters have returned. He's having the home repaired."

"A home of that magnitude would take years to repair," he said.

"Perhaps not with a staff the size of his," I said. "He has offered me room and board with a small salary, and that is more security than I've ever had."

"It's better you're safe than at the mercy of your brother," he said. "I need to get back to the shop and help Vater."

We returned to the boardwalk, and he turned to me and took my hand and held it in his. "Try to stay out of trouble, as it does have a way of finding you." He winked.

"There may be some truth in that." A warmth settled in my belly as I smiled up at him.

He squeezed my hand and returned my smile before stepping past me and taking off at a jog.

I stood rooted to the boardwalk, staring after him until Flicker said behind me, "Still daydreaming, are ya?"

I swung to face him. "Hush."

"Well, I can see you didn't become a meal, as everyone has been saying."

"Shh." I grabbed the shoulder of his tattered brown coat and pulled him back into the shadows. "No, I haven't, but it appears you weren't the least bit worried. And to think I call you a friend." I feigned a pout.

He lifted a hand to push his far too large hat back from his eyes. His face split with a lopsided grin. "I guessed you probably outwitted that clod. You're the one with the wits."

"Is that so? Well, I'll take that as you saying something nice to me for a change."

He looped his fingers in his vest and rocked back on

his heels. "I get my share of listening to women's ramblings at home. Makes a man wish his hearing weren't so good." He bounced on his toes, finding much joy in his musings.

"You're impossible," I said with a roll of my eyes. "I must get back before I'm missed. I wanted to let you know that I'm safe, and you needn't worry about me."

"I was already aware," he said.

"But I just told you."

His teeth flashed. "Ya did, but I got my sources."

"Is that so?" I folded my arms across my chest. "Would it be too much to assume your informers may be the earthmen I see from time to time?"

He shrugged. "One does not reveal one's sources." He wiggled his thick chestnut brows in the way he often did to cheer me up.

I laughed and informed him of my new position, which he also appeared to know about. Although confused by his desire to keep watch over me, I appreciated the depth of his love. "Have these sources seen my brother?"

"Not a trace of him; but don't worry, I put out the word—if any earthmen see or hear of him, they're to report back to me immediately."

I felt a surge of love and admiration as I looked down at him. "Thank you."

"For what?"

"For always being there," I said.

He waved a hand in dismissal. "It ain't nothing you wouldn't do."

I embraced him, and he squirmed. I smiled to myself, knowing how he detested signs of affection.

After we said our goodbyes, I raced back to the hatter's shop.

Yara glanced at me when I entered, breathless and flushed. "Did you find what you left?" she asked when I came to stand beside her.

I held up the receipt I'd tucked into my purse before leaving the dressmaker's shop. "Indeed."

Her brow furrowed, and I avoided meeting her gaze. She had caught me in my lie. Instead of outing me, she carried on as before. I suspected I'd receive a knock on my chamber door after the rest of the house slept.

CHAPTER 15

In the Alps—The Thief

THE OUTSIDER STOOD AT THE MOUTH OF THE cave and nervously looked back over the sleepy village nestled below. Humans had forged a treaty with the dwarves, agreeing not to enter the mountains uninvited, but the voice had summoned him. The man had awakened as the sun cracked through the canopy of spruces. He lay naked and shivering in a nest of boughs with no recollection of how he'd gotten there.

The new voice suppressed the usual inhabitant's ramblings and sequestered itself deep inside the man's mind. Most of his life, he had smothered the daunting voice saturating his head with confusion, but in recent years it had become more insistent, and he believed it responsible for missing clips of time. The inhabitant fought to seize command of his body, mind, and soul, and the knowledge disquieted the man.

A lammergeier landed on a crag and displayed its cinnamon chest while eyeing him. The man turned and walked into the cave, pulling the coat he'd taken off the traveling peddler's body tighter around himself. He swung around at movement behind him, and the picturesque view of the village and snow-covered mountains vanished. He swallowed the nerves gripping his throat.

"I am here." His voice reverberated in the dank darkness of the cavern. He heard the scratch of a claw on stone, and a floating orb of fire lit up the narrow passage.

Do not delay. Follow the light until it goes out. Hot breath tickled his ear, and he whipped around to locate the owner of the voice but found no one. His insides quivered.

The flame shepherded him along the tunnel and farther underground. In the distance water trickled, and the humidity pasted the shirt to his chest. When the fire ceased its movement the man halted, and his heart lurched into his throat. Below, the floor gave way to a raging underground river. He teetered on the edge, and his arms flailed as he tried to regain his balance.

You never know when your road will end, a sinister laugh came.

"You could have warned me," the man said with a grumble.

Silence, you imp.

The man clawed at the invisible hands cutting off his breathing. Veins in his temples bulged, and he felt himself fading. And then his breath returned as the fingers relaxed. Wheezing, he bent and rested his hands on his knees, trying to catch his breath. The harrowing demonstration of the newcomer's abilities made his heart pound in his chest.

"What is it you want from me?"

So many questions, human, it said. Move.

A force pushed him forward, and he stumbled before catching himself. He'd become clay in the newcomer's hands.

Ahead of him, the rattling of chains and the crack of a whip cut the air, and the guiding flame flickered and swept from side to side, providing a view of where the ground fell away. Below, wall torches lit the pit that vibrated with movement. Shackled humans and dwarves struck the stone with pickaxes. They pushed wheelbarrows piled high with gleaming gems, enough to satisfy the greed of any man, into oversized carts hitched to oxen and driven by dwarves. The dwarf masters barked orders and slashed their whips on the bare backs of slaves.

"What is this?" the man asked.

Prisoners of war. Does it offend you?

"No."

For decades, we've built our kingdoms on the backs of humans and dwarves alike. If you don't do as I command, I will see you're imprisoned here for the rest of your days.

The man gulped.

Now, move. Keep to the wall, or you will surely meet your death this day.

A blow to the back of his head sent him staggering forward, and he gripped the wall to keep from plummeting to his death below.

He trailed fingers along the damp wall until he arrived at a ledge only a handbreadth wide. He gripped the stones that projected from the wall here and there, his breathing rapid and sweat beading his forehead. He lost his footing on loose pebbles and he grasped at a rock, trying to catch himself. His fingers found a secure anchor and he regained his feet. Heart thrashing against his ribcage, he closed his eyes and sighed in relief before gathering himself and sidling onward. He reached the other side without further mishap, and descended the stairs leading into the pit. As he reached the bottom, the flame flickered and went out.

The man hid in the shadows, observing the slaves. Anxiety pinned his feet to the bedrock. What did the newcomer want with him? A cart of gems rolled past, and he stepped out to grab one. He held the jewel in his hand and a warmth washed over him. Its radiance pulsed the blood through his veins faster and faster. He licked his lips and regarded his reflection in the gem. The mines held the means for a better life. He could become lord of a castle in the heart of Europe, with servants to wait on him and maidens to warm his bed. The thrill of such a life thundered in his chest.

A whip snapped, and the wind of its passage breezed by his face. He jumped and dropped the gem and it clunked at his feet before fading into the shadows.

Do you think you can steal from me? It will be the last thought you will have, the voice boomed in his head, and he covered his ears to quiet the shrill echo. Move, or I will slit your throat where you stand.

The man stepped into the midst of the toiling slaves. Clothed only in rags, their bodies greased with grime and sweat, the men and women moved mechanically, their gaunt faces devoid of emotion. An older man with a hunched back and straggly blond hair straightened and walked toward him. *Vater?* Tears congregated in his throat. *No.* He searched the man's face as he drew nearer. *Vater!*

He grasped the man's arm as he passed, and it felt frail under his grip. "Vater, it is me." The man looked at him with blank eyes, no recognition reflected in his gaze. "Vater, it's Orell." He gestured at himself.

"Move along," a voice said. A whip split the air and tore the flesh of his vater's back, scarred with years under the lash.

Orell caught him before he hit the ground, and a soft whimper escaped his vater's lips. *How did he get here?*

"Get up," a dwarf master said. "You!" The whip came again, and Orell screamed as the blow found his back.

Orell helped his vater to his feet, then whirled on the dwarf who stood on the driver's seat of the cart. He clutched the earthman's throat in his hand and squeezed. Tighter and tighter. "I'll kill you for this."

The dwarf's face reddened as he struggled for breath. He scratched and slapped at Orell's hand, but it was the earthman's glazed yellow eyes that gave him pause. The dwarf looked through him, as if a spirit didn't exist in his body. He was as much an empty puppet as the slaves.

Enough, the voice roared.

Orell released the earthman, and he landed on the ground in a heap. A jarring pain shot through Orell's head, and he clasped it with both hands as his knees buckled.

How dare you come into my kingdom and attack my men.

"Stop. Make it stop! I will do as you say," he cried.

The chiseling in his head stopped, and he stood and cast a glance at his vater, lying on the ground, a heap of bones and flesh. He bit down hard and turned and strode out of the pits. Silent tears streamed down his face. Hate erupted in his chest for the darkness that had summoned him, but like a moth drawn to fire he trudged on, smothering the sob wavering in his chest. *I will come back*, he promised.

Soon you won't care if he lives or dies, the voice said.

Never!

The underground river came into view and grew still as he reached it. Burning golden blocks floated upon it, paving a way to the other side. A woman with waist-length, silver-white tresses who wore a swirling gown of blue flashed, then faded, before reappearing, as though she were a spirit that haunted the caves. She held a scroll that glowed like the sun had set upon the Earth. The intensity in her violet eyes spoke a warning. "You must not give in to him. He will use you for his purposes and leave you a corpse."

The emaciated face of his vater seized his mind, and Orell ignored her warning and crossed to the other side. "Go away," he said.

She strode—or floated, he couldn't tell—to stand in front of him. "No, you must listen. All of creation is in danger. King Gian uses black magic to make his tribesmen masters over your kind." Her skin shimmered like the glistening of a first snowfall. Intrigued by the ethereal being, he hesitated.

She summoned him with crystalline fingers. "Come, let me show you something."

As though in a trance, he followed. The wraith stopped when she came to a cavity in the wall and moved back. "See for yourself."

A chamber expanded before him, and he shrank back. The tower of human and dwarf corpses rose as far as the eye could see.

"All his failed subjects. You will be next if you don't heed my words," she said.

Do you want the life I've promised you? A life where you want no more, where hunger doesn't tear at your belly and cold doesn't chew through your bones? The voice battled for its position in Orell's head.

The celestial and the summoner appeared unaware of the other's existence.

She stepped forward and touched his arm. He sprang back at her touch, which ran cold, then hot. "Please, heed my warning." As sudden as the celestial appeared, she vanished.

The guiding flame glided down a serpentine tunnel that ended at a lava moat surrounding a small island. In the center stood a hooded figure cloaked in dark furs, flanked by two towering lava sentinels with hollow black eyes and gnarled staves.

"You've made it, Seelenfresser," the voice said. "Come closer, so I may look upon you."

Seelenfresser? Curiosity pushed his feet forward until he stood before the cloaked figure. The heat radiating from the guards made his flesh tingle like the flair of a sunburn. The hooded being kept his head lowered.

"Who are you, and where is the treasure you promised?" Orell asked.

"Shouldn't you be asking what it is I want from you, Seelenfresser?"

"I know not who you speak of, but I am Orell Fürst, son of Timo Fürst. A man that went missing ten years ago."

"I recall this man."

"You should, you have him imprisoned in your mines." Orell took a step forward, his hands clenched at his sides. The lava sentinels flared and forced him back.

An eerie chuckle crackled from the confines of the hood. "And he's lucky of that. We found him trying to steal from us, and as a punishment I condemned him to a life sentence in the mines."

"And what of his wife? You want me to believe a woman that healed the sick and cared for the poor while singing of virtue until her children's ears bled was also a thief?"

Silence fell. After moments passed, the cloaked figure spoke again. "Yes, there was a woman around the time we captured the man, but she was already dead. Gutted by her own husband."

Orell envisioned his mutter's blood painting the mountain's earth. "Nothing less than she deserved. She was a nit that needed squashing."

"One who hates his own mutter so is a man without a soul." The cloaked figured sucked back a sharp breath of pleasure. "I've been watching you, wondering if you would be the one to help me. The seed of darkness that inhabits you is the final element in the unification of the Zwilling and Vormacht."

"Seelenfresser. Zwilling. Vormacht. What the hell are you referring to?"

"We believe you hold an element of the Zwilling power."

"Me?" Orell pointed a finger at himself, then threw back his head and laughed.

A throaty rumble came from the cloaked figure. "What is so funny?"

"If I had any power, I'd have figured it out by now. Don't ya think?"

"Not if you were unaware it existed, or mistook it for something else."

"All right, say I appease you and I am this Seelenfresser. What power am I supposed to possess?" He was desperate for a turn of luck. Valentina had run off, or had become prey to creatures of the forest, and the small fortune he would have received from Helias had gone with her. If he found her alive, he'd break her delicate neck himself.

"If I am correct, you are the darkness. The devourer of souls." The cloaked figure lowered his hood.

Orell narrowed his eyes before breaking into laughter. "You're a dwarf! And a blind one at that." He turned away and kicked at the flagstone with the tip of his boot. "You had me there for a moment. Almost had me believing your blabbering." He wiped a hand over his face and cursed himself for the flicker of hope that had buoyed in him. The dwarf had taken advantage of his shake of lousy luck and his desperation.

"One does not need eyes when they have magic to show the way," the dwarf hissed. Scars ran from the earthman's nose to his ears and blue-haloed irises shone through his milky corneas. Ropes of black hair moved like live roots creeping over the forest floor. "My enemies thought they would weaken me by poking out my eyes. And they did for a while, until I found black magic in the Totholz forest, in the land where men roam the earth as beasts and the beasts become men."

"What black magic?"

"The magic to raise the Vormacht. The supreme power."

Orell frowned and shook his head in confusion. "Your dwarf voodoo has no meaning to me. What do you want with me?" he snapped.

"Humans act with their hearts, and that makes them

susceptible. That weakness of the mortals will always be their downfall. Tell me, Seelenfresser, do you wish to roll in the muck with pigs, or do you desire to sit amongst gods?"

The dwarf's words stoked Orell's hunger for power. He thought back to the day in his boyhood when the desire for control first consumed him. He'd been chasing after his ball, which stopped at the base of the ancient pine that overshadowed his family's cottage. On the ground, a Pine Grosbeak chick that had not yet found its wings lay keening for its mutter. He had picked up the bird and the vulnerability in its small body sent a rush of adrenaline pumping through his veins. He recalled the warmth and drumming in his chest. He had squeezed gently at first and then tighter, and with the crunching of bones waves of ecstasy overtook him.

"You possess darkness, unlike the others. Darkness not yet fashioned. I can teach you all that you need to know to become more powerful than you could ever imagine."

"How?" Ignoring the heat of the sentinels, Orell leaned forward.

"By giving in to the voice inside you. You must set aside your wish to control it and allow it to step into the light. Never again will you be vulnerable to your human flesh. You will not bleed or fall to human diseases. All the wealth and women you desire can be yours."

A thrill rushed through Orell, and desire burned in his gut. "Why would you help me? What do you seek to gain?"

"To rid the world of humans. Together we can cleanse the Earth of them once and for all," the dwarf said.

"And why would I need you?"

"Because you're still human. You carry the Zwilling power, but it's a seed that needs cultivating. Humans have no records or knowledge of the power. It hasn't been seen in hundreds of years. The Zwilling was only granted to my ancestors. Left in the body of a human, it can never fully flourish without the training and magic of dwarves."

"You say I have this ability, but how do you know?" Orell said.

"Watching from the forest, I saw it take form when you tried to drown your own sister. And, recently, why you woke up in the alley next to the dead streetwalker, covered in her blood. And the travelers along the road."

The dwarf perceived too much. "I don't recall killing them, only the aftermath."

"Because your humanity blocks out your acts of brutality, while another part of your mind knows you should feed off the ones that won't be missed."

"Feed?" He gulped in disgust.

"You have much to learn. Your stamina needs nurturing, and only when the seed is watered with the blood of the innocent will it sprout and the dark magic of the Zwilling will come into its true form. Do you wish to know how?"

Orell nodded.

The earthman straightened and held out his arms. "Then follow me. You have much to learn."

CHAPTER 16

Kingdom of Himmelart

PRINCE SIXTUS AND GENERAL CRISPIAN WOVE their mounts through the crowd of hawkers and peasants in the central square as they rode toward the palace gates, responding to the king's summons. Harlots leaned in the entrances of cathouses and over balconies, waving colorful handkerchiefs and calling out invitations. Beggars, young and old, sat on stoops and lounged on corners while pickpockets floated in the shadows.

As they rode past a merchant's cart, the prince drew his sword and neatly skewered an apple from the display before tossing a coin toward the merchant. The woman grinned and caught the spinning coin. "It's good to see you, Your Highness," she said.

He nodded before sinking his teeth into the apple,

and its sweet juices ran over his tongue. "Home at last," he said to the general around the mouthful, nodding toward the gates up ahead. "We've ridden through those gates together many times, but after that insufferable length of time spent in the village it somehow feels sweeter today."

General Crispian sat with a hand resting on his thigh and his shoulders back, his ginger mane gleaming against brass armor. "Need I remind you that we are here on business at the king's command and not for your delight in the palace wenches?"

Sixtus glowered down at Crispian, who was shorter by a foot or so, but broader. *"It's the human blood in your veins that gives you the advantage,"* Crispian had jeered when they were boys, knowing that part of Sixtus's origins irritated him when, at first, the prince had used his height to defeat Crispian in fencing duels. Not to be outwitted, Crispian had trained in secret until he became a champion at the sport and exceeded the prince's abilities. "If our friendship hadn't started in boyhood, I might not let you get away with such forwardness," he warned.

Sixtus looked over the crowd of peasants and tribesmen, and a sense of kinship swelled in his chest. The weeks in human territory had been dreary and the brotherhood he'd once felt between Crispian and himself had become strained by the general's ever-evolving annoyance at him. If he were to trek into an unknown region he would have none but Crispian at his side, regardless of his newly claimed sour disposition and loss of rank and title.

Ahead, the daughter of the blacksmith stepped out

from under the thatched roof of the open-air forge and raised a hand in greeting. Sixtus smiled, recalling the scar that ran the length of her inner thigh. The horses clip-clopped past the baker's shop and the baker's twin daughters, Anouk and Anaïs, reached out to him. A low rumble rose in his chest as he recalled how their hips had moved with unbridled passion against him as they fornicated amongst the sacks of flour in the shop's storage room. He inclined his head and rode on. Yes, it was indeed good to be home. Even if it was only for a few hours.

Crispian grunted with disgust. "Your unruly ways will one day catch up with you."

"What horse shit do you spew?" the prince retorted. "Does the boredom of having a wife fill you with jealousy?"

"When your manhood shrivels with disease, you will wish you had taken a wife. The time has come for you to think of producing an heir to succeed your vater and you."

"I've told you, a wife and running a kingdom aren't for me. I yearn for freedom," Sixtus said.

"A selfish desire that can never be yours. Your people need you to step into your rightful place as the successor to your vater."

"In due time. For the time being, I will enjoy these years before I too become a political bore like my vater."

"You're looking at your duty all the wrong way. And to think he put you in charge of the mission."

"A mission I wanted nothing to do with, if you recall."

"I do. But what I don't understand is why you made me endure your anger at your vater."

The prince laughed and reined in his horse before the golden stairs rising to the palace. He dismounted and handed the reins to an equerry.

Crispian dropped to the ground with a thud and focused again on the prince. "The camaraderie between us should not enter into this situation. We have a duty and having me in my best form at your side is crucial."

"But don't you see, my friend?" Sixtus placed a hand on Crispian's shoulder. "You are." He erupted with laughter and turned and mounted the stairs.

A chain of curses from the general followed behind him. "I will pay you back for this," he said.

"I look forward to it," Sixtus threw over his shoulder.

Inside, the pair marched through the corridors, their armor clanging as they followed the king's steward to the inner domed courtyards. The king, cloaked in an ankle-length cream robe, sat on a stone bench in the center of the lush gardens, reciting passages from a scroll.

"Your Highness," the steward announced. "Prince Sixtus and General Crispian are here."

"Thank you, Lio." The king lifted a jeweled hand and silently dismissed the servant, who bowed and backed away.

Sixtus and Crispian bowed. "Your Highness," they said.

King Jörg set the scroll on the bench beside him and extended a hand to his son. "Do you bring news of the girl?"

Sixtus kissed the hand his vater offered him. "We do."

"Then don't hesitate, tell me what has transpired," the king said.

"As hoped, she's employed at the estate and seems to be determined to stay."

Worry lines creased the king's forehead. "Any sign of the brother?"

"No, Your Majesty. When we arrived at the homestead he was gone, and only his friends remained." *With a heap of clothing at their feet, unfortunate bastards.* Sixtus stifled a grin. He and Crispian had watched from the forest as the men exited the cottage cloaked in furs and blankets and started their journey to town.

The king glowered at his son and lifted two thick fingers to rub his temples. "I sent you to do a job, not to play your games. Those men could have died of hypothermia. Need I remind you that we don't wish to harm the humans?"

"The men deserve what they got." Sixtus rested his hands on his hips.

"Says who?" The king's face turned a deep violet shade. "Do you decide now? Do you forget who is king?"

Sixtus dropped his hands. "I meant no disrespect, Vater. I may be all the things you say, but I don't abide a man mistreating a woman."

"Since when? Do you not play with women's emotions then discard them to move on to the next pretty face?"

Sixtus's protest caught in his throat. He had never considered it in that light. Or maybe he had, but had whisked such considerations aside.

"They roughed the girl up, Your Grace," Crispian said. "And then the brother offered his sister up like a golden goose on a platter to that bungler Helias."

The king regarded the general with a look akin to respect.

"You should be thankful we took care of them." Sixtus's arrogance returned.

King Jörg grunted and rose from the bench to walk the gardens. Sixtus and Crispian fell into step behind him. "Maybe I should have sent a man to do the job instead of a boy." He stopped and eyed the general. "I expected more from you. You may be my son's friend, but you're also a general in my army. A position you shouldn't take lightly."

"Yes, Your Highness." Crispian placed a fist to his heart and inclined his head. "It won't happen again."

"Let's hope not." He turned and continued on. "Sixtus, you must conduct yourself as a prince would and use the wisdom I believe you possess in that numb skull of yours."

Sixtus had grown tired of his vater's whining. "You asked us to watch the girl and to see she found the advertisement, and we have done that."

"I don't have the time or patience to quarrel with you over how I should run my kingdom. Besides, more urgent concerns have arisen." The king ran a hand over a flower that was limp and dying, and it sprang to life as though recently bloomed.

"What is it?" Sixtus asked.

"Tribesmen bring news of unexplainable deaths

happening throughout the kingdoms. Yesterday they found a shepherd boy and his flock, all gutted," the king said.

Sixtus drew himself up and looked solemnly from the king to Crispian.

"Now I have your attention." Displeasure darkened the king's face.

"Crispian and I will aid your men in their search for the culprit." Sixtus clutched the hilt of his sword.

The king whirled around. "You will do no such thing. You're to watch the girl. It is your one and only order." His demand echoed off the dome ceiling.

In the past, Sixtus had pushed his vater to the point of threatening to lock him in the dungeons until he learned his station. But never before had he seen concern etched so profoundly in his vater's eyes. He gave the king his full attention. "Why is she so important to you?"

"Animals that have roamed our lands for hundreds of years are now gone. There are only carcasses with dead-end blood trails—these are reasons to believe the Seelenfresser has awakened. Until we understand what part she plays in this, we need to keep her out of her brother's grasp. Animal blood no longer satisfies the incubus. I worry that it is evolving and now thirsts for the lifeblood of our tribesmen and village folk."

"We will return home," the prince said. "We must protect our people from this creature."

The king shook his head and clapped a hand on his son's shoulder. "Where is this man of honor when I need him? A man willing to defend his people against all the odds." Sadness tinged his voice. "Now, son, I need to count on you more than ever. Watch the girl and don't let her out of your sight."

Their footsteps echoed down the corridors as Sixtus and Crispian took their leave of the palace.

"I'm a warrior and the Prince of Himmelart, yet he has given me the lowly task of watching the girl," Sixtus grumbled.

Crispian gave him a sideways glance. "There must be a reason he has chosen to do so. His majesty is a wise and good king."

"He's weak. His perpetual litany about the virtue of humans and that we should all live in harmony is foolish. Humans' avarice and lust for power will be a hindrance to us all."

"What do you think is at play here?" Crispian said as they descended the palace stairs.

Pulling on black elbow-length riding gloves, Sixtus registered troubled eyes on his friend. "I'm not sure. We will do as ordered for now, but we need to be on the lookout."

Crispian nodded in agreement. "The king said he will send word to King Gian and arrange a meeting."

"And we will accompany him." The prince clasped his friend's shoulder. "See your family. Then meet me at the palace stables in two hours."

CHAPTER 17

Valentina

My duties at Chateau Winslow kept me busy until late in the evening, and my life before coming to the estate felt like a lifetime ago. My frame started to fill out with two square meals a day, my cheekbones didn't look so gaunt, the dark circles under my eyes faded, and my cheeks had a rosy glow.

"What a lovely creature you are." Her arms full of linens, Mrs. Potts stopped in the doorway of my chamber one evening as I stood in front of the looking glass. She looked at me strangely, as if pondering something. "A temptation for sure," she said, then continued down the corridor.

Lady Zuna became a ray of sunshine in my days, while her sister proved to be anything but. Each day she set out to defy me, and each day became a battle. At night

I'd return to my chamber defeated and flabbergasted, wondering why the child was so miserable.

"There, there, lass, don't let the child defeat you," Mrs. Potts said one day as I burst into the kitchen and plopped down on a chair at the table. As the tears started, she shooed everyone out.

"It's hopeless. The child hates me." I buried my face in my hands and allowed myself a pity cry.

Mrs. Potts stood quietly until my tears subsided and I dropped my hands and looked at her, pleading. "I try to be attentive and kind, but she continues to fight me at every turn."

"Did she do that to you?" She pointed at the wet stain on my blouse.

My shoulders slumped.

"Don't lose heart. That one has been going around here with a puss face since we arrived."

"She must have been a dreadful baby," I said, my foot tapping the floor with building agitation.

She replied with a low chuckle. "No, she was a delightful baby, to my recollection. It seems her da and she have come down with a case of melancholy since our arrival. Give it time; it will pass. Now you dry those tears and go back out there and rein the lass in." She nudged her head at the doorway.

There was nothing I wanted to do less. I wanted to bolt out the back door and escape into the sanctuary of the forest. The birds' melodies and the whispers of the woods had often soothed the despondency that had always followed me. But I stood, blotted my tears, and wiped my hands on the fabric of my skirt. I breathed determination into my broken spirit and strode from the room.

"Got spunk, that one." Mrs. Potts's mutter drifted after me.

I returned to the music room where I'd left the children after Farrah had thrown her morning tea at me.

"You've returned for more?" She focused her gaze on me as I walked into the room.

Although my insides shook, I looked her directly in the eye with more courage than I felt and said calmly, "I may be employed by your vater, but you will not treat me as though I am deserving of such ill-treatment."

"I shall do as I wish," she said curtly with a tilt of her chin.

"Then I will speak to your vater about you staying behind when Zuna and I explore what adventures the forest holds."

Leaning forward in her chair, she wrinkled her nose. Her eyes glinted. "And I will tell him you pinch me when no one's looking!"

"You will do no such thing." My knees trembled under my skirt, but I stood unwavering.

"And I will tell Papa that you lie." Zuna pushed back her chair.

"You will not." Dismay flickered in Farrah's eyes at her sister's willingness to go against her.

"W-will too," Zuna stammered.

"You always were a little snitch." Farrah leaped to her feet and grabbed for her sister's plait. The child screamed, and Farrah tackled her. They hit the floor hard.

"Get off me!" Zuna pounded her with her fists.

I grabbed Farrah around the waist and pulled her off the girl, then held her tight as she unleashed a tantrum. She reached for my hair, but I blocked her with my arm. She tried to kick me in the shin with her heels, but I avoided her again. In my struggle to keep ahold of her, I dropped to the floor and sat with my legs and hands pinning the child down.

"What has gotten into you? Calm down. There is no need for all this fussing," I said, my breathing heavy from exertion.

Her eyes flashed with anger, her mouth gaped, and white teeth flashed as she snapped for my cheek. I craned my neck to avoid her bite, but she freed one of her hands and clawed my cheek. My face burned as her fingernails peeled back layers of skin. I trapped her flailing arm with mine. Was the child possessed?

"Breathe, Lady Farrah. When you calm down, I will release you."

"No!" she screamed.

Had I done the right thing by restraining the child? I was unsure, but to release her now would be like releasing a wild animal. "You mustn't work yourself up so."

Insubordination shone in her eyes. Sucking in a deep breath, she held it until the muscles on the sides of her temples pulsed and her face turned purple. Fear coursed through me, and I let go. She released her breath and scrambled to her feet, and I quickly followed.

"You stay away from me," she said with a deadly glare. "I will tell Papa what you've done, and you will be gone before nightfall."

"What is the meaning of this?" Lord Winslow's voice thundered, making us all jump. We stood facing him. No one spoke. Zuna hurried to my side and cuddled into the curve of my hip. I put an arm around the child to ease her trembling, and she whimpered.

"She tried to kill me." Farrah rushed to his side.

His mouth sagged open as he looked from her to me to Zuna. Then he demanded, "Miss Wolf, I expect an answer."

I fought to still my quivering lips. Summoning what courage I had left, I met his gaze. "Very well, I will tell you. Lady Farrah believes that, if she tests me long enough, I will leave. But she doesn't realize that I'm not going anywhere." I squared my shoulders with all the confidence I could muster, but they slumped just as fast as I added, "Unless, of course, you relieve me of my duties. What I mean to say is, nothing she does will see me leave this house of my own accord."

A gleam of reverence, as minuscule as it was, flashed in his eyes before he straightened. "What caused this uproar?"

"Farrah threw her tea on Miss Wolf for no reason at all. Then she pulled my hair and knocked me to the ground." Zuna crept forward. "Miss Wolf tried to stop her."

"Did she do that also?" He jutted his chin at me.

I lifted my fingers to touch the dampness trickling down my face and held them out to see the crimson stain. I remained silent.

He turned and gripped the child by the shoulder. "You will go find the stable master and ask him what task he has for a child that doesn't know how to respect those in charge of her well-being."

"But—"

"Not another word," he said sharply. "Now go, before I change my mind and forbid you your afternoon rides and strolls in the gardens."

"Yes, Papa." She hung her head, and with hunched shoulders, she left the room.

He turned back to Zuna. "You go find Mrs. Potts and tell her I wish to see her in my study."

The girl hurried from the room without a word.

He watched her go before walking to stand in front of me. He lifted my chin and grimaced as he peered at my cheek. "Nothing that won't heal." He freed my chin. "You did well, controlling the child. Maybe there is some spirit in you."

More than you know, I said to myself.

"I think it will serve you well to find other tasks for the rest of the day."

"Yes, my lord." I curtsied.

He left, and I stood wondering if I'd received my first nod of approval from his lordship. The thought gave me hope.

CHAPTER 18

Some weeks after the incident, Mrs. Potts was helping me change the linens on the children's beds.

"That lass has always been too bold for her own good. A lot like her da, one may say." She tossed the pillows on the floor. "You're learning not to back down from the child. This is your best plan of action. A firmer hand with his lordship would've done him some good when he was a lad."

"You know stories of him as a boy?" I asked.

"That I do." She squared her broad shoulders. "His mum died when he was very young, and his da did his best to raise him with the help of his nursemaid and servants. But his lordship was stubborn and spoiled. He had the servants running around like Christmas geese when he beckoned. Thought he owed nothing to nobody, and he was adamant about making his own mark on the world."

"How long have you known the Winslows?"

"Since I was a wee one myself." Her gaze drifted, as if a memory had snatched her mind. "His lordship and his best mate used to get in heaps of trouble. His da threatened to send him to a monastery to be raised by monks until he could learn to conduct himself as a man worthy of his title."

I pulled the linens back with her help and discarded them on the floor. "I suppose the duties that come with a person of importance could become quite dreary. Always having someone looking over your shoulder and telling you to behave in a manner that does not bring reproach upon the family."

"Some people ain't got many choices," she said. "Children born of aristocratic families do seem like a dreary lot, don't they?" A smile crept onto her face.

"Lady Zuna is quite lovely."

"Always been a delight, that one," she said.

I shook out the bedsheet and gave her a corner. "And their mutter?"

Mrs. Potts's body stiffened. "It's best to not talk of the dead." She tucked the corner of the linen under the mattress.

"Forgive me," I said, regretting my forwardness.

"Don't fret, it's all right." She reached for the coverlet folded on the footboard. "You never say much about yourself. What is your story, lass?"

My nerves hummed. "There isn't much to tell."

"Got a man?"

"If I did, I wouldn't have left him to travel to this canton." Dampness coated my palms, and I turned away to avoid her gaze. I strolled to a rocking chair and busied myself with arranging the slumped-over dolls. Nisse's face appeared in my mind.

"Ever been in love?" When I didn't answer, she said, "Don't be shy, love."

"I suppose one could call it that." I moved on to fiddle with a lopsided drape.

"So, you're still in love with him?"

"It wouldn't matter if I was," I said, keeping my back to her. "He may never see me as more than the pathetic child that followed after him, thinking he was the smartest, most interesting boy in the village."

"I know love when I see it. And no turned back will hide the true feelings inside you," she said.

I dropped my hand from the drape and turned to face her.

"You consider marrying the lad?"

"No—well..." My face burned. "You see, my mutter told me once to make sure that the man I chose as a husband was a prince and only a prince."

"She wanted you to marry for money?" Disapproval and judgment registered on her face.

"No. She wanted me to have a man who would love and care for me."

"She seems like a wise woman. But you talk of her like she is..."

"She died when I was little. She was the kindest

human I've ever met. Always looking to do good and spread joy to all those she met and loved." Pride expanded in my chest.

"I'm sorry to hear that," she said. "It appears life ain't been that easy for ya."

"One doesn't get to choose the life they're given, but I intend to make the best of the one I was handed."

"I see the wisdom and goodness of your mum have passed to you."

Mrs. Potts's words struck me straight in the heart. I felt as if she'd embraced me in a massive hug. "Thank you." I blinked away unshed tears. "You're too kind."

She walked to my side and laid a hand on my arm. "Got to admire a girl alone in the world who can make a go of it on her own. That is something that takes valor and guts." She dropped her hand. "Now, dry those tears. You tidy up in here and then go on down to the washhouse and help the laundress with the washing."

"Yes, Mrs. Potts." I curtsied.

She grunted in her usual manner and left me to tidy the room. I finished and gathered the bundle of linens from the floor.

Downstairs, I went to retrieve the basket of dirty washing cloths I'd left in the parlor earlier. On my way past Lord Winslow's study, I paused at the sound of male voices within.

"The girl isn't like most. She is special."

"So I've been informed. What is your point?" Lord Winslow sounded agitated.

"Tread lightly around her," the stranger said. "Handle her with care."

Was I the girl the men spoke of? I leaned closer to hear.

"I received word that requires our immediate attention," Lord Winslow said. "I'll meet you in the meadow within the hour. Until then, don't you have matters that should occupy you?"

"Very well. But do remember what I said."

"Yes, yes. Be gone." Lord Winslow's voice rose. A chair scraped back.

I darted into the parlor and pressed myself against the wall to keep from being spotted. The study door opened and closed, and then somewhere in the house, another door closed. I waited, not daring to move or breathe. The clock in the room ticked, and I counted each strike. When I thought it safe, I slipped from the parlor and raced to the washhouse.

CHAPTER 19

Nisse

I PLACED A TIN PLATE OF EGGS, CHEESE, AND BREAD before my vater and lowered myself onto the chair to his right. His loyal companion whined and eyed the plate from his position at Vater's feet. When I'd brought the bright-eyed, wriggling ball of fur home, Vater's eyes had welled up, but he'd told me to take the dog back, stating he didn't have any need for a dog. Since I had been contemplating leaving and didn't want him left alone, I told him I'd take the animal back by the end of the week. And, as I'd hoped, he decided the dog could stay.

Our small apartment above Vater's watch shop was filled with trunks of old watches, mechanisms, books, and treasures he'd collected throughout his life. His greatest treasure, though, was my mutter, who had died when I was seven, and although the memory of her had faded long ago, Vater kept her alive in my mind and heart with tales of their love story.

Ten years younger than Vater, my mutter had been a street urchin of only seventeen when she'd walked into his shop and tried to steal from him while he was preoccupied with a customer. The gentleman had seen her slip the watch into her pocket and grabbed her before she could escape. He had demanded they report her to the authorities, who would take her hand for her thievery, but Vater had interceded and held her arm until the customer finished his business and left. After he departed Vater fed her, and during that meal mutter had shared with him how she'd ended up living on the streets. It was then that he offered her a job sweeping floors, washing windows, polishing, and dusting the display cases.

Not long after he'd hired her, he recognized her interest in the mechanisms of a watch. Soon she was tinkering on watches and fixing them for customers. People had given him grief for not hiring a male apprentice, but Vater wouldn't turn her away for the mere fact she was a woman. She became his greatest apprentice. In the years that followed, she earned the respect of the village people.

I dreamed of a love like my parents'. Out of that love, Mutter had borne three children, but I was the only surviving child to carry on the Strasser name. The pride I took in being Tobias Strasser's son had guided me throughout my seven and twenty years.

Before me sat a glimmer of the man I'd left behind. Years had weathered Vater's flesh, strong shoulders now hunched forward, and his once-vibrant blue eyes had dulled. Since I'd returned, I noted the faint yet persistent trembling of his hands. The rapidly advancing disease of his lungs was taking its toll on him. Each day since my return, I questioned if I'd done right by him when I'd left him behind to pursue my faraway adventures. If I'd stayed, maybe he wouldn't have deteriorated so much. In his letters, he'd concealed from me how far the sickness had advanced.

"Flicker and I will meet the supplier in the next village. We should be home before nightfall." I dug my fork into the eggs.

"That is good. I don't think I can handle the journey today." Vater pulled a handkerchief from his pocket and held it up to his mouth as another coughing spell erupted.

My muscles tensed as I waited for it to subside. "They seem to be getting worse. We must consider selling the shop and taking the council's offer."

"Nonsense. I won't hear of it." He folded the handkerchief, but not before I spotted the ruby stain on the cloth.

"You're a sick man. Doc says warmer weather will give you a chance at a quality life in the years you have left."

"Son." He placed his hand on mine. "If I'm to leave Switzerland, I will go home to Austria. I won't venture across the ocean to a foreign place in the middle of a civil war. I'll take my chances here." He regarded me, long and hard. "I wish to see my homeland before I die. It's been too long since my eyes have beheld its beauty. Would a son do this for his vater?"

He had been a force of strength and structure in my life, but he also provided the gentleness I'd expect of a mutter. Our bond as vater and son had never faltered, and I loved him more than I'd ever loved anything. He had integrity and honor, traits I strove to embody. One day, when I took a wife and we had our first son, I would name him after the man who'd been both mutter and vater to me.

"I'll do anything you ask of me." I covered his hand with my other and gently squeezed.

"That's my boy." He smiled before his expression turned solemn. "I wish Mutter could have seen the man you've become." His jaw quivered. "Sometimes I miss her so bad, the ache is like a sword to my chest."

"I know, Vater, but all we have is the here and now. And each other."

He lifted the handkerchief to dry his tears. "You're right, my son. I know I shouldn't dwell on things of the past."

"You loved her, and it's only right that your heart would ache for her."

"I suppose if you were to marry, you could give me other reasons to find joy in the years I have left." His eyes lit with amusement and a thread of hope.

I leaned back in my chair as a grin broke. "And am I to assume you have a wife in mind?"

"The one I've thought would make a good addition to this family for some time."

"She may never see me as a man worthy of marriage," I said.

Since returning home, a face often stirred in my thoughts: eyes the color of the Aegean Sea, dark hair that gleamed with tiny threads of gold, and full pink lips that puckered into a pout when she was displeased. The young girl I'd taken on as my duty to protect had grown into a woman of striking beauty. Vater's letters had spoken of her trips to his shop when she'd come to the village to trade. He'd written about her with fondness, and shared his concerns about her well-being. *She is no longer the wide-eyed girl that walked in your shadow,* he'd written. And often, as I had settled in whatever cave, forest, or meadow I'd found for the night, I'd dream of the woman he spoke of and how her kindness had helped assuage his yearning for my return.

"Time will tell." He bent over and placed his plate on the ground so the dog could lick it clean.

I rose from the table and took my dish and the empty one the dog had licked of any last morsel and dropped them into the basin of warm water.

"I need to get downstairs and open the shop. Herr Schneider is coming to have his pocket watch fixed." Vater hobbled to the doorway beyond which a narrow flight of stairs descended to the shop below. "Stop and greet him if he is here before you head out."

A short time later, I joined Vater and Herr Schneider downstairs. The men had been good friends since Vater had come to Switzerland when he was scarcely twenty.

Vater's leather pouch of tools lay rolled out across the counter, and spectacles now teetered on the bridge of his nose. Herr Schneider held a glass of whiskey in his hand and leaned close to observe my vater at work. Vater glanced over his spectacles at my arrival, and Herr Schneider swerved to greet me. He held his crystal glass in the air.

"It isn't too early to be hitting the whiskey?" I beamed as I closed the distance between us and embraced the man who'd become like family.

He clapped my back with his free hand. After his wife had passed some time back, the men had become that much closer. He'd been there the day I'd decided to leave, saying, "Don't worry, young Nisse. Your vater will be fine in your absence. He has me to be a pain in his arse." Though his words were humorous, his face always wore the same tight, unsmiling expression.

"You tell that swine Signor Barnone that I've waited long enough for him to find the Louis Audemars timepiece he promised me."

Vater snickered and continued his work with profound steadiness.

The chime over the door sounded, and Flicker stomped his feet outside on the boardwalk and entered the shop. He removed his fur hat, revealing his frosted chestnut plaits. "Good morning, gentlemen. It's a cold one out there today." He blew on cupped hands to warm them up.

After a quick introduction, I left Flicker talking to

the men while I retrieved my pistol from the back room. I strapped the holster around my waist before putting on my furs, and stuck my head out the doorway. "If we intend to get back by evening, we need to be on our way. Bring your mount and meet me in the livery down the way."

Flicker waved a hand in acknowledgment and continued chatting. I said my goodbyes and exited through the back door. The sun sulked behind the clouds, and I blamed it for the eeriness that settled on my shoulders. I shook the uncanny feeling off and strode out the back gate and down the alley to the livery.

"Good morning." The livery master, smelling of horse shit, greeted me in the yard. "Off so early?"

"I've supplies to pick up for Vater and wanted to get a jump on it."

"It's good you came back. That stubborn old coot would never tell you how much he needs you." The livery master had visited our apartment many times to drink and play a friendly game of cards with Vater and his friends.

"He never told me he'd gotten worse," I said.

He adjusted the brown leather patch masking the eye damaged in a tavern fight between him and a mining dwarf. "Didn't want you to come home on his account. He wanted you to see the world. To behold all the mystery and magic reported to exist beyond this canton." He craned his neck to eye me, his expression serious. "Tell me, is it as they say, what lies beyond those mountains?"

"Most of it." I strode past him to saddle my horse.

"Fire-breathing dragons?"

"As real as I stand before you now." I grinned. "I've met a Barbegazi. Helped me out of a bind once. Quite a friendly creature."

His eye widened. "It isn't so!"

"You better believe it. There are plenty of adventures to keep a man away for a lifetime."

He thrust his hands in the air in exasperation, the yearning for adventure born in every man alive in his face. "Then why return?"

"Grew weary of life on the road, sleeping under bridges and sharing lairs with whatever creatures lived within while sheltering from the rain."

I saddled my horse and led it from the stables as Flicker rode in on his steed. The animal's head reached only to my horse's chest.

The livery master's countenance darkened. "We don't offer service to dwarves."

"He is with me," I said.

"You're hanging out with the likes of them now, are ya?" He turned his stony expression on me.

"Flicker and I've known each other for years. He's a friend of mine."

"Well, you better get him out of my yard. You know how I feel about the bastards."

I pulled myself up on my mount. "You can't blame every dwarf for the scoundrel who stole your eye." I inclined my head, wished him a good day, and urged my horse over to where Flicker waited.

"What's his problem?" He nudged his chin at the livery master.

"One of yours left him without an eye."

"Then he must have earned it," he said under his breath, keeping a straight face to avoid upsetting the man further.

"Any word or sighting of Orell?" I asked Flicker as we left the village behind.

"Nah, and I can't say I'm disappointed. Valentina had good reasons to abandon the place. I ran into a man claiming to work at the Winslow estate, and he said she was faring well."

"That's good to hear. I'm waiting for the day Orell will show his face and cast her life into an uproar." Indignation centered in my gut. As boys, Orell and I had hunted together. Reflecting on those years, I recognized the evil filling him. I bore a scar from the day he'd come undone over my choice to let go a mother doe.

"He won't hear of her whereabouts from me." The muscles in Flicker's face grew taut. "She should have left years ago."

"And go where?" I looked at him as our mounts plodded along.

"Anywhere is better than being within his grasp. Maybe now she will have a life where she doesn't have to fight for every meal. She worked herself almost to death, trying to keep the homestead running, even when there was no hope. I tried to help her, but she refused most offers."

"She told me of the ruby," I said.

"Did she now?"

"It's an honorable thing you tried to do for her."

"She didn't see it that way. You'd have thought I'd emptied the mines, the way she reacted. I have little coin of my own with my mutter and siblings to care for, but Valentina is like family," he said.

The next hours passed with light conversation. As we reached the outskirts of the next village, we came across the gruesome blood trail spattering the snow.

"Whoa," we said in unison and reined our mounts to a halt. We cast a look at each other, and the jitters that had chased me all morning manifested on Flicker's face.

"What do you figure it was?" he asked.

"I don't rightfully know."

Flicker stood up in his stirrups and pointed at something on the ground about ten yards away. "Look there."

I nudged my horse forward to investigate, and upon reaching it, my stomach lurched. A human hand, shredded at the wrist, lay in the snow.

"Well, what is it?" Flicker pulled up beside me. Seeing the hand, he gagged.

I lifted a hand to shield myself from the stench that threatened to spew the contents of my own stomach. Tension pulled at every part of me as I scanned the banks and forest skirting the road.

"It's the work of the Seelenfresser," Flicker said.

I swung back to him. "What makes you say that?"

"The tribes talk of a creature that feasts on the

innocent and vulnerable. Our ancestors foretold that the beast comes into his true form when the devil awakens within him."

"Have your people spotted the creature?" I'd seen my share of monsters in my years abroad, but our canton had remained safe. Although rumors of the creature that lived in the face of the mountain surfaced from time to time, no actual proof to back up the tales existed.

"No, but this isn't the first of its victims." He enlightened me on happenings in the dwarf kingdoms as we followed the blood trail into the forest.

"But how does the beast get beyond the kingdoms' barriers?"

"Magic, we assume," he said. "The beast's evolution is of grave concern, and our tribesmen will not rest until it is destroyed."

The trail dried up where tree branches hung snapped, and the snow was trodden down as though an oversized animal had thrashed about trying to make a bed.

"Let's leave these woods. We need to report this to the village, finish our business, and hit it for home," I said.

"I am with you. I don't seek to be on the roads after dusk." The gravity of our discovery was etched on his brow.

We pushed our mounts at a gallop toward the village and informed the authorities of what we'd found on the road before tracking down my vater's associate to tie up our business.

CHAPTER 20

Kingdom of Schattenberg—Mining Kingdom

Sixtus and King Jörg had traveled hours into the dank bowels of the Kingdom of Schattenberg to speak with King Gian. Now they stood before him, at the bottom of the stone steps to his throne. Posted on either side of him were his loyal subjects, creatures with the faces of gargoyles, their humanoid bodies covered in black feathers, like oversize hybridizations of ravens. They observed the prince and his vater with slitted citrine eyes, their snake-like tongues flicking out. One gurgled, then hissed.

Shadows stretched across the cave floor, cast by creatures that soared overhead in the infinite cavern canopy, awaiting the signal of their king. The air was heavy with the pungent scent of iron and brimstone from the flames that burst forth with their rasping cries.

"What have you done?" King Jörg's voice reverberated off the red-stone walls glittering with gems of various colors and sizes.

King Gian's long nails clicked repetitively on the skulls of his enemies, fashioned into end caps on the sleek arms of his copper throne. "It is as I stated, cousin: the power belongs to me." His tone remained calm, but his gnarled face twisted with hatred for King Jörg.

King Jörg's mouth gaped before he snapped it shut. "For how long? I knew you were capable of such corruption with your hatred of humans, but do you feel no allegiance with your kinsmen?"

"To rise, it must devour souls, and the blood of the innocent has been proven to accelerate its mutation." His insinuation was unmistakable.

Bile rose in Sixtus's throat as he recalled the aftereffects of the Seelenfresser when he and Crispian had investigated a tip. "Our informant notified me of the creature's trip to the human village."

"It is young and not yet tamed. The man was an obstacle. Consider him target practice. You needn't worry, I'll see it's trained appropriately."

"You will cause the destruction of us all." King Jörg's hands clenched at his sides. "Greed and the need for dominance have fueled your actions for too long."

"We must defeat the monster before there are no dwarves or humans left," Sixtus said.

King Gian cocked his head at the sound of Sixtus's voice. "Don't tell me you feel pity for the humans."

Sixtus grimaced. "I hold no love for humans, but it isn't only humans that are in jeopardy."

A sinister smirk rippled across King Gian's face. "Dwarf magic stands no chance against what is coming."

Sixtus's hand moved to his sword, but his vater stopped him. "Speak what you know," King Jörg said.

King Gian's laughter thundered. "Has your mind dulled with age? Why would a commander reveal his strategies to the enemy?"

"We are enemies now, are we?" Spittle sprayed with the force of King Jörg's words. "It is no secret, the animosity we feel for each other, but we are kinsmen. It is our duty to our tribesmen to put their interests and that of our kingdoms above our rivalry."

"Do you think I'm still bitter that the people of Himmelart chose you to be their king, and I was elected to rule Schattenberg? Then you're more of a gull than I thought. This place has grown on me." He raised his hands. "You've underestimated me, cousin. While you sang to your flowers and grew fat, I've spent years researching and searching for the Totholz forest."

Sixtus inhaled sharply as cold panic washed over him.

"No! Tell me it isn't so." King Jörg careened forward, grabbing the hem of King Gian's robe.

The wardens struck their staves on the ground and let out an ear-ringing protest. King Jörg was thrown back with so much force he hit the ground and grunted in pain.

"Vater!" Sixtus bolted to his vater's side and cradled an

arm around his shoulders, never letting his eyes leave King Gian. Befuddlement enveloped him as the curtain over his eyes parted, then he saw King Gian as his vater did.

King Gian rose from his throne, descended the steps, and hovered over them. His crystalline eyes blazed. "You see, my wretched cousin, I do not seek to possess benevolent dwarf magic. No, such magic is inadequate. When the Seelenfresser comes into his own, I will meld his power with the vial of our ancestors' blood—"

"And raise the Vormacht and become immortal," King Jörg finished for him as Sixtus helped him to his feet.

"Yes." Exhilaration shone in King Gian's face. "We are warriors, and our hearts and swords thirst for blood. The battlefield is where we belong."

"You seek to unleash a war?" Sixtus felt sickened that he'd ever defended the king against his vater.

"If you won't join me, you're my enemy. I will not rule this kingdom while the gods and men like you nestle amongst the clouds." Venom dripped from his words.

"No," King Jörg declared, with more vigor than the prince had witnessed in decades. "We fight for what is right. For all folks. We fight to protect our universe from the deformity and covetousness of men like you. If we are to survive, we need to preserve what was bequeathed to us to protect. Our lands grow barren, famine sweeps our canton, and species are vanishing. Now you wish to massacre dwarves and humans alike. What is this world to us if it has no life forms left?"

"I will create an army more powerful than all the ones recorded in the scrolls of our ancestors." He held out his hand and a dark, globular mass whirled and stretched with the movement of his fingers. The ball revealed iron-clad monsters marching along mountain paths, and the biggest amongst them turned and peered at the human village below. The vision changed; now the prince saw a nation engulfed in flames, prowled by aliens of demonic creation.

King Gian clasped his fingers closed, and the globe disappeared, taking with it the vision. "You will remove yourselves from my sight and go back to the comforts of your sector."

His guards escorted Sixtus and his vater to the mouth of the cave. They struck the floor with their staves, and the barrier wall rose. The creatures shoved them forward. Sixtus swung around as the barrier closed, sealing off the entrance of the mines with an illusion of a snow-covered cliff.

"Your Majesties, I'd begun to worry about you," Crispian said. He and the king's men had stationed themselves near the entrance to await their return.

"Ready my men and bring my mount," Jörg ordered. Weariness hunched the king's shoulders. "We ride back to Himmelart without delay."

"Right away, Your Highness." Crispian thumped his armor with a fist and went to do the king's bidding.

Sixtus stared after him. He turned when his vater placed a hand on his arm. "If he succeeds in melding the Seelenfresser with the Vormact, we stand but one hope."

"What is that?" Sixtus said.

"The Reinheit."

"Valentina?" The prince's pulse pounded in his ears.

"She does not know the power that sleeps within her. You see, my son, your assignment is not an easy one. The existence of all folks depends on her safety until her time comes, when she must make the greatest sacrifice of all."

CHAPTER 21

Nisse

THE *TEUFEL ON THE RAMPAGE*, THE NEWSPAPER headline announced in glaring black print, and beneath it the illustrator had sketched a hideous-looking monster. Dread settled in my soul, and my body stiffened. I laid the paper down and peered around the empty shop. Months had passed since the morning Vater had set out to visit his friend who lived outside the village limits. Later that day a wagon tore through the streets, taking down anything or anyone in its path. Hearing the pandemonium outside, I'd stepped out onto the front stoop of the shop as Herr Schneider reined his team to a halt.

"Nisse." His eyes had been bright and feverish with fright as he'd jumped down from the driver's seat.

"Herr Schneider, what's happened?" Fear clutched my chest.

"It's your vater. I found him on the road." He seized my arm to stop me as I rushed to the back of the wagon. Disregarding his warning, I threw back the tarp and gasped at the sight of my vater's mangled body. A sight that still woke me night after night, leaving me trembling and drenched in cold sweat. Vater had asked me to go with him that day. If only I'd gone, maybe together we could have fought the creature off.

I folded the newspaper and shoved it in a drawer under the register. The shop had remained closed since Vater's passing, and a layer of dust had settled over the counter and glass display case. Moonlight crept through the wooden slats of the closed shutters covering the storefront windows.

A decree had gone out, banning people from roaming the streets at night or venturing beyond the village limits. Our once somnolent village turned into a ghost village as fearful townsfolk took to their homes, barring their doors and windows. The priest offered a prayer for the farmers, who refused to abandon their homes and seek shelter in the village. I searched for Valentina's face amongst the folks pouring in daily, but to no avail. No word had reached her of my vater's passing, or she would have come. As the days blended together, thoughts of Valentina and the Winslow household being slaughtered left me in a state of turmoil. Patrols blocked every road from the village; I tried to slip out daily, only to be apprehended every time. Nevertheless, I'd come up with a new strategy, and no matter the risk of traveling alone and at night I would use the cloak of twilight and the changing of the guard to step into whatever awaited me beyond.

When I found Valentina I'd take her far away, with or without her consent. Once she was safe, I'd return to search for the cave in the face of the mountain and slay the monster who'd killed my vater. Flicker had spoken of the Seelenfresser, and after seeing the condition of Vater's body, I wondered if such a beast had finally come to Schläfrigz. Past the barriers of our canton, all the mythical creatures in the fairy tales mutters and vaters read to children were very much alive.

I strapped the leather scabbard at my waist, and my sword took its rightful place at my side. I moved to retrieve my cloak from the peg by the back door of the shop and froze as Vater's scent wafted from his wool coat hanging next to mine. A sob clogged in my throat as I lifted the jacket from the peg and pressed it to my chest. The scent of his pipe captured my breath. Vater's smell lingered in every crevice of the apartment and shop, haunting me. Each time I'd inhaled it, a pang of guilt hit me. He hadn't deserved to die in such a horrific way. I punished myself for the years I'd spent fighting against the beasts overtaking foreign lands. *"A young man needs to get the adventure out of his system,"* he'd said.

"I'm sorry. So very sorry," I muttered into the solace of his coat. Life had stolen the most incredible man I'd ever known. A man who'd shooed imaginary fiends from under my bed when I was a boy. Before I'd grown old enough to wield my sword to rid the world of trolls, ogres, and similar vermin.

I replaced his coat on the peg and wrapped my cloak around my shoulders. Lifting the hood over my head, I took one last look around before exiting through the back door and hurrying to the livery. I saddled my horse while keeping an eye open for anyone seeking to report me.

I kept to the shadows of buildings, weaving through alleys and streets until I came to the edge of the village. A bonfire shot high into the night sky and sprayed light for several feet into the darkness beyond. At their stations, guards conversed amongst themselves while keeping their eyes alert and weapons handy. I retreated into the shadows to wait. Minutes felt like hours until the church bell struck the twelfth hour, signaling the change of the guard. The wives of villagers came into sight, carrying covered baskets filled with food for the guards. I had but minutes to escape into the darkness beyond before those with fresh eyes would relieve the sentries, and another day would defeat me.

I shrouded my face with the hood of my cape. My heart pounded fiercely against my ribcage as I led my mount into the narrow space that was the guards' blind spot, and my only chance of slipping by unnoticed.

"You there," a man called out.

A chill ran through me, and I quickened my pace.

"Stop that man."

I grabbed the mane of my mount, swung myself up, and kicked my heels into his flanks. Hands yanked at my cloak, trying to seize me, but my thighs gripped the horse, and I held on as he charged through the barricade at the entrance of the village and into the unknown.

The black night blanketed me and swallowed the lights of Schläfrigz. Though I was sure no one was fool enough to come after me, I waited until I was a safe distance away before I reined my horse to a stop and dismounted. Using the full moon as my guide, I searched the roadside for a branch to use as a torch. After unearthing one that would suit, I removed a tinderbox containing fire steel, flint, and char cloth from my saddlebag.

I urged my horse to a gallop toward the Winslow estate. Upon reaching it, I guided my horse down the carriage lane. A few yards in, I came to a fallen tree obstructing the road and turned my horse up the bank into the woods before circling back to the lane. I rode until the canopy of trees sheltering the road gave way to the house. Tall weeds clogged the circular drive, and moss and vines had engulfed the begrimed stone walls. The unkempt gardens and hedges in front of the mansion had probably at one time been strikingly beautiful. An uncanny quiet hung over the place.

When no one came to greet me, I escorted my mount around to the stable yard. There I was welcomed with the same disturbing lifelessness. Not a critter stirred. I lowered the torch to examine the ground for wagon tracks or footsteps in the snow and found none.

I dismounted and secured my mount to a hitching post. Watering troughs were filled with debris, snow, and ice. In the carriage house, an old buggy sat propped up on wood planks. My puzzlement grew when the servants' living quarters appeared not to have been slept in for some time. Out in the yard, I gazed up at the broken windowpanes of the home and found no flickering of lanterns or shadows from people moving within. The hour was late, and the family and servants would be asleep. But why were there no indications of life?

I cupped my hands and called, "Hello."

The mountains echoed my voice.

I walked around to the front of the house, to the doors that hung crooked and partially open. I knocked, and the door moved under my hand. "Hello," I said.

No answer.

I pushed on the door, and it swung on the hinge keeping it mounted. Inside, heavy velvet curtains embellished the eyes of the home, which scattered silvery moonlight over the rubble littering the flagstone floors. Holding the torch aloft, I strode through the hallways and rooms. Cobwebs draped sleeping walls and stretched across doorways like traps in a witch's lair. I swiped a hand to remove the silky threads from my face. Around me, the house shuddered and shivered, and cinders coated in layers of dust lay on the hearthstones.

I searched each room for confirmation that the family had returned and ended back in the foyer. My bafflement amplified. Hadn't Flicker said he'd run into a man claiming to work at the estate? I climbed the stairs to the upper floor—the first shifted under my boot, and I gripped the railing to keep from falling into whatever lay below. I scoured each wing of the home until my torch had burned low, and the urge to leave whatever hex bound the house overcame me.

Then, like a floating whisper, I heard her voice, and my feet rooted in place as though ropes now bound my ankles. I looked back down the corridor.

"How does one keep from drowning?" Valentina said.

"It won't be filled. You add just enough water to get you cleaned up," a woman said.

I broke from the trance imprisoning my feet and moved toward the voices. Stopping at a room the voices drifted from, I pushed open the door to find a bedchamber. No life stirred within, and once-white sheets still covered the room's furniture. I strained to listen, but no voices came. Had I imagined things? I was sure I'd heard her voice.

In the stable yard, I mounted my horse and nudged him forward. Voices rose again.

"What are you still doing out here?" a woman said. "The children need tending." This female sounded older than the last.

"I've not finished the task." Exhaustion echoed in Valentina's voice. I shifted in my saddle to search the shadowy silhouettes in the yard and jerked as the woman spoke again.

"Come now, lass, up you go. Don't let him see you cry or give him the satisfaction of your defeat," she said.

But then the voices dwindled.

Valentina. My lips moved, but no sound came out. I lifted a hand and swept it through my hair. Had I lost my mind?

In front of the home, I studied the exterior and the surrounding property. The estate stood in the condition I'd expect of a place neglected for years. If Valentina didn't work at the estate, where had she gone? And why would she lie about taking a position at Chateau Winslow? Valentina had said she'd taken the Winslow children to the dressmaker's shop the day I'd seen her. I'd start there and then inquire with the livery master and at the general store. Surely the earl's staff or he had purchased supplies for the estate.

A cold chill ran through me, and I kicked my heels into my mount's flanks. I felt the breath of the property raise the hair on my neck as I rode off. Was the place cursed, or was someone bent on destroying the Fürst family? I grasped but one thing: I wouldn't rest until I found out.

CHAPTER 22

Valentina

AFTER I TOLD THE CHILDREN A BEDTIME STORY and tucked them in, I picked up the lantern and strode to the door.

"Do you believe in fairy godmothers," Farrah said as I grasped the door handle. Zuna slept with an arm slung over her sister, and soft snores rose and fell.

"As a little girl, I did."

"And now?" she asked.

"I like to believe there's someone that watches over us all." I thought of the earthmen who scurried in the shadows.

"Do you think my mum watches over Zuna and me?" She propped herself up on an elbow, her expression perplexed.

I smiled. "Yes."

Her expression softened. "Why do think Charles Perrault gave Cendrillon glass slippers instead of golden?"

I laughed. "So many questions. And I'll answer all of them in the morning."

"Very well, but I shan't forget." She lay back against the pillows with her auburn ringlets fanned around her.

"No, I don't expect you will. Good night, Lady Farrah," I said.

"Good night, Miss Wolf."

As I closed the door to the children's chamber, I considered how Farrah had forgotten she'd declared me her enemy and became engrossed in the story. When I was a child, and my headaches would come, Mutter would sit by my bed and tell me tales. I'd imagine I was the stories' characters setting out on grand adventures of my own making. Goblins and giants would storm the castle gates to kidnap the princess, and the prince would fly in with his sword raised. The worlds inside the pages of Mutter's stories took me far away from the pain to a make-believe life where vaters were kind and princesses had only sisters. A world where Mutter laughed and planted endless kisses on a vater whose eyes were brown and tender like those of a foal. A vater that loved me as she did. Inside a fairy tale, all the cares of the outside world faded, and it became the place I'd liked best. A place where I had powers to defend myself against the creatures that scurried in the dark and against evil kings who looked to acquire my magical skills. I had lived inside my head so much, I'd gotten lost between what was reality and fantasy.

However, I'd outgrown such tales and cast them aside

after my parents' disappearance, and life proved it wasn't a fairy tale where I could overpower bad men and control my destiny. No. Such tales were best left as bedtime stories that gave children their farewells to the lands where dreams come true.

I descended the back stairs to the main floor. As I walked by the library, I noticed his lordship sitting in an armchair facing the fire and I quietened my steps.

"Mrs. Potts, please bring me some of my best brandy," he said without turning.

I searched for Mrs. Potts but found the kitchen dark, except for the fire in the fireplace that cast a glow over the cinder maid who lay asleep near the hearthstone. After I checked the other rooms and saw no sight of her, I returned to the corridor. Footsteps echoed behind me, and I held the lantern high to observe who approached.

"You looking to blind me?" Yara grabbed my wrist and lowered the lantern.

"I'm looking for Mrs. Potts. Lord Winslow has requested that she bring him his best brandy."

"You're out of luck. Mrs. Potts retired early with complaints of an upset stomach. You had better serve his lordship yourself. Best not to keep him waiting. You don't want to get on his bad side. Trust me, no one wants that."

"I don't know the first thing about brandy. Or where I would look for it," I said.

"Well…" A cheeky smile captured her mouth. "You got just the girl for that." She spun on her heel and marched deeper into the house.

At a narrow door she pulled on the handle, and it fell off in her hand. "Blimey, the blacksmith still ain't fixed it." She stuck a chubby finger into the hole to maneuver the latch. The tip of her tongue curled over her lip as she worked the lock. *Click.* "There we go. There ain't a lock Yara Appleton can't pick." She grinned. "Hand me that lantern."

I followed her down a cramped staircase. Dampness and mildew hung in the air. At the bottom she turned a corner, and we came into a small room with floor to ceiling shelves that held various bottles of liquor.

"This should be to his liking." She moved to a shelf in the center. I presumed it wasn't her first trip to the cellar, but then I recalled the story of her sneaking drinks with her lover.

She pushed the bottle at me, and I clasped it with both hands. *Jules Robin 1789 Cognac,* the label read.

Yara lifted the skirt of her blue frock and made her ascent, and I trailed behind her.

"You don't appear as though you're going to bed," I said.

"'Cause I ain't. I'm meeting my man in the stables."

"In the stables? Can't you find a place more suitable for your lovemaking?"

She stopped mid-stride and twisted to face me. I held up a hand to shield my eyes from the lantern. "A woman has needs as much as a man," she said with a hand on her hip. "Besides, he says his wife is becoming suspicious." She continued up the stairs. "He says she would never go to the stables because she's terrified of horses. One almost trampled her to death, so she stays clear of them." She closed the door after us and replaced the door handle. "You know where the glasses and tray are, right?"

"Yes," I said.

"I'll leave you to it then," she said in a clipped tone.

"Yara." I grabbed her arm, regardless of her displeasure with me. "Be careful."

The tightness of moments ago faded, and her expression eased. "Don't you worry none about me, love."

"It's just I don't want to see you heartbroken when—"

"He breaks my heart and returns to his wife," she said.

I nodded.

Her shoulders slumped. "I suppose I've always known this would end with heartache."

"But why do you still go?"

She shrugged. "Because a woman gets lonely." And with that, she turned and walked down the corridor and disappeared.

I stood staring after her, my heart heavy because I'd offended her.

"Mrs. Potts." Lord Winslow's voice was sharp with the curtness of impatience.

I retrieved a silver tray and placed the brandy and a glass on it and hurried to the library.

"It's about time. What took you so long?" He directed his gaze to where I stood. "Miss Wolf, what are you doing here, and where is Mrs. Potts?"

"She wasn't feeling well and has retired for the night. I've brought you the brandy you requested." I walked to the small table that sat between the two armchairs and set down the tray. I removed the brandy cap and looked up to find him studying me with unmasked interest. "May I?" I asked.

"Please." He gestured at the glass.

I filled the bottom.

"Won't you join me?" He tilted his head at the other chair.

"It isn't fitting," I said. "Others will talk." I'd overheard the whispering between servants at the special treatment I'd received from his lordship. A chamber fit for a lady and four outfits worth a year or two's wages.

"Let them talk. I insist. Sit."

I did as he requested. He took a sip of the amber liquid and released a sigh. I glanced at him as he sat with his gaze captured by the flames, my fingers knotted in the folds of my skirt. He had a way about him that sent my belly into knots. In my time at the estate, he'd managed his home with firmness. His servants and children alike marched like soldiers in an army. He'd never been unkind to me but he was reserved, never engaging on a level one would consider social or friendly. Dark lashes touched his cheeks, and laugh lines creased the corners of his eyes. I wondered when he ever laughed. A long scar curved from the side of his temple and disappeared behind his ear. Long legs clothed in dark blue trousers stretched out in front of him on the woven rug. He'd removed his cravat and undone the first few buttons of his white shirt. I realized it was the first time I'd seen him in a relaxed state. He seemed almost approachable. His beauty, luminous in the firelight, started a fluttering in my stomach.

"Do you like what you see," he said.

I blinked and found him looking at me. Amusement flashed in his eyes at catching me staring.

"My apologies, my lord." Heat licked my cheeks, and I lowered my gaze.

"Do you like it here?"

"Yes, it suits fine," I said.

"Perhaps in time, you will come to find it better than fine."

"I'm grateful for your generosity—"

"Please look at me when you speak," he said.

I raised my gaze.

"The eyes are a glimpse of all the emotions one holds. And your eyes tell me you may not fear me as you once did," he said.

"I-I," I stammered.

"You need not explain. It was hard for me to come here."

"Because of your wife?" I asked.

He didn't answer right away, and I worried I'd offended him.

"That, and my daughters. It isn't easy being a vater, and without a woman to help it becomes a challenge. Farrah is a difficult child, and you have handled her with more kindness than I would have thought possible." He lifted the bottle and refilled his glass.

"Thank you, my lord."

He crossed his legs and adjusted himself in the chair to face me. "So, tell me, what is your true story?"

"What? I told you—"

"I know what you told me, but I believe there is more to it than that. What or whom were you running from when you came here?"

"I-I…" I couldn't tell him the truth. What if he set out in search of my brother or Helias and told them of my whereabouts?

"A husband?"

"No." I squirmed.

He swirled the liquid in his glass. "The authorities?"

"No."

"Then what?"

"It's not as you presume," I said. "I've done nothing wrong. I wanted a change of life, and with my vater's passing I set out to find something more. One can seek blame for their situation or take matters into their own hands, and that is what I did and nothing more."

"And have you found that something more?" He lifted the glass to his lips and swallowed, his eyes observing me over the rim.

"More than I've had in a long time."

"But you don't have all you seek?"

The silhouette of my mutter, her face long faded, flashed before me. Then the memory of Nisse, the day in the forest when he'd lowered his face to kiss my cheek and how I'd wished it had been something more.

"Is there a lover?" he asked, as though reading my thoughts.

"No."

"Then why do I sense hesitation in your voice."

Nerves twisted my stomach. "I do not seek to offend, but I don't wish to discuss such matters."

"I offer my apologies for intruding." He stood. "Perhaps it's best if we retire for the evening." He held out a hand, and I slipped mine in his as he helped me to my feet. His hand lingered on mine, and I glanced up at him. "It's been a pleasure, Valentina." He pressed his lips to my hand, kissing it. The gentleness in his demeanor sent a rush of warmth over me.

"The pleasure is all mine, my lord." I allowed him to guide me from the room with his hand on the small of my back.

At the doorway, he paused, and his gaze held mine. I saw longing in his eyes. "Good night," he said and released me.

I curtsied and departed.

Upstairs, dressed in my nightclothes, I pulled back the linens on the bed and slipped beneath the covers. I stared up at the pleated fabric enclosing the bed and thought on the mysterious man I considered cold and aloof. Tonight he had lowered his barriers a smidgen and let me glimpse a man who wasn't as frightening. I drifted off to sleep with his lordship's face whirling about in my mind, and my dreams that night became complex and tangled.

CHAPTER 23

Nisse

IN THE DAYS THAT FOLLOWED, I PAID A VISIT TO THE dressmaker. When I questioned her about Valentina and the Winslow children's visit to her shop, her brow had puckered. "The Winslows haven't visited my shop in years. They returned to England years ago. No one has heard or seen from them since. Never could understand why the earl would just up and leave with no groundskeeper to maintain the place."

At the general store and the livery, I asked if they'd conducted business with anyone from the estate, and they answered no, not in some years. Perplexed, my suspicion rising, I escaped the blockades and returned to the estate during the day. I found the place in the same condition as I had that night. Afterward I went to the Fürst homestead to check if Orell had returned and found the cottage empty and dust-laden. No one had been there in months. I kept an eye out for Flicker in town, but he never came.

Over the next months I joined the patrols in hunting down the beast, and we returned empty-handed. Others never returned at all. The council had sent word to King Jörg of the mountain dwarves, seeking his help, and he obliged, sending earthmen to strengthen our numbers. Nonetheless, the valley became the feeding ground for the beast, and the dwarf magic failed to conjure the monster from concealment.

At night I paced the floors, mulling over what to do next. My turmoil was exacerbated by the increasing suspicion that something superior was at work, and that the earthmen understood more than they let on.

Spring had come to the valley, and wildflowers speckled the hillsides the day I walked into the tavern, feeling depleted, my mind riddled with turmoil.

"What can I get you?" the tavern owner asked as I dropped onto a stool at the counter. "Although I ain't sure I got enough to heal what ails ya."

"Ale. And keep them coming," I said.

As he sauntered away, my eyes swept over the place and halted on two earthmen sitting at a table in the corner with their eyes trained on me. I returned their gaze, and they busied themselves with a newspaper spread on the table in front of them. With my suspicions still on my mind, I strolled toward them. The clicking of my boots on the plank floor warned the earthmen of my approach. The gray-bearded fellow leaned in and whispered to his mate.

"Something I can help you with, gentlemen?" I cast a glance at the newspaper heading, which read *Victims of the Teufel on the Rise.*

"What is it with you humans? Always thinking we are up to something. Can't a couple of mates enjoy a drink?" the older of the pair asked.

"Why are you scouting me out?" I asked.

He leaned forward, and anxiety shadowed his countenance. "What is your interest in the old Winslow place?"

I bristled inside but kept my composure. "I'm looking for someone."

"No one has lived there in years. Not since the Winslows—"

"Yes, I know. The same story I've been told for months." I restrained my building impatience. "Any chance you know much of the family?"

"Not much, except Lord Winslow showed up here with a young wife heavy with child. Pretty little thing. They were very much in love, from what I recall. He was a collector of sorts. After his wife died, he returned to England with his daughters."

"Collector of what?" I asked. *Bodies?* My imagination raced with images of his lordship in the cellar of his home, wielding black magic. The rumors surrounding the death of his firstborn and wife came to mind. Had he returned to England? Perhaps he was responsible for the deaths of his family and the bodies piling up. My thoughts veered to Mary Shelley's character, Victor

Frankenstein, the Swiss student who wanted to mimic the power of the gods by creating an anomaly made of corpses.

"Artifacts that have no business being in human hands." The dwarf with a pox-scarred face spoke for the first time.

I raised a brow. "Care to explain yourself?"

The older dwarf silenced his mate with a stony glare from his deep-set eyes. "He tinkered with relics containing metaphysical energies. Artifacts belonging to our forefathers that have no place in the inadequate hands of the humans."

"Am I to believe there was bad blood between the earthmen clans and Lord Winslow?" I asked.

"I warn you, mister, you stay away from the estate. The place is cursed, and you're no match for what is out there." He jumped down from his seat, and his mate followed. They waddled through the tables and out the back door.

Mystified by the new information, I returned to my seat as the tavern owner placed a mug of ale before me. "Friends of yours?" He nudged his head at the empty table the earthmen had occupied.

"Never saw them before. They come in here often?" I lifted the mug and guzzled back several gulps.

"In recent months, with the hunting parties coming and going, I've had a slew of earthmen in here. Can't recall them all," he said. "Looks like you haven't slept in weeks. Your vater was a good man, and we miss him too."

"Much appreciated," I said.

He set another mug before me. "What's on your mind besides what has got us all on edge?"

"You wouldn't believe me if I told you." I stared at the foam seeping over the rim and trickling down the side.

"Give me a go. You never know."

I reiterated Valentina's claim and my findings, and by the time I'd finished, he stepped back with his thick arms crossed, looking befuddled. "See, I told you there's no sense to any of it," I said.

He rinsed a mug and picked up a cloth to wipe it. "No more sense than this creature carrying us off one by one."

"We are sitting prey, ripe for the plucking," I said. "Do you remember much about the Fürst family?"

"I grew up with Timo. A right looker, he was. A shrewd fellow that gained his fortune and lost it just as quick. Then he went off to Italy and got himself married and brought Piera back here. Never knew what she saw in him. Became one of his victims, I suspect. Had a way about him that could fool you into believing he was a man of integrity—he could charm the leeriest of folks. Biggest fraud to wander these parts. Too bad he set his sights on Piera. Poor soul dedicated her life to trying to make up for his wrongdoings.

"Then, when Timo moved her to the country after it was rumored he had to sell their home to cover his debts to the mining dwarves, she became pregnant with that abomination, Orell. The boy has caused nothing but chaos since he came into this world. Watching him and his sister after Timo and Piera disappeared was like their parents had been reincarnated. The oddest thing was what happened to Piera when she became pregnant with the bastard."

"What?" I asked.

"Piera was a stunning woman. But during her pregnancy, she stopped coming to the village. Then, one day, I stopped by the homestead to deliver the kegs Timo had purchased. She greeted me at the door, and I stumbled back in shock at her condition. She was nothing but a rack of bones. It was as though the fetus had sucked the life from her. Her eyes were sunken into their sockets, and her once luminous locks were all scraggly and thin. Her hands were bandaged with cloths that seeped blood. Yet her stomach swelled with a babe of seven months or so. But it was her behavior that I remember after all these years."

"Well, out with it!" I slammed my mug down, impatient with anxiety.

"Fear," he said.

"Of you?"

"No, I'd always been good to her. And she knew I didn't mean her any harm. I asked her that day if Timo was withholding food from her, and she pulled her shawl tighter around herself as if she was unaware of the shock her appearance would cause. She said the pregnancy had taken its toll on her. Although she played it off as trifling, the look in her eyes told me she was scared. Downright terrified."

"If Timo isolated her in the country, maybe she worried about delivering a babe without a midwife or another woman for miles," I said.

"It was more than that. She looked like a walking corpse," he said.

I tried to sort the clutter of information. "But she lived, and managed to give birth again."

"See, that is where it gets bizarre. When she was pregnant with the girl, Piera blossomed, as most women do when they are with child. I met her in the street, and she told me she felt better than she ever had."

I swiped a hand over my face, my mind spinning with confusion. "I think the dwarves know more than they are letting on. They appease us by joining our hunt for the monster, but I've studied them and how they gather together and speak on things they feel we're incompetent to address."

He wiped the counter with a cloth. "What makes you say that?"

"Because a friend of mine, a dwarf, made mention of a Seelenfresser. A creature that feeds on souls. Yet the earthmen trudging through the forest and countryside with us have never made mention of it."

He straightened, his gaze probing. "Have you questioned your friend further?"

"No, he seems to have vanished too."

"That leaves you with one option." He slung the cloth over his shoulder.

"State your meaning."

"The answers you seek may be in England."

"But I can't leave the valley when there is so much apprehension," I said.

He nodded. "With the amped-up attempts of the council to protect the villagers, access in and out is restricted. Word has spread of the beast that terrorizes our valley, and shipments are being delayed. I, for one, am not looking to have my soul sucked out. You ain't doing anyone any good here. If you've managed to get outside the gates twice already, you may be able to do it again. Get yourself on a ship and go get the answers we all seek."

Moments later, I stepped out onto the boardwalk and glanced around my beloved home. I needed answers, and scouring the woodlands for a creature we had never seen was squandered time. If I were to assist the village, my time was better spent elsewhere. I'd journey to England to inquire of Lord Winslow's whereabouts in hopes of gaining insight into what was at stake. Only then would I be of service to my village.

CHAPTER 24

Valentina

SPRING HAD COME, AND THE ALPS' TEARS cascaded down the mountainside, causing floods in the valley. Melting snow dripped steadily from the roof tiles and droplets splashed on the windowsills. The curtains in half-cocked windows in the library ruffled in the breeze, chasing away the stale air of the winter months.

The Winslows had left for the afternoon, and with the servants awarded the day off in the family's absence, quiet encompassed the estate. I strolled the floor of the library. Book-lined shelves extended to the ceiling and I regarded them in wonder, trailing my fingers over the bindings with care, afraid they would evaporate into powder at any moment. I removed one from the shelf and flipped through pages dense with text and maps. A hunger to learn kindled in me. My studies had terminated with the loss of my mutter, and responsibilities at the farm had consumed my time. Nonno had provided Mutter with the best education, and like the Winslow children, she had a private tutor. Mutter and Vater couldn't afford a tutor for us, so she took it upon herself to educate Orell and me. I thrived under her tutorship, but Orell protested, and when he turned eleven, Vater permitted him to resign from his studies to work alongside him in the fields.

"Valentina."

I shifted to the reedy servant tasked with managing the household while Mrs. Potts was away with the family on their outing. "What is it?"

"There's an odd little fellow in the foyer who says he's a friend of yours," she said, finishing with an inquisitive lilt. "He says his name is Flicker."

My nerves hummed. What was he doing here? "Thank you." I strolled past her and down the corridor to the foyer. Flicker stood with his hat in his hands, inspecting the crumbling plaster of the ceiling.

"There you are," he said. "It appears there's still a fair amount of work required to get the place in order. But it's coming along. Lord Winslow has outdone himself."

"Shh!" I glanced over my shoulder before marching to the door and swinging it open. Gesturing for him to follow, I stepped outside. "Let's take a walk, shall we?" I said when he joined me.

After we reached the forest, I slowed my pace. "What are you doing here?"

He leveled a scowl on me. "Checking on you, of course. With it being Sunday and all, I figured you'd have part of the day off for a little visit with a friend." He brightened.

"How do you suppose I'm to explain having acquaintances here when I've only left the estate once in the months since I came here?"

"I noticed fresh carriage tracks on the main road, coming from here. Did a little spying, and the place seemed lifeless."

"And you're lucky it was," I said.

He postured. "I see nothing to worry about."

"I mean it. You mustn't show up without me telling you it's safe."

He grunted and waved a hand in defeat. "Fine. As you say. Now, are we going to enjoy our time together, or will you continue to scold me like one of your wards?"

I linked my arm with his. "I'm thrilled to see you."

He bent, picked an alpine snowbell, and held it out to me. When I elevated an eyebrow, he grinned and said, "A peace offering."

"Charming and clever." I shook my head and tucked the flower in the waistband of my apron.

We bantered back and forth, and the tension of his arrival vanished and my heart lightened in his company. All came to a halt when an earth-shattering howl permeated the air and I dropped to my knees, clutching the sides of my head. Pain ripped through my skull, and the blood coursing through my veins burned like fire. Flicker gripped my shoulders. My eyesight blurred, and tears spilled as my body convulsed with agonizing pain. *Help me! Please!*

Then the misery withdrew, and I gasped and sagged against Flicker. He rocked back but steadied himself and draped his arms around me. His words were muffled by the ringing in my ears. When the world stopped spinning, my hearing and vision cleared.

"W-what was that?" I said, my voice quavering.

His heart thundered against my ear. "I don't know." Fear echoed in his voice.

My strength returned, and I clambered to my feet and glanced in the direction the scream had come from.

"Don't even think of it." He grabbed my arm.

The thrashing of my heart hammered in my ears, and I swung to look at him. "Did you not see what just happened?"

He swallowed hard and stared at the forest over my shoulder. "You aren't safe."

The agonized cry rose again and my knees buckled, but Flicker dashed forward to catch me. I clutched the sides of my head. I couldn't breathe. *No, no. Make it stop.* The force of the wail paralyzed my body, but as the scream silenced the pain retreated. I clambered to my feet, pushed away from Flicker, and trotted farther into the forest.

"Are you crazy?" He clutched my hand.

I pulled my hand free and raced on as I regained control of my senses. I had to find where the noise came from before it struck again.

Flicker jogged after me. "Valentina, stop. You mustn't go near it."

The scream cut through the forest, and birds fled in panic. I clung to a tree trunk to stay upright and pressed my forehead against the bark as I fought through the agony. *What is happening?* Terror clawed at my throat.

The cry released me from its grip, and I gasped air into my lungs. I bent to rest my hands on my knees as I struggled to catch my breath. I eyed Flicker, who stood gawking into the woods, his face drained of color.

I continued on, Flicker trailing.

The trees parted to reveal a meadow. I stood at the tree line and scoured it for movement until my gaze halted at the edge of the forest to our left. Cold fear settled in my core as I gaped at a dark form writhing on the ground. A massive humanoid hand with long talons stabbed at the heavens, followed by a colossal head with a white mane as the creature rose. It was as tall as the surrounding trees. It staggered, and the earth trembled under my feet. Amber eyes blazed, and it arched back, its mouth unhinged, exposing glistening ivory fangs as it threw back its head and vented its rage.

I covered my ears and planted my feet as I fought against the intense pain that blurred my vision. I lost all sense of reality, slipping between what was real and the stories of my youth. The cry ended, and my vision cleared. Trapped in a realm between reality and dreams, I rubbed my eyes to remove the illusions. But the beast remained.

It fell to its knees, and its mass began to shrink. The

creature transformed into a man before my eyes. His blond locks shielded his face as he rose to his feet, naked and trembling. He hesitated, as if getting his bearings, then swiveled to gaze at us.

Orell? I lurched back in horror and disbelief. My brother stared at me as though not truly seeing me. Then he spun and scampered into the forest. I fell to the earth, sobbing. *No, no, no.* It couldn't be real.

Flicker pulled me against him as sobs racked my body, offering hushed words of comfort. "Valentina, you must listen to me." He pulled back and looked me hard in the eye. "We can't stay here."

"What is happening?" I grabbed fistfuls of his shirt, and he winced and struggled against my attack.

"You must calm down. I can't hold on much longer," he said through gritted teeth.

I rocked back on my knees and gawked at him as my brain reeled in confusion.

"There is a lot you must know, but it mustn't come from me," he said.

"What is it? You know. Tell me." I lunged forward. He put his hands up to shield himself, and I froze in mid-movement, dumbfounded by his reaction. "Flicker?" Tears tattered my voice. "I'm not like him. I'm not capable of harming anyone."

He lowered his hands, and a solemnness that was foreign to him altered his expression. "It has awakened."

"What?" I asked.

"The power within you."

"Power? What power?" I said, on the brink of hysteria.

He pushed to his feet and held out a hand. "Let's get back."

My mind raced. "What are you keeping from me? You're supposed to be my friend, and we promised to never lie to each other."

He winced. "I am your friend. And I'm begging you to trust me." He grabbed my hand and yanked me around and darted back the way we had come.

Wake up, you must wake up, my mind screamed. Branches whipped my face and chest, but the numbness dominating my body and mind made them seem like windblown hairs brushing my face. We bolted across the grounds, then up the stairs to the main door before Flicker paused and looked over his shoulder. He threw open the door and shoved me inside.

"Flicker?" I twisted and gripped his shirt, holding onto the one person that I trusted with all of my being.

"Stay here and don't come out. I must check the grounds." He slammed the door.

I charged at the door and pulled on the knob. It wouldn't open. "Flicker, open this door at once." I pounded on the door.

"Valentina, what seems to be the trouble?" I jumped at the sound of Lord Winslow's voice and whirled around to find him and Mrs. Potts staring at me in amazement.

"When did you get back?" I asked. Expecting their bodies to contort and change into creatures I conjured in my mind, I looked around for an escape route. Fresh tears spilled as my panic rose. Their voices closed in on me.

"It is all right. You have nothing to fear," Lord Winslow said.

"You aren't real. Stay away from me." I backed up until my back pressed against the door, but Lord Winslow advanced. "No, no, no." I shut my eyes to force the hallucinations away.

Fingers, gentle and reassuring, touched my face. Arms embraced me as my legs gave out, and my world went dark.

CHAPTER 25

M Y LIDS OPENED. THE DARK OF NIGHT encompassed me, and I adjusted to my surroundings. A fire crackled and flickered nearby, and I gazed at the familiarity of the canopy above the bed in my chamber. I rolled onto my side and drew a sharp breath at the sight of Lord Winslow standing at the fireplace with his hand resting on the mantel, staring into the flames. He rubbed a hand over his face and muttered to himself. I propped myself up, and he glanced up at my movement.

"You are awake. We've been worried about you." He strode to the nightstand and lit the lantern.

I looked down and found myself fully clothed, but my shoes had been removed. What was he doing in my chamber? And where were the children? I moved to swing my legs off the bed, but he leaned down and stopped me with a hand pressed on my shoulder.

"Rest. All is taken care of." Tenderness glimmered in his eyes.

The fog in my brain shifted, and I remembered the incident in the foyer when he and Mrs. Potts had cornered me. A shiver scurried over my limbs. Orell? Had it all been a dream? It felt so real. I glanced at Lord Winslow, whose hand remained on my shoulder, and I touched his face with the tips of my fingers. "You are real?" I searched his face for confirmation.

His mouth curved into a smile. "As real as you are."

And the meadow…was that real? Or the beast that had evolved into my brother…I wanted to bombard him with the questions racing through my head, but I feared he'd think I'd lost my mind. And I wasn't sure I hadn't.

"But how did you get back?" I asked, and when he looked at me in confusion I hurried to explain myself. "You all were gone, maybe an hour or two. And a trip to the village takes a good part of the day."

He straightened. "Yes, well, we didn't make it to the village. The carriage wheel hit a rut and broke clean off before we made it a few miles. We returned on foot, and I wasn't aware you'd left until you bolted through the door with that strange fellow."

"His name is Flicker. I'd written to him to inform him I was safe and where I was staying. I sent the letter when I was in town; I hope you don't mind?" The lie poured from my tongue.

"Not at all," he said. "He is a friend of yours?"

"Yes."

"And you don't mind that he's a dwarf?" he asked.

I sat erect as defensiveness stirred in me. "What does that matter? He is honest and good. And he's someone who means everything to me." Panic clutched me as I spoke the truth I'd believed of Flicker, but after what had happened…. But what had happened? I swung my legs to the floor and scampered off the bed.

"Steady now, you had a terrible scare from the looks of you when you turned up here." He reached out to steady me. His touch was gentle.

I shuffled to the looking glass with him holding my arm, his other hand pressing lightly on the curve of my back. My heart surged with gratitude for his kindness. As I stood in front of the glass he released me, and I regarded my reflection. Leaves and debris matted my hair and mud caked my frock. Threads of red ran through my eyes, the lids swollen from past tears. Welts marked my cheeks from the lash of the tree branches.

"Looks like you took a tumble," he said, peering at me through the glass.

"Yes." I veered from the mirror. "Thank you for your kindness and understanding. If you don't mind, I'd like to change and check on the children."

"Very well. I will leave you." He strode to the open door, but paused in the hallway. "Will you be all right?" Concern haloed his face, and the way the flickering light from the corridor sconces illuminated his flesh licked at my heart.

I pressed my lips together to hold back the sobs

gathering in my throat and nodded. Perhaps I had taken a tumble.

He rested a hand on the doorframe. "Are you sure you're up to caring for the children?"

I smiled. "They keep my mind busy and off what lies beyond these walls."

His footfalls faded in the corridor, and I closed the door and retrieved a clean dress from the wardrobe. Behind the privacy screen, I wiggled out of my stockings and reached around to untie my apron when I spotted the withered flower. My chest pounded, and with trembling hands I removed the flower. Flicker. The meadow. The beast…my brother. It was all real. The flower fell to the floor and I stumbled to the bed, clutching the bedpost to keep upright. All of it came rushing back. "*It has awakened,*" Flicker had said. My stomach knotted. Would I too become a monster like Orell?

CHAPTER 26

Later that night, after I'd put the children to bed, I retired to my room.

"Are you sure you don't want me to stay with you?" Yara stood outside my chamber. "Lord Winslow gave his approval."

"I will be fine. I wish to be alone," I said. Reading the concern in her eyes, I stroked her arm. "I will see you in the morning."

"If you're sure." She didn't appear keen on the idea but didn't push the matter further.

"I'm fine, truly," I said. "It's nothing rest won't cure." I'd played the incident off as though I'd hit my head when Lord Winslow and Mrs. Potts had eyed me suspiciously, after I'd changed and joined them downstairs.

That night I tossed and turned, my dreams filled with my mutation into a grotesque creature that unleashed horrors throughout the valley. I awoke in the early hours of the morning, before the household stirred, and dressed. I tiptoed down the back stairs and into the kitchen to retrieve a blade before slipping out the door and racing to the stables. Once there, I saddled my mare and swung up onto her back, and without glancing back, I rode down the lane to the main road. It was only a matter of time before they noticed I was missing. Leaving without permission meant I was jeopardizing everything. But I didn't know where else to turn—I had to find Nisse, and tell him about Orell and what Flicker had said. Alert to my surroundings, I rode the mare hard in the direction of Schläfrigz. The image of my brother in the meadow revolved in my head. What had happened to him?

As I approached the village some hours later, I reined in my horse at the sight of the blockades across the road. A quilt of silence had extinguished the usual vigor of townsfolk as they went about their day-to-day business. The delectable aromas that usually hung in the air above the bakery and the chocolatier's shop were missing. Melancholy shrouded the quaint village with its transformation into a fortress. Lookouts hunched on rooftops, maintaining surveillance of the Alps and forest. The uncanny sensation that something terrible had happened made my stomach drop.

Taking in the scene before me, I realized they had prepared for battle. But the patrols had no idea what they stood against. The beast towered over the height of the walls and could clear the lot of them with one sweep of its arm. I had to find Nisse and tell him what I'd witnessed,

He would prepare the villagers for what lay beyond the comforts of Schläfrigz. I nudged my horse on with light touch to her flanks.

"Who goes there?" a voice called from behind the barrier.

"It is me, Valentina Fürst," I said.

Silence followed until the gate screeched open a crack, and the bellow came again. "Dismount and come here. Let me look at you."

I strode to the gate.

Signor Zesiger, the butcher, clad in armor fashioned of wood planks and metal, revealed his face. "It looks like you, but one can never be too sure. Come closer," he said.

Again I complied, walking until I stood within inches of him. He gripped my face in his beefy hands and stared into my eyes as if expecting to glimpse the reflection of a monster.

The intensity of his scrutiny relaxed, and he released me. "Is it really you?"

"It is me, signor," I said.

"Where have you been? Everyone's been wondering what happened to you and your brother after the beast tore up your home."

"I took a job in another canton. Only returned when word reached me that there was trouble." Guilt gripped me at the lies I continued to weave.

"You shouldn't have come back," he said. "You were safe outside of the valley, and to travel here alone was dangerous. Maybe you're the fortunate one of the Fürst lot."

The statement kicked me in the stomach. My family was gone. Each and every one of them. And as a new contemplation surfaced, I quivered. What if the beast was responsible for my parents' disappearance? Had Orell killed them?

"Are you all right?" Signor Zesiger asked, plucking me from the troubling thought.

I gulped back tears. "I need to check on a friend."

"No one is allowed in or out. Council's orders. I shouldn't be letting you in, but I never got to repay your mutter for saving my boy from the fever. Once I give you sanctuary, I can't let you out." His warning clear, I nodded.

I had to get back to the estate and beg Lord Winslow to keep me on, but at the moment the dire need to seek Nisse's counsel took precedence over all of my concerns. If Lord Winslow found out my brother was a monster and the one wreaking havoc in the valley, he'd send me on my way as quick as nothing.

Signor Zesiger granted me entry and dragged the gate closed. I walked past the guards posted throughout the streets, and the solemnness that had settled over Schläfrigz was unnerving. Merchants and townsfolk had retreated inside and boarded the windows of their homes and shops. Even the poor had vanished. The eyes of the ones hiding in the sewer peered at me from the openings in the cobblestone. Fear hung over the rooftops and flooded the streets and alleys.

At Nisse's vater's shop, I found the place in the same state as the others. I pulled on the door, but it wouldn't budge. I beat on the door with an open palm. "Herr Strasser? Nisse? It's me, Valentina." I waited, but no answer came.

"Well, well, if it isn't the little minx that slithered away," a voice purred behind me.

I spun around to face Helias and took a few steps back. "You stay away from me. The answer remains the same, I won't marry you. Not now or in another lifetime."

He laughed. "No need to worry, I've moved on. Got me a wife that met my vater's approval. Though she isn't as intoxicating as you." His gaze was feverish.

"I mean it, you stay away from me." I yanked the blade from inside my cloak and jabbed it at him as he advanced.

His eyes widened, and he stopped in his tracks. "You got some nerve, pulling a blade on me. I could gut you right here and scream 'Teufel,' and no one would think anything different."

"I'd rather be gutted spleen to throat than be touched by the likes of you," I said, my nose twitching with disgust.

"You come looking for the watchmaker's son?"

"What if I have?" I said.

"You won't find him. He took off some months after his vater died."

"Herr Strasser is dead?" My blade faltered at the news. "What happened?" I failed to hide the anguish in my voice.

"The beast got him. Shredded him like paper. His son went out on patrols with the rest of the men and pestered villagers with endless questions before he just took off one day. The tavern owner said he was headed for England."

Nisse. A chasm opened in the pit of my stomach for his loss. I shook at the vision of his vater's brutal death. "What for," I said.

Helias shrugged his broad shoulders. "Most likely saw his chance to escape and took it."

He wouldn't leave without saying goodbye. My throat thickened. "He's an honorable man. He wouldn't just pick up and leave when his home is in turmoil."

"Grief can do strange things to a person. Besides, why do you care if he left anyway? You take a fancy to him?" His gaze was sharp and assessing.

"No."

"Don't lie to me." He strode forward, and I thrust the blade toward him.

He wailed and clutched his side as blood blossomed on the fabric of his shirt and dripped on the cobblestones. He gaped at me. "You little whore, y-you stabbed me."

"And I'll do it again if you move an inch closer." Heat flared within me. But, reluctant to back down, he came again. "I mean it, stay away, or I will leave your body on the cobblestones." I took a step forward.

Alarm lit in his eyes, and he halted. A muscle twitched in the corner of his eye. "You win this time, but beware, I won't forget this."

I straightened my shoulders and glared at him while my insides trembled. "No, I'm sure you won't."

Helias retreated, and I lowered my blade and released my pent breath. I leaned back against the wall of the shop to steady my trembling body. I'd been a fool to come. Nisse was gone, and I'd risked everything to achieve nothing. Teardrops stained the front of my cape. What was I supposed to do now? Signor Zesiger had said no one was permitted in or out. I regarded my surroundings, feeling despondent before my gaze halted on the slot in the cobblestones. The sewers. That was my only option.

I sat down on the front stoop and removed one of my stockings before slipping the shoe back on and tying the cloth over my nose and mouth. "You have to stay here," I said to the mare as I caressed her muzzle.

I lowered myself down into the sewers, and hands reached up to assist me. As I splashed into the waste and darkness, my stomach roiled, and I fought to keep its contents down. People huddled in the dark, and somewhere a babe cried. Guilt weighed in my chest at the suffering caused by my own flesh and blood. I had to repair my brother's depravity and set everything right, but how?

I waded through the underground tunnels, asking directions to the point where the sewers emptied into the river. Daylight flickered ahead, and, eager to put the stench behind me, I pushed my weary legs onward.

At the egress, guards drawn from the ranks of the impoverished eyed me warily as I approached. "Halt." A man blocked my exit with his staff. "No one comes in or out."

"My children are out there," I said, lowering the

stocking masking my face. "Our rations ran out, and I risked all coming to the village in hopes of finding food, but I didn't have enough coin. I'm their only hope, and without me, they will surely perish." I started weeping, drawing on the hole in my soul that had grown with my admission into Schläfrigz and the discovery of Nisse's absence.

"Let her go." A woman stepped from the shadows. "If she is fool enough to go out there, then she deserves to serve as food for the beast. Better her than us."

I concealed my shock at her callousness, but as the man stepped aside she grabbed a fistful of my cape and shoved me forward. Then I was free-falling over the side of a cliff. Panic seized me, and I flailed my limbs as the air snatched my breath. *Calm yourself, Valentina, or you will die on impact,* a woman's voice said, as clear as though she sailed with me toward certain death below. The currents of the river raced to meet me, and I prepared myself for impact.

I met the water with a flesh-separating smack, but I didn't have time to reflect on the pain as I went under. I clawed for the surface, and as my head broke through I gasped and inhaled before the current captured me. The water thrashed my body. *Stay calm,* the lulling voice urged. I emerged a few times, and each time my hands flailed for anything to grasp onto. Submerged, I clutched a tree root protruding from the bank and held on as I struggled toward the surface. In the shallows at last, I climbed up the riverbank and sprawled belly down on the ground, gasping, my chest burning with the intake of water.

When I recovered, I pushed to my feet and got my bearings before I began the long journey back to the chateau. Worry at what awaited me churned in my stomach.

I'd walked for hours before I detected the earthmen's mounts charging down the road toward me and then, as if spotting me, they reined in their steeds and veered off into the woods. When I walked by the area where they had vanished, I called out, "You could at least accompany me home, after you took all the trouble to track me down."

I heard a curse, but they didn't reveal themselves, and I continued along the main road, their presence, as limited as it was, providing me with some solace.

When I arrived at the estate minutes before dusk, I took a deep breath and entered the servants' door. As I'd expected, Mrs. Potts and Lord Winslow awaited me.

After Mrs. Potts left, I stood shivering in my soiled clothing in the middle of the study.

"What were you thinking? You gave us all a fright." Lord Winslow stood before me, and I looked away under the pressure of his gaze.

I felt utter despair. "I can only offer my apologies, my lord. I thought myself unfit to care for your children and got the fool idea to leave."

"Care to explain the stench spewing from you?"

Taking a calming breath, I said, "I fell into the river the village sewer flows into. If you wish for me to leave, I will not hold it against you."

He scoffed. "I would think not. You act rash, and such behavior isn't acceptable. What has gotten into you?"

"I don't know, my lord. But if you can find it within you to bestow on me another chance, I won't mess up again."

"I'd hope not," he said. "I don't paint you as a rash person. A little tumble that caused you to imagine things is no reason to send us all into a panic."

But it wasn't my imagination. It was real. Very real. I wiped my palms in the folds of my skirt. "Again, I apologize."

He paced the room. "What am I to do with you?"

"I'll work in the stable yards, or whatever you find suitable. But please hear me when I say it won't happen again." I crept forward, and he held up a hand to stop me.

"You reek of sewage," he said. "Your trial had ended and I'd hoped to keep you on, but with your recent shenanigans I question if it's wise."

"Please, I beg of you." I detested the desperation in my voice, but I had no choice. On the journey back to the estate, I realized that I had to bide my time. And with no place to go, I needed the refuge of his estate.

"Mrs. Potts!" he said.

The door creaked open, and Mrs. Potts stuck her head into the room. "Yes, my lord?"

"See to it that she is bathed, and get rid of her clothes. And send someone to clean up the filth dirtying the floors."

"Straight away." She pushed the door open and beckoned to me.

I glanced at Lord Winslow and he jutted his chin, signaling me to leave. I hurried to the door.

"Miss Wolf," he said, and my heart skipped.

I swiveled back. "My lord?"

"This is your one and only chance."

Tears brimmed in my eyes. "Thank you, my lord."

Mrs. Potts gripped my arm and stifled a gag before leading me from the room. She remained silent as we climbed the stairs. I'd given a promise, which I aspired to uphold until I could sort out what had happened to me in the meadow. Why had Orell's cries afflicted me so? And what power had Flicker referred to?

CHAPTER 27

"Miss Wolf, Zuna and I wish to go down to the river to skate," Farrah announced as she marched into the room with her sister on her heels.

I glanced up from the maple chiffonier I dusted. Wiping the pearls of sweat from my brow, I rose from the floor. "You stay away from the river. The ice is thin and will not hold." The river, unlike the one by the village, sat capped in ice.

"But we wish to skate," Farrah said.

I walked to her and placed a hand on her shoulder. "It's past the season for skating. You're to stay away, do you hear me? Study the lesson Mr. Evans set out for you, and then after I'm done helping Yara, we will seek whatever adventures the grounds hold for us. Agreed?" I thrust out a hand.

Zuna shook it eagerly.

"The grounds? There is nothing of interest here," Farrah said with a stomp of her foot, but I'd grown used to her ways. "What about the forest?"

"No!" I shrieked, and they jumped at my response. Not wanting to frighten the children, I'd decided not to speak of the dangers that lay in the woods. "You're to do as instructed." I wiggled my outstretched hand at Farrah, and although reluctant, she took it with one eyebrow raised in apprehension.

"Go on now, do as I say, and the day will be one in your favor." I smiled.

"Very well," Farrah said with a huff. "If you promise to take us after you've finished."

I crossed my fingers over my heart. "Promise."

"See, Farrah? She will. Miss Wolf always keeps her promises," Zuna said.

After the girls' footsteps faded down the corridor I finished my dusting, then stepped out onto the back portico. Rugs and tapestries from various rooms lay in a heap at my feet. The door squeaked, and I turned as Yara entered. Together we stood gaping unhappily at the rugs.

"We will hack up our lungs before we're done this chore," she said. "Let's put this one behind us, shall we?" She bent and hoisted a rug into her arms and marched down the stairs. Mud from the yard caked the hem of her dress as she waddled to the clothesline.

I hurried after her, mud squishing over the top of my shoes to soak my stockings and feet.

Some time later, we pinned the last tapestry to the

line; I lifted my carpet rod from the ground and caught a full view of Yara. Her blonde brows and wisps of stray hair had turned snow-white, her lips dust-powdered and dry; a sight that would scare anyone if they were to come upon her at night. "Ghost of Christmas Past," I said with a laugh.

"Too much Charles Dickens for you." She pretended to pout and struck the tapestry with a powerful blow.

The dust blasted me in the face. I coughed and sputtered, and brushed away the dirt with my sleeve. Yara erupted in laughter, a manly sort of sound that wobbled her fleshy parts. "You look a sight, you do."

I planted a hand on my waist. "I'll get you for that one." I grinned, tasting the dust coating my teeth.

Our merriment evaporated when screams pierced the afternoon air.

"Help! Someone, please help." Farrah raced up the bank toward the house.

"Fetch Lord Winslow," I blurted, then flew across the yard, through the side gate, and on toward the child. Fear knotted my stomach. The beast had come! My feet pounded the ground as I tried to pump my legs faster. Farrah had left the safety of the house against strict orders not to, and where she was her sister wasn't far behind. I peered past her for a glimpse of the child and found no movement.

I caught up with her and gripped her by the shoulders. Sheer panic shone in her face. "Where is your sister?" I asked.

She trembled under my fingers. Tears flooded her cheeks. "She's fallen through the ice."

"What—" I released her and charged down the hill. My frock snapped in the wind as I sprinted toward the river. My chest ached, and my legs felt leaden as I tried to gain speed. *I'll never make it.* My stomach roiled with grief.

I arrived at the river and discovered the black gap in the ice. There was no sign of the girl. My heart battered against my ribcage as I stepped onto the ice, and with little care for my safety I hurried on, until the sound of cracking stopped me.

"Zuna!" Tears blurred my vision, and I wiped them away with the back of my hand. *She can't die.* I pressed on until I stood over the opening in the ice. I dropped to my belly and thrust my hand into the black hole. The cold of the water sent pains up my arms as I groped around in the hole for the child.

"Please!" Grief built in my soul. "Help me." I lifted my head and scoured the woods. Where were they? The earthmen who kept to the shadows. I took a deep breath and plunged my face into the water. Panic seized my chest, and the cold burned through my skull. I searched the black depths for the girl. My hands thrashed in the water, and then I gripped fabric. Zuna. I pulled, and the weight attached to the material moved toward me. Maybe it wasn't too late.

A movement spun the water, and then I saw it—a skeleton with the body of a fish and its claw outstretched as it swam straight at me.

No, no, no. I tugged with all my strength and fell backward with a jaw-rattling thud against the ice. The object within my grasp landed next to me. Too pained and stunned to move, I rolled my eyes toward it. Zuna, lying next to me. Her flesh was tinged blue, and her chest did not rise and fall. I scrambled to get up, but something grabbed my foot and dragged me backward. I twisted and came face to face with the river monster that had seized me by the ankle.

"Come to me, little one. I will take care of you." Its voice lulled me.

"I'll take care of the child. You get the girl," a male voice said behind me.

"Release her at once," another man said.

Drawn to the croon of the creature's voice, I couldn't break my gaze, and before my eyes its face changed, and my hand went to my throat. "Nisse, is that you?" A sob caught in my throat. He hadn't left.

Nisse glided from the water, his beard frosted, and his gray eyes bright with affection. "Yes, little one. All is well. I've been looking for you." He walked toward me.

"But, you left," I said.

"You're mistaken. That is what they wanted you to believe."

"They?" I asked.

"The dwarves. They're the enemy. You can't trust them. I am here, my love."

My love?

He held out his hand and warnings sounded in my head, but my hand reached for his.

"Valentina, no!" A sword swept out in front of me, and a dwarf dodged between Nisse and me. I recognized him as the uppity dwarf from the market. What was he doing here?

Again, he slashed his sword in warning.

"No, he's a friend." I gripped the dwarf's arm, but a squeal rose, and I dropped to my knees, gripping the sides of my head. Currents of pain zapped in my skull. Nisse and the river monster had vanished, and in their place stood my brother in the form I'd seen in the meadow. The dwarf lifted a hand, and a visible translucent barrier charged with electric current rose between us and the beast.

"Don't think you can stop me, Sixtus," it said.

The dwarf helped me to my feet and turned to the creature. "You will not succeed. The girl's protected."

"Your magic can't defeat me."

"You will lose today," the dwarf said. I gawked at the dwarf, and he gave me a sideways glance but kept his eyes trained on the creature. "The barrier won't hold. Go relieve my man," he said.

I looked behind me to find another dwarf with unruly red hair kneeling over Zuna. I recognized him from the market, too. He breathed air into the child's lungs like the man at the river had done when Orell tried to kill me. The child coughed and sputtered and let out a wail.

I raced to her side and pulled her into my lap, pushing back her wet hair from her face. "Lady Zuna." Tears streamed down my cheeks.

"Valentina?" She looked at me with dazed eyes.

"Can you carry her to the house?" the earthman asked.

I nodded, biting my lip to cease its quivering.

"Then go. I must help the prince." He drew his sword and ran to the prince's side.

I clambered to my feet with the deadweight of Zuna and staggered toward the bank. Yara, the stable master, and other servants gathered at the riverbank, waiting with outstretched arms. The ice crackled and popped beneath me, and fear squeezed at my chest as I felt it move. It broke, and I screamed as my legs split apart. I clutched the child to my breast as I struggled to stay upright.

A blade struck the ice behind me. I looked back at the dwarf Orell had referred to as "prince" as he struck the ice again. A crystalline blue beam chased the crack in the ice and sealed it like a weaver zigzags a needle in a garment. The gap pulling at my legs closed, and I breathed my gratitude while fighting back the tears.

When I reached the shoreline, the stable master took the girl from my arms. Yara covered her with furs, and the man turned and bolted toward the house.

Yara threw a blanket over my shoulders. "You did good." Her arm weighted my shoulder.

"Why didn't she listen? Lady Zuna has never disobeyed me," I said as we climbed the bank.

"It is a bit strange." Her voice reflected my puzzlement.

"Out of the way." The stable master pushed his way past the concerned servants crowding the work yard. Lady

Farrah burst through the back door, and I broke away from Yara to go to her.

Her eyes fastened on the bundle in the stable master's arms, then turned to me. "Zuna?"

"She is alive." I pulled her into the curve of my side. "Come, let's get the child inside."

"Yes, Miss Wolf." The stable master didn't hesitate; he dashed up the back steps and into the house behind us.

"Here, bring her here." I led him to the settee in the library. "Lay her down. Lady Farrah." I lifted her trembling chin. Her face was red from crying. "You fetch a nightrobe and stockings for your sister."

She darted from the room.

"You," I said to a chambermaid hovering on the threshold. "Go get blankets and cloths to dry her off. You—" I nudged my head at the girl behind her "—stoke the fire and bring her warm milk."

Echoes of "Yes, Miss Wolf" followed.

"I'll leave you ladies to it," the stable master said and departed.

Yara and I stripped Zuna, whose lips were purple with cold, and her teeth chattered. A chambermaid returned with Farrah behind her. We dressed Zuna and wrapped her in fresh blankets. The chambermaid picked up the furs and clothing and took her leave.

I sat at Zuna's side on the settee, rubbing her limbs. She lay with her lids closed, blonde lashes kissing the tops of her cheeks. "Why did you go to the river? Your sister could have died," I said to Farrah.

"I didn't, I swear it. We were in here as you instructed. She took the chair by the window, and I lay on my belly by the hearth, practicing my arithmetic as you requested. My eyes grew heavy, but I rested only a moment." Her eyes pleaded with me. "When I awoke, she was gone. I called for her, but she didn't answer, and then from the window, I saw her crossing to the riverbank. She looked strange. By the time I caught up with her, she had reached the river and stepped onto the ice. You'd told us the ice was dangerous, so I stayed put. I called her name again, and she turned and looked right at me, but she looked to be asleep. Then I heard the crack, and the ice broke, and she…" She threw herself into my arms. "It wasn't my fault."

I smoothed her hair and kissed her temple as she lay against my chest. "I believe you."

"Farrah, please don't cry," a soft voice said.

Farrah pushed back, and we looked at her sister, whose eyes were open. She held out a hand to her sister.

"Zuna." Farrah pulled her into a hug. "I thought I'd lost you."

Zuna looked past her at me. "I'm sorry, Miss Wolf. I tried not to listen. But it called to me, and I couldn't stop. My feet moved toward the river, although I knew I wasn't supposed to go there."

"What voice?" I asked, remembering the creature and its luring voice.

"I thought it was you." Zuna dropped her eyes. "But then it wasn't, and then it was. I tried to turn back, truly I did."

"Zuna. Farrah. What happened?" Lord Winslow burst into the room, hopping as he fought to get his boot on. His hair was tousled and his shirt untucked, and fear shone in his eyes. I scooted aside as he dropped to his knees beside his daughters and gathered them into his embrace. A tear fell from the corner of his eye as he kissed each of their cheeks.

I reiterated what the girls had said, and told him about the dwarves that had come to our aid.

"If I see them, I will thank each properly. Yara," he said, "I will take Zuna to her chamber, and I want you to sit and watch over her."

The servant girl returned with the tray of milk.

"And I'll read to her," Farrah said.

Lord Winslow hoisted Zuna into his arms and headed for the door. "Valentina, change out of your wet clothing, and I expect you to be here upon my return."

"Yes, my lord." I swallowed back the worry thickening my throat. Again, I'd failed him, and my chances at Chateau Winslow would come to an end.

The servant girl took my arm. "Come, let's get you changed."

I permitted her to steer me upstairs, numbed by the realization that the world we lived in contained creatures that roamed amongst us, for my brother couldn't be the only one. I wanted to lower the curtain that had veiled me from what I'd experienced lately.

Changed, I returned to the library to find Lord Winslow pacing the floor with his hands planted at his waistline. He glanced at me when I entered and dropped his hands. "Have a seat." He gestured at the settee. I obeyed, and he sank down next to me.

I waited.

When he finally spoke, he turned and leaned forward. Taking my hands in his, he rubbed the chill from mine. "Thank you for risking your life to save Zuna's. I don't know what I would have done if it had turned out differently." Emotion clotted in his voice, and he cleared his throat before releasing my hands.

"You believe Lady Zuna's claims, don't you?" I asked.

"Yes."

Buoyed by hope, I breathed a sigh of relief. He didn't think I was crazy.

"You can understand the gravity of my concern." He leveled troubled eyes on me. "You must stay close to the house where you're protected. Keep the children within your sight. I'm releasing you from all duties, so you can supervise them at all times."

"You mean, you're not letting me go?" My heart sang with delight.

"This wasn't your fault. Until I can find out more about the creature and why it came here, you must heed my words and keep your eyes open," he said. "For now, Yara will watch over the children. Why don't you retire to your chamber and rest? You look ready to collapse."

I nodded.

"Go now. I have matters to attend to." His gaze became distant, as though he was occupied.

I rose and walked to the door. At the threshold, I rested my hand on the frame and turned back to say something, but found him leaning forward with his elbows on his knees and his face buried in his hands. Quietly, I turned and left him to his thoughts.

In my chamber, I sat on the edge of the bed, staring at the closed door. The heart-wrenching feeling that had haunted me since I'd discovered what my brother had become consumed me. What had happened to him and for how long? He had tried to kill the child in order to get to me. But why? What was my part in all this, and why were the dwarves protecting me? My thoughts turned to Nisse and the loss of his vater. Nausea rose in my belly with the understanding that Orell was responsible for his death.

CHAPTER 28

Kingdom of Himmelart

"KING GIAN KNOWS ABOUT THE GIRL." Sixtus stood in front of his vater in the Great Hall.

Alarm flared in the king's eyes. "How can you be certain?"

Sixtus stifled his nerves and leaned on his palms on the grand table, letting the sapphire embedded in the table's surface capture his gaze. "He lured one of the children to the river, and she went through the ice."

"What?" The king leaped to his feet, and his chair clattered to the floor. Sixtus straightened and regarded his vater, whose face had become ashen. "Tell me the child is all right."

"She is fine."

"Well, thank the gods for that!" He paced the room, treading heavily, his footsteps pounding the marble floor.

"You were to watch them all." He halted and turned to glower at Sixtus. "Were you off frolicking with a scullion?"

Sixtus threw his hands in the air. "Is that all you think of me?"

The vein at the king's temple pulsated. "Have you given me any reason to think otherwise?"

"The child was a ploy to get Valentina to the river."

"And did she go?" the king asked.

"Of course, and with complete disregard for her safety. If we hadn't interceded, Gian would have succeeded in his plan to have the Seelenfresser drain the life from her." What if he and Crispian had been too late? The mere thought awakened something primal inside of him. "There was something about the Seelenfresser that summoned her."

"Perhaps the meshing of the two pieces the siblings hold."

"No, it was something else. She regarded the beast as though he was someone she loved. Her fear vanished, and her face softened with tenderness. And we are aware of what she's suffered at her brother's hands and that there is no love lost between them." Sixtus lifted a magnifying glass and aimlessly studied the map unrolled across the table. Carved stone horse heads were placed strategically by villages and cities. "I can't be certain, but she seemed to be seeing something the rest of us did not. There's no doubt Gian's subject grows stronger."

"Gian possesses the ability to control their minds. He called to the darkness born in the Seelenfresser, and in doing so, he was able to suck any thread of humanity from him," the king said. "Our one hope lies with the girl. She holds the Reinheit portion of the Zwilling power. These years have been hard on the girl, but still, she perseveres. She's proven she has a strong spirit that isn't easily swayed from her internal compass."

Sixtus turned and rested his hip against the edge of the table and met his vater's gaze. "But did she need to suffer so? You speak of your love for humans and how our ancestors fought at their side. How we helped them when they were in need. You could have intervened at any time, but yet you wouldn't allow it. Why?"

"What are the virtues of an undefeated warrior?"

"Strength," Sixtus said with conviction.

"Yes, but I do not refer to physical strength." The king jabbed the side of his temple with a finger. "It is in here. And in here!" He thumped a palm against his chest, passion blazing in his eyes. "The beauty and the danger of humans lies within their minds. It is their strongest weapon and the battlefield where their greatest struggles are fought. A warrior finds strength when faced with adversity and forges courage when all is lost. It is not upon mountains where lessons are learned, but in the shadows of the valley. Hardships force one to trample the forest alone, and only those that seek out the light can rise to the warrior within themselves. The girl is unaware of the warrior that flourishes within her. The twin power survives on the likeness it finds within its host."

Valentina's eyes, a mirror of the turquoise ice that

sheltered the mountain, scrolled through Sixtus's mind. Neither malnourishment nor her small stature had stopped the girl from carrying out the tasks assigned to her, that first day at the chateau. As his vater believed, he too had come to consider her a human worthy of a better lot in life.

"Are you any closer to discovering how we can stop Gian from awakening the energies of the Seelenfresser?" Sixtus asked.

"We have searched the writings of our ancestors for years. The Zwilling power manifested in dwarves is one thing, and we understand its strength and weakness. Existing within humans, it has exhibited traits contradictory to all the teachings in history."

"And the woman?" Sixtus said. "She hasn't found anything?"

The king dropped his gaze and sighed heavily. "She depletes herself with examining the scrolls I bring her. My trusted subjects have traveled to remote parts of the world to uncover teachings about the twin power."

"You can't keep her in that tower forever. If your intuition is right, she too plays a part in ending all of this," Sixtus said.

"I concur. But until we comprehend how we can defeat Gian and end his plan to free the Vormacht, it's unsafe to drop the veil and release the tower from the spell. Because once I do, and the Träger steps through into our realm, King Gian will know she lives. And if you're correct in assuming he knows the girl carries the Reinheit, he will seek to unite the twin power to wake the black magic of the Vormacht. If he finds out about the Träger, he will stop at nothing to possess her, because in her lies the ability to hold both the Seelenfresser and the Reinheit in one form. Fused with the Vormacht, it would make him unstoppable." The king's knuckles turned pallid where they rested on the back of a chair, and fear flickered in his eyes.

"And what is Valentina's part in all of this?" Sixtus asked.

"We assume, although the girl's abilities haven't been nurtured, she and the Träger embody the purity of the power, and together they can extinguish the darkness Gian has nurtured in the Seelenfresser."

Sixtus slammed his fist on the table. "There are too many uncertainties when Valentina's life is at risk. Tell your men to move faster. We are running out of time. Twice, the beast has come too close to her. If it wasn't for the girl's friend, the mining dwarf, King Gian might have already succeeded."

"That is why you and Crispian must keep her in your sight until we have definitive answers. Now that the Seelenfresser has become its true self, King Gian will turn his attention to the Reinheit."

"And he will die trying," Sixtus said with conviction. "His head will roll at my feet if he so much as cuts a strand of her hair."

The king crossed his arms over his chest and studied him. "You speak forcefully. Am I to assume you harbor feelings for the girl?"

"No." Sixtus's voice hitched. "I will not see our kingdom fall or our tribesmen slaughtered."

His vater gave him an all-knowing look but said only, "Of course not."

Sixtus brushed off his vater's insinuation, but as he rode out of Himmelart he recalled his vater's words and laughed out loud.

Crispian shot him a sideways glance. "What seems to have festered under your skin?"

"It is nothing," Sixtus said and clucked his tongue to spur on his steed.

CHAPTER 29

Valentina

SUMMER BLOSSOMS PERFUMED THE EVENING AIR and painted the front gardens with color. In the distance, the river, swollen by mountain streams, raced toward uncertainty. Overhead, the moon spied on me from its perch in the velvet sky as I strolled through the gardens. Gas lanterns, now in working order, lit the stone paths, and their shadows climbed the walls of the mansion.

My thoughts dwelt on Nisse and where he had gone. Although my heart told me he would never abandon our village, I understood how grief could affect a person. What if he never returned? If he did, would he ever look at me the same way? Such thoughts played with my mind until I thought I'd go crazy. Each day the questions and uncertainties continued to accumulate, and with them came the feeling that I was trapped. And what of Flicker? Where was he? I hadn't seen him. He held the answers I needed, and with each day my frustration heightened. The fear that I'd observed in the village had found its way to Chateau Winslow. After the incident at the river, Lord Winslow had hired men to protect his household, and the place had become a fortress with guards posted everywhere.

"So deep in thought," he said behind me, and I turned to squint into the shadows of the gardens.

"Good evening, my lord. I do not wish to intrude. I'll leave you—"

"Please don't." He stepped into the light, dressed in dark slacks and a cream cotton shirt, and my heart raced. The glow of the lanterns glistened off his dark locks. "Do tell me, what has your face contorting with so many emotions?"

"It is nothing, my lord." I inclined my head.

"It didn't appear as nothing," he said, his tone revealing a foreign warmth.

Taken aback, I lifted my eyes to find him observing me tenderly. "Thoughts of home, my lord." Despite my frustration with Flicker and my confusion over Nisse leaving, they were the only sense of home I had.

He smiled. "Home does have a certain pull on the heart, doesn't it?"

The curve of his mouth and the gentleness in his eyes made my heart flutter. He was even more beautiful when he smiled.

"Won't you join me for an evening stroll?" he said, offering his elbow.

I looked at the mansion. "I should go."

He grabbed my arm, and when I glanced at his fingers, he eased their grip. "Have I given you cause to fear me?"

"No, my lord," I said.

Perplexed, he frowned. "Have you suffered while serving in my home?"

I shook my head.

"Then why do you fear me so?"

"I don't fear you so much as choosing to proceed with caution," I said, and when his eyes widened, I went on to explain. "If I may speak frankly, my lord?"

He gestured. "Please do."

"You aren't the approachable sort."

He sucked back a breath, and I cocked my head to look at him. "Go on," he said with surprising calmness.

"I don't suppose you've had much fun in your life," I said, and as quickly as it left my lips, I wished I could take it back. My mouth agape, I waited for a wave of insults, but he made a funny sound as though stifling a laugh.

He cleared his throat. "Please continue. I'm finding this conversation rather enlightening."

"Well, most days, you seem bored to tears."

"How so?"

"When we engage with you, it is as though we're obstacles in your way," I said.

He winced, and I clamped my lips shut. I had said too much. What was I thinking?

"And what else is on your mind? Please don't hold back on my account."

"Nothing, sir. Forgive me." My shoulders slumped. It wasn't the first time my honesty had gotten the better of me.

"A good dose of healthy criticism is good for you, my father used to say." He played with his cufflink before eyeing me. "Continue."

"But, sir—"

"I insist."

My heart pounded, and I swallowed hard before saying, "Very well. I wonder, do you simply exist in life, or do any emotions stir in you at all?"

His mouth unhinged, and he stood gawking as if genuinely seeing me for the first time. "The situation is difficult. But yes, I assure you I feel like anyone else. I suppose life has taught me to be guarded."

"I understand wanting to protect oneself. But how can we truly love and find peace in this life if we don't allow others to give us comfort and happiness?"

Interest flickered in his eyes. "Do I sense you speak from experience?"

"I've never had much, but the little I've had I treasure," I said. "One thing life is teaching me is everything can change, and there is nothing we can do to stop it."

"There is a purity about you that is alluring. Sincere honesty that makes people reassess themselves."

Filled with guilt, I lowered my eyes and clasped my hands in front of me. "You're wrong," I said. "I've not been fully honest with you." My eyes settled on the tips of my shoes. "Please, forgive me, but I was scared…"

"Of what?"

"Of my brother finding me, or the man he betrothed me to showing up to claim me." I sighed and lifted my head. The nonjudgmental way he looked at me gave me the courage to continue. "I am Valentina Fürst, daughter of Piera and Timo. My parents vanished ten years ago. I grew up here in this valley, and my family's homestead is a short wagon ride away."

"And where is this brother of yours?" His voice was tight.

My body tensed, and regardless of the honesty he credited me with, I wasn't ready to tell him of the beast that had swallowed my brother's humanity. "He disappeared the night I left to seek work, hoping to find refuge here. When I took your daughters to town, a friend told me that rumors spread that the beast from the river came and took us."

"And you said nothing?" he said.

Tears welled in my eyes, and my shoulders sagged again. "I thought it was my chance to be free of my brother and a future married to a man as vulgar and demeaning as Helias."

"I had wondered why a woman of your beauty hadn't married. I thought perhaps you'd sworn off men."

I hugged myself to ward off the unpleasant memory

of Helias's attempts in town. "Because one man is a liar and a thief, it doesn't make another less of a man."

"There is truth in what you speak," he said. "Tell me. How does one so young become so wise?"

I shrugged. "Sometimes hardships make one see life through a different lens. Am I to judge all men by Helias and my brother's shortcomings?"

His eyes grew distant, as though his thoughts captured his attention. "I suppose that would be unfair of one." He focused on me. "You are extraordinary, Valentina Fürst, and I thank you for your honesty." He lifted my hand to his lips and softly kissed it before releasing me. "It's been a pleasure. Good evening." He bowed gracefully at the waist before turning and walking back toward the mansion.

I stood in shock at his sudden bluntness. Had I gone too far? Said too much? At the end of the path, he paused and turned back to look at me, then vanished into the shadows from whence he came.

CHAPTER 30

"JUST ONE MORE STORY, MISS WOLF," ZUNA said between yawns. Tiredness glazed her blue eyes.

Since the incident at the river, she'd awaken with night terrors. The first few occurrences, Lord Winslow and I'd met in the corridor in our nightclothes, his eyes wide with panic and my heart pounding. Once we understood what was happening, he left me to care for the child.

"Not tonight. You must sleep." I sat propped against the headboard with a girl snuggled into either side of me. Farrah had softened toward me and extended an occasional smile. The sisters had grown closer, and the way Farrah doted on her sister warmed my heart. Often, when I observed them, I wondered what it would be like to have a sister. To have someone to share your confidences with and who'd look out for you.

The girls lay peering up at me, and I gave them both

a gentle squeeze. "Tomorrow I've planned a picnic in the gardens. And I will share with you my favorite fairy tale of all."

The sisters looked at each other, and Zuna squealed.

"How does that sound?" I asked.

"Delightful." Farrah removed her head from my shoulder.

"Very well," I said, kissing the top of her head and then her sister's. I clambered off the bed before pulling the linens up under the girls' chins. "Sleep well, princesses." I dabbed each of their noses, and they grinned.

I gathered their clothing from the floor and had turned to blow out the lantern when Farrah said, her voice heavy with sleep, "We love you, Miss Wolf."

Tears caught in my throat. "And I, you, Lady Farrah." I blew out the lantern and walked toward the door.

Hurried footfalls echoed in the corridor, and I stepped into the hallway as his lordship's door closed. I crossed to my chamber and paused just inside as I caught sight of the red brocade gown laid out on the bed. I frowned and moved to the bedside. Next to the dress sat a pair of ruby satin shoes. A folded piece of parchment lay on the frock, and I unfolded it. The pattering in my chest galloped as I read the script:

Miss Wolf,

It would be my great pleasure if you would join me in the ballroom.

Sincerely,

Brett Winslow

I set the parchment on the bed and stroked the silk fabric of the frock, then the full, delicate lace-trimmed sleeves.

"He asked me to assist you, and I suggest we make it quick," Yara said. I turned as she entered the chamber and closed the door behind her.

Behind the privacy screen, I undid the buttons of my blouse and removed it and my skirt. Standing in my camisole and petticoats, I waited as Yara retrieved a corset from the wardrobe. After I'd slipped the undergarment on, she yanked on the strings, extracting a yelp from me. When she had finished, I felt like my ribs would crack at any moment.

"Why do the wealthy subject themselves to such torture?" I grumbled, longing for the cloth bindings of days past.

"Because it sucks away all the jiggly bits and snatches your waist while making your breasts sit like inviting little pillows of temptation for menfolk," she said with a wicked grin as she buttoned the back of the gown.

My cheeks burned and my mouth dropped open at her brashness.

"You wait until a man knocks that innocence outa ya. Then you'll wish you never waited so long to make love to a man," she said.

"Yara." Mrs. Potts's displeased voice made her jump.

My heart knocked. We hadn't heard her come in and turned to face her.

"Can't you see you are embarrassing the lass?"

"Aw, Mrs. Potts, I ain't meant no harm. I was just informing her about the facts of life."

Mrs. Potts's thick brows furrowed. "Because Valentina doesn't speak candidly about facts best kept private doesn't mean she isn't aware of what goes on between a woman and a man. Now, let's not dillydally. Fix her hair and get downstairs." Mrs. Potts left Yara to finish up.

Minutes later, Yara stood back to admire her work. "You sure are a sight. I'd never know you were the same rack of bones that showed up here all those months ago."

Dressed, my hair pulled back with jeweled combs and hanging long down my back, I murmured, "Thank you." Nerves churned my gut at the thought of spending an evening alone with Lord Winslow.

"Don't look so scared. He ain't the beast, looking to make you a bedtime snack." Yara gave me a sideways glance as we strolled to the door. "He's never done this before for a woman. Somehow you've managed to thaw his heart. I never thought it possible," she said, her voice tinged with respect.

Downstairs, I walked to the doors that had remained locked during my time at the estate but now stood open. Inside, massive crystal chandeliers lit the room in a rainbow aurora that splayed across the walls and oak floors. In the corner, a quartet played an enchanting melody.

"Shall we?" Lord Winslow appeared at my side and offered his elbow.

"I'm afraid I don't dance that well." I thought of the times when my mutter and I would laugh and dance in the fields as she tried to teach me. The ache for her squeezed my chest.

"Follow my lead, and all will be well." He thrust out his elbow, signaling me to slip my hand inside, and when I did, he placed his hand over mine. The tiniest of wings fluttered in my chest.

We danced to song after song, and he was a patient teacher as I continued to stumble and step on his toes. When he released me, I was breathless. I lifted a hand to pinch the stitch in my side.

He waved a hand in the air, and the butler strode into the room, carrying a tray of refreshments.

"Miss?" The butler offered me a glass with a white-gloved hand. Beyond parched, I accepted the glass and drained it greedily, then patted my lips with my fingers as Lord Winslow eyed me with amusement.

"Wore you out, did I," he said.

I replaced the glass on the tray. "You are quite good." I realized how much I'd enjoyed myself.

He drained the contents of his glass, returned it to the tray, and gestured for the butler to leave. "You challenged me. And what was a gentleman to do," he said with an impish smile.

I craned my neck to peer up at him. "How so?"

"A fortnight ago you told me you didn't believe I knew how to have fun, and I took it upon myself to show you that I do indeed appreciate a good time."

My cheeks burned. "I didn't mean to offend you, my lord."

"On the contrary; I like a good challenge." He touched my arm.

I drew back, confused and mortified. "All of this was to prove me wrong?"

He sobered, and the intensity in his gaze kept me from racing from the room. "No. Well…not all of it. I enjoy your company, and I wanted to give you an evening of enjoyment. Now I feel I've offended you. Please accept my deepest apology."

"All is forgiven. If you'll excuse me, I'm tired." I turned to go, but he reached out to stop me.

"Please don't leave." The tenderness in his eyes made my heart race.

"I think it's best," I said.

He released my arm and nodded. Without another word, I retreated to my room.

CHAPTER 31

Liverpool, England—Nisse

MUD SPLASHED OVER MY SHOES AND TROUSERS AS I raced across the cobblestone street, dodging omnibuses and private carriages while threading between people and mystical entities that had abandoned their lands and coexisted with humans. The pungent effluvium from factories, workhouses, and sewage hung in the afternoon air. My weeks in Liverpool had proven useless. I'd plodded the streets inquiring on the whereabouts of the Winslow family, and so far, I'd come up empty-handed. As my frustrations grew, images of Schläfrigz and what could be transpiring in my absence plagued me, but the disappearance of Valentina and the entire Fürst family urged me forward.

"Winslow? Earl Brett Winslow. Do you know where I can find him?" I asked a gentleman coming out of the town hall with his top hat tucked in the crook of his arm.

"Never heard of him." He dodged past me and climbed into a private carriage driven by a smartly dressed troll with gleaming gold teeth.

Deflated, I moved on down the street and stopped two women exiting a coffee house. I smoothed back the wisps of hair escaping the ribbon at the nape of my neck and directed my question at the brunette. "Excuse me, fräulein. May I have a moment of your time?"

"Why, yes." She pressed a hand to her chest and smiled warmly. Too warmly. Her dark eyes roved over me, and she gave her friend a pleased nod. "What is it we can help you with?" Her mouth curved seductively.

"I'm looking for a gentleman by the name of Winslow," I said.

"There are several Winslows around these parts," her blonde friend said. "You will have to be more specific than that." She eyed me uncertainly.

I offered her my full attention, and her brunette friend heaved a dejected sigh. "Earl Brett Winslow. His wife was from France. A Lady Risette. She died—"

"Took her own life, from what I heard," the brunette said.

"Yes, that is the one." Hope buoyed. "Do you know where I can find the family?" I regarded the brunette and victory gleamed in her eyes. She seemed pleased to have secured my attention.

But it wasn't to last, as the blonde spoke. "My cousin is betrothed to his lordship."

The brunette touched my arm and cocked her head,

looking at me through thick lashes. "But what is it you will do for us?"

"Pardon me?" I looked from one woman to the other.

With unnerving coyness, the wayward daughter of one of Liverpool's finest, I assumed, drew closer. "We gave you something of value. Now it's your turn to give us something we seek."

I didn't have time for games, but I stifled my irritation. "What is it you seek?"

"Nothing." The blonde woman placed a gloved hand on her friend's arm and glowered at her before looking back at me. "What is your business with the Winslow family?"

"I need to speak to Lord Winslow about his estate in Schläfrigz. It's urgent."

Her keen eyes studied me, and I felt my insides squirm with discomfort as I waited.

"You seem like a stand-up sort of fellow," she said. After we exchanged a few more words, she gave me an address. I thanked her and raced to a nearby carriage and hired the driver to take me to Winslow's countryside residence.

The brownstone mansion resembled a castle on a hill, overlooking a large pond. Meticulous hedges and gardens in full bloom surrounded the home. Private carriages lined the lane, and to the left of the house, a horse race was underway. The sunbonnets and umbrellas of onlookers speckled the field. Women clutched their gentlemen's elbows, and cheers rose as a brilliant chestnut thoroughbred crossed the finish line.

The carriage stopped in front of the home, and a giant clad in black and white livery descended the stairs. The driver climbed down from the carriage seat.

"His lordship isn't expecting any guest," the steward said in a deep voice.

Through the gap in the curtain, I saw the driver shrug before walking to the carriage door. When he opened the door, I ducked my head and disembarked.

"Good day, sir," the steward said. The fabric of his white gloves strained to contain his massive hands, held stiffly at his sides. "What is the purpose of your visit to Risette Estates?" His acquired refinement seemed odd in a giant. Remarkable! Bloody remarkable. Who would have thought the cannibals could be tamed?

"I came to speak with Lord Winslow on matters of his estate in Schläfrigz." I kept my eyes honed on him, alert for any sudden movement. I imagined myself hogtied and slung over his mammoth shoulders and taken to the kitchen to be stewed by his one-eyed wife.

Recognition glimmered in the giant's eyes, though his brow drew down, tugging at his sparse hairline. "You've come all this way?"

"That is correct." I squared my shoulders.

He sized up my appearance, and as if perceiving I wasn't one of his lordship's highfalutin acquaintances, he said, "His lordship is busy with a previous engagement."

I nudged my head at the field. "Am I to assume that he and his engagement are out there in the fields?"

He peered down the bridge of his crooked nose,

probably broken at some point in his life, and advanced on legs like tree trunks until he stood towering over me. The breath coming from his nostrils ruffled my hair.

Not about to let his size intimidate me, I said, "I suggest you go and fetch him and tell him the matters I have come about can't wait. They will be very concerning to him."

"Very well, I will speak to him." His breath, redolent of onions, roiled my stomach. But I stood, gawking with befuddlement. It was believed impossible for giants to live in harmony with humans, let alone manage a household. "You will wait in the parlor. Filibert?" he said over his shoulder.

Behind him, the flowers in the flowerbed swayed, and dirt flew in the air and collected with speed on the cobblestone drive. "What do you want now, Ingo?" a crackling voice snapped.

I leaned to the left to look past the steward at the dirt pile, beside which a pint-size gnarled man with a hunched back and a plaited white beard now stood. I took a second glance. Well, I'll be! A Barbegazi living amongst humans.

"See to it our guest is made comfortable in the parlor while I go and inform Lord Winslow of his arrival," the steward said before marching off with surprising grace.

I turned my gaze back at the thump of heavy footsteps to find the gnome squinting up at me. "Filibert?" I asked.

He puffed out his chest. "That's right. I'm the personal treasure keeper of the House of Winslow."

"His lordship keeps his treasures underground?"

He scowled, and his lip curled up in one corner. "Why you asking?"

I lifted my hands in peace. "You divulged, and I inquired."

He snorted and elevated a brow. All the while, I saw the gears turning in his head, as if he wondered if he'd said too much.

I cocked my head and studied him.

"What," he said. "Ain't you ever seen a gnome before?"

"Yes, but in the mountains, where they guard their own secret treasures. Any gnomes I've run across aren't too fond of socializing, and they certainly aren't footmen in humans' homes."

"I don't live with humans. I keep to my underground tunnels. But when Ingo calls, I assist." He turned and marched toward the stairs and heaved his feet up them. "We sort of took to looking out for each other since the master brought us here."

Master? "Lord Winslow is your master?"

He turned and glowered at me as he reached the landing. "No more questions." He stretched on tiptoe to reach the doorknob.

Inside, the fluttering of wings greeted us, and I spotted a fiery-haired fairy perched on the back of a pigeon, coming at us. "Greetings," the fairy said, pulling back on the leather reins.

"Bring something for our guest to quench his thirst," Filibert said before continuing down the corridor.

I inclined my head at the fairy and followed after him.

In a room stranger than any parlor I'd ever stood in before, Filibert gestured for me to take a seat on an embroidered armchair. After he left, I rose and examined the room embellished with treasures superior to any I'd witnessed on my crusades. Items one would have to dicker with thieves in back alleys or venture into lands not intended for humans to obtain. A glass dome caged a creature with hundreds of jagged teeth and oversized watering, eyes that pleaded with me to release him.

"I wouldn't do that if I were you."

I turned as the fairy approached on the pigeon. A glass of water hovered in midair and moved toward me. As the glass drew near, I reached out and gripped it, holding it to inspect the magical enchantment.

"Are all of Lord Winslow's servants magical creatures?" I asked before bringing the glass to my lips and gulping back its contents. Fire raced down my throat, and I frowned and held out the glass to inspect it as the taste of brandy warmed my belly.

Her musical laughter danced about the room. "Most guests require a stiff drink to endure time spent at his lordship's home." She winked. "His appetite for collecting is quite extraordinary. But to answer your question, no, not all of us are marvelous beings that some humans seek to possess while others run from in terror. His lordship does employ a few predictable humans."

I turned back to the dome. "And you don't mind that he keeps your kind caged?"

She hovered beside me. Her delicate fingers traced the dome. "That is a Kjøtt eater. They inhabit the tree canopies in the Weeping Forest in Norway. The slice of his tongue will sever your flesh and inject deadly poison that will infect your blood first, then as it moves through your body, devour your muscles and then your organs, leaving your brain for last. They are a threat to all living things. Above all, they crave fairy blood and have an appetite that is never satisfied. So, to answer your question, no. I care not what my master does with his kind."

"Are you a slave in this household?" I gave her a sideways glance.

Her face softened, and a small smile touched her ruby red lips. "I stay of my own free will. Most all do." She eyed the creature trapped in the glass. "Lord Winslow found me wounded and nursed me back to health. Brought me back here because I had nowhere else to go." Her fingers tightened on the dome, and it shook under her grip. I heard a cracking sound, and a hairline fracture appeared in the glass. "The Kjøtts invaded our homes and slaughtered us, and the few of my kind that remained fled to other regions."

"Peony!" A voice reverberated behind us. The fairy veered her mount backward and hung her head, not out of fear, but out of reverence. A dark-haired sweaty fellow with mutton chops strode forward and covered the dome with a larger one.

"I'm sorry, my lord. But I hate the sight of the little demon," she said with downcast eyes.

"I understand. But his kind is also becoming extinct. If we go around killing off each other, there will be none of us left."

"I disagree, my lord. The strong will always defeat the powerless." And with that, her mount flew out of the room, leaving an undeniable scent of peonies in her departure.

The man I assumed to be Lord Winslow stood staring after her with his hands resting on his hips. After a moment, he turned to me, and his hooded gaze disappeared, and curiosity took its place. "I heard you bring news of my estate in Schläfrigz."

"I do. I'm Nisse Strasser." I held out a hand, which he shook cautiously.

"Tell me, Nisse Strasser; what is this news you traveled so far to bring?"

My heart pounded. "Are you indeed Lord Brett Winslow?"

"I am."

"If you don't mind me asking, how long has it been since you were in Schläfrigz?" I asked.

His brow furrowed. "Close to ten years, I would guess. Why do you ask?"

My throat tightened. If the man that stood before me was Lord Winslow, then who was the man Valentina had spoken of? Panic seized my chest. "A woman has gone missing. The last time I saw her, she informed me she had taken on a job as a maid and governess at your estate."

The wrinkles in his brow deepened. "That's quite impossible, as I mentioned."

"I gathered as much, because when I visited the estate it was in disrepair. It was as though you had abandoned it without a thought for its maintenance during your absence." I raked my fingers through my hair. What had happened to her?

Lord Winslow lowered himself down into the armchair I'd occupied moments ago and gestured for me to take a seat on the settee. "Missing, you say?"

I sat down. "Before she went missing, it was her brother, and some years before that, her parents vanished."

"Strange indeed." He steepled his fingers at his nose, his dark blue eyes probing me.

"You may know of them. The Fürsts?"

"Yes, of course. The Fürst family were my neighbors. I caught Timo in my house, trying to steal my best silver. Slimy bastard. He had a boy with him that I learned later was his son. Felt kind of sorry for the lad to have been fathered by Timo, until I peered into the boy's eyes."

"Why?" I leaned forward and rested my elbows on my knees.

"His eyes were like looking into a demon's eyes. Empty and unnerving." He shivered at the memory. "I've seen my share of demons and creatures, but something about that boy stuck with me."

"There is a beast the dwarves call the Seelenfresser that has come to our canton. A hunter once made claims he'd seen the beast. Some believe it is the reason the animals have been disappearing. The creature's victims are becoming numerous, and my vater was one of them." I choked back the emotions that admission conjured. "The people of Schläfrigz are not skilled enough to take on the creatures that exist outside our borders. Most choose to dismiss tales their sons bring home from their crusades and those of travelers as stories made up to entertain children."

"Did you say the Seelenfresser?" He had blanched.

"You know of it?"

He wetted his lips then stood, strode to the stand, poured a glass of whiskey, and swallowed the amber liquid before following it with another. He set down the glass and stood with his hands on either side of the tray, his head bowed. "May the gods help us all," he said. "He succeeded." A guttural groan rumbled from him.

"Who?" I stood. Fear enveloped me like it had the day I'd gripped a mountain ledge to pull myself over and saw my reflection in the iris of a dragon.

"King Gian of the miner dwarves." He turned, and I saw the fear in his eyes. He knew something. Something grave.

"What is it? You must tell me." I strode forward and gripped his arm. "My village may lay slaughtered and the woman I-I love…" My voice cracked. I couldn't speak the words.

"Sit, and I will give you the answers you seek." He returned to his seat. After I sat down, he continued. "When King Gian learned of my travels and adventures into forbidden lands, he and his entourage paid me a visit. It was during our evening meal. My wife, Risette, was heavy with child. At first he thought he'd persuade me with mediocre artifacts and treasures, but when I declined, his ego convinced him that it was because his offering wasn't substantial enough for a man who possessed so much. He threatened me with the life of our unborn child. Said he'd use his black magic to ensure the babe never drew breath. Afraid, Risette begged me to go in search of the power he sought."

"What power?"

"The Vormacht. It is a power he thought, when combined with the Zwilling, would surpass all magic," he said.

"Did you go?"

"I didn't. I could not leave my wife in her condition, and I didn't believe he would do what he threatened because he needed me. My pride got in the way, and because of it, after our child was born, he played with my wife's mind. She envisioned a rat scurrying in the bassinet with the babe. She…" Tears welled in his eyes. "She threw our child over the balcony, thinking he was the rat she was disposing of." Sobs convulsed his body, and he buried his face in his hands.

Nausea gripped my gut. I sat quietly until he collected himself. "I'm sorry for your loss," I said, my own grief surging in my chest.

"The guilt never gets any less. If I hadn't witnessed it myself, I'd never have believed she'd done it. I screamed at her, and she turned with unseeing eyes and walked past me to our chamber. Like a fool, I'd raced down the stairs in hopes of saving the babe. But I arrived to find my servants standing in a circle, and when I pushed my way through…" He paused. "I-I saw my child, lying on the ground, his bones crushed." Silence blanketed the room. He picked at invisible lint on his trousers and tried to steady the quiver in his jaw.

"When I returned to the chamber, my wife lay asleep on the bed as though nothing had happened. I sent for the healer that lived by the healing springs in hopes she'd cast out whatever spell had overtaken my wife. When Risette awoke she went to nurse our child and, finding him gone, she panicked. It was then I forged the story that the healer had gone crazy and dropped him. I couldn't bear for my wife to know the truth, so we buried our son and allowed the villagers to burn an innocent woman at the stake because they also wanted someone to blame for the Fürsts' disappearance."

I recalled the girl he spoke of, and her screams mingling with the cries of ecstasy of the crowd. I had stood with my vater at the window in the shop. The glow of the flames had lit the evening sky. Vater's hands had clenched at his sides, and following muttered curses, he'd said, *"They've gone crazy."* Chills clawed over my arms at the unnecessary act that had ended a life.

"King Gian paid me a visit soon after to inform me of what he'd done to my wife and again stated his desire. Afraid he'd stop at nothing to obtain this power, I went in search of the Totholz forest, where the Vormacht magic was rumored to be hidden. I searched for two years before returning home. And soon after, my wife became pregnant with our daughters. She had never recovered from our son's death, and our fear of what he'd do if I didn't find the power consumed her." Voice ragged, he wrung his hands as painful memories awoke. "She pleaded with me to return to the forest. And this time, I was successful. I brought him back the power, and by then my wife had given birth. And for a while we were happy, until the day King Gian paid us another visit and revealed to Risette what she had done. There was no end to his cruelty against my family.

"The fear of what she could do to our daughters drove her crazy. She refused to mother them in any way, and I had to hire a wet nurse from the village. One day after I'd returned from town, a servant informed me that Risette had requested she be chained in the cellar to protect the babies from her. I convinced her that she needed time away from the estate and to return to her family in France. Soon after, I received word that she had taken her own life.

"It was at this time that King Gian amped-up his quest to control the Zwilling power. King Gian ventured into the monastery in the Himalayas where a dwarf king had entrusted the monks with hiding the scrolls. By the time Gian's men had finished his massacre, only one monk remained. They tortured him, but still he wouldn't talk. It was when they discovered the monks' sacred writings hidden in a crypt that King Gian threatened to wipe their teachings and history from humans forever. The monk revealed there was a dwarf keeper entrusted with the scrolls that they'd given sanctuary. No one was permitted to look upon the scripts but the keeper. They scoured the monastery for his body and didn't find him. Suspecting he had escaped into the mountains with the scrolls, King Gian sent his men after him. But…"

"But what?" I said.

"The monk said the scrolls and the keeper were protected by a magical spell conjured by the Reinheit. The keeper was never found. From that day, Gian believed that if the dwarf Reinheit had entrusted humans with the scrolls when the Zwilling revealed itself, it would be in them. He began using humans as test subjects."

"Testing them how," I said.

"He sent his men into hamlets and cities, scouring them for humans with any physical abilities believed to be beyond what is normal for humans. He tried to summon the Seelenfresser, but their skulls could not sustain the force of his mind control, and their brains disintegrated."

I gulped back my horror. "How do you know this?"

"I saw the corpses in his mines. The ones he didn't kill in his attempts, he imprisoned to work his mines. He uses his tribesmen as overseers for his human slaves, against their will."

"How can you be certain?"

"Because the same unseeing gaze my wife had in her eyes the day King Gian killed my son shone in theirs." His eyes misted.

"Does King Jörg know of this?"

"No, not even Gian's own people know of his crimes," he said. "The tunnels he performs his sorcery in are undiscovered by his tribesmen."

I felt a frisson of anger. "Why didn't you warn the villagers of his activities?"

"Because I believed, as long as they remained naive, they were safe."

"You didn't think to seek the help of the mountain dwarves?"

His gaze shifted downward. "After what I saw in that mine, I knew I had to protect my daughters. I was all they had left. So, after I was escorted from the mines that day, I packed up my household and fled back to England."

"What made you think he wouldn't send his men after you?"

"I didn't," he said. "But I hoped with the distance and his obsession with summoning the Seelenfresser, he'd forget me. Besides, he wasn't the only one seeking magic. After King Gian used my family as blackmail against me, I spent my time while searching for the Vormacht seeking protection against him. As you can see, my home isn't typical of men of my station. Magic fills every crevice, and it provides protection not only for me and my children, but for mystical beings that have been hunted to exploit their magic. Together we are stronger. Together we have established a fortress to keep out those wishing us harm."

"That is all well and good, but what of Schläfrigz? You must come with me and expose King Gian. With your help and that of the mountain dwarves, we may stand a chance."

He heaved a sigh. "If I'm correct in my assumptions that King Gian has succeeded in animating the Seelenfresser, then I'm afraid nothing I can do will stop what he has planned. However, I feel I have no choice but to return and try to set right the wrongs of my past."

CHAPTER 32

Farrah and Zuna sat on the blanket spread on the grass in the garden with their necks craned and their eyes regarding me with anticipation.

I placed a hand on my chest, evoking passion and yearning from my audience as I told the fairy tale I'd woven in my head since I was a girl. "Time was running out, and Küni rode his steed urgently toward the farm. If he didn't confess his love for the girl, she would marry another." My voice cracked with feigned emotion.

"But he can't. Prima is his true love," Zuna said with a sorrowful expression.

"Yes, but she doesn't know this," I said. "She believes he will never see her as she sees him. She worries that she will spend her life always loving a man that will—"

"Never see her as the woman she has become." Tears welled in Zuna's eyes.

Farrah's hands twisted the blanket. "But Prima must

have Küni because, without him, she will die of a broken heart. She already lost so much. Her mum, her papa, and her sister." Her brow furrowed, and her eyes flashed. "This is a dreadful story. I shan't listen to it anymore. You said this was your favorite story of all."

I smiled and lifted a finger. "You must wait and hear how the tale ends."

Zuna used the back of her hand to wipe her tears. "Please, tell us more."

"Küni arrived at the homestead to find the prince, his royal carriage, and entourage waiting in front of the cottage. Prima stepped outside. She had foregone her rags and was now adorned in silks and jewels fit for a princess; she was more beautiful than he'd ever seen her. But the look of sadness on her face puzzled him. He dismounted and raced to her.

"'Küni,' she cried. 'What brings you to my doorstep?'

"'You can't marry the prince,' Küni said, and grabbed her hand and held it over his heart. 'It is I you love.'"

Farrah and Zuna groaned and awed, holding on to my every word.

"'But you do not love me,' Prima said, and tears brimmed in her eyes.

"'You are wrong. I've loved you for some time, but I'm a simple man without treasures and servants to wait on you,' Küni said.

"'I care not for those things,' she said."

The girls leaned closer.

"'I would love and provide for you until my body

breathes its last breath,' Küni said, his stormy gray eyes holding hers.

"'Can it be true?' Prima clasped her hands to her chest. 'Do you return my love?'

"Küni nodded and wrapped Prima in his arms, and they shared a kiss, and for the first time in her life, she felt whole. When they broke from the enchantment of love pounding in their hearts, Prima told the prince she couldn't marry him, and though brokenhearted, the prince departed."

The girls squealed. "And Küni and Prima lived happily ever after?" Zuna asked.

I laughed. "That's right. Prima finally finds the love she has always wanted, and Küni and her live a long life together."

"And they had lots of children?" Hope beamed on Farrah's face.

"Five, in fact," I said.

The girls linked arms and lay on the blanket, staring dreamily up at the sky. "Do you suppose we will marry princes," Farrah said to her sister.

"I don't care if he is a prince, as long as he loves me like Küni loved Prima." Zuna twisted to look at her sister.

I pushed to my feet. "Come now, we must get back to your studies."

"If we were princesses, we'd never have to worry about arithmetic," Farrah said with a huff.

"Head inside, and I will be along shortly," I said.

After the girls had entered the house, I folded the

blanket and gathered the picnic basket. As I turned to head back, I noticed Lord Winslow and Mrs. Potts engaged in what appeared to be a heated discussion. I'd met his lordship in the corridor that morning, and although he'd been gracious, he had spent the rest of the morning avoiding my gaze when our paths crossed. I'd wondered if my early departure the evening before had offended him. I studied them a moment longer, and as Lord Winslow turned to look at me, I lowered my gaze and hurried on toward the mansion.

CHAPTER 33

The Valley—Lord Winslow

"Y OU'VE BEEN GOING AROUND ALL DAY LOOKING miserable," Mrs. Potts said to him from where she stood at his side. "What happened between you and the girl?"

He glanced at the garden as the children stood and walked toward the house. Then his gaze settled on Valentina, and his heartbeat quickened. "I let my pride get the best of me and offended her in the process."

"I warned you she isn't like the maidens of the kingdom. She is the Reinheit for a reason. She is pure of heart. Much too good—" She caught herself.

"Why hold your tongue now, General? These human illusions haven't stopped you from speaking what is on your mind before."

She straightened and arched back her shoulders.

"With all due respect, sir, she will never be your bedmate to discard when you've finished. She has a higher purpose to fulfill."

He glowered at the general. "I don't think of her like that. I grow tired of this mission and seeing you enrobed in women's clothing."

"Need I remind you, sir, that your vater has requested our presence at the castle," Mrs. Potts said.

He stood looking at Valentina, and an ache formed in his chest. Her beauty and the innocence within her heightened his desire to protect her. The yearning had become suffocating. His time in the valley had made him soft.

As Valentina's eyes met his, he choked back the mixture of emotions stirring in him and turned to Mrs. Potts. "We will go, but ensure your men are in place in our absence. Twice the Seelenfresser has managed to get past the barriers and enter this realm. If your men fail again, I will make an example of them for all to see."

"As you request, Your Highness," Mrs. Potts said and left him.

He looked back at Valentina as she walked toward the house, and he broke into a jog to catch up with her. "Valentina."

She turned at his call and stopped to wait for him to catch up. "Good afternoon, my lord."

"And to you as well," he said. "I feel a bit of a fool for allowing my pride to ruin a night that was planned with good intentions."

"I appreciated your thoughtfulness. I don't recall a time that I've had so much fun. You never lost patience with me regardless of my poor dancing skills," she said with a laugh. Her eyes gleamed like the prettiest of jewels, and the weakness inside him drew his gaze to her full mouth. Damn him for allowing a human into his heart.

"It was an evening I will remember," he said. "I will be gone for a few hours, but you and the children have nothing to worry about. The guards will be on full alert."

"I thank you for your protection," she said sincerely, looking at him.

As a tendril of hair fluttered across her cheek, he wanted desperately to reach out and caress it away, but he had come to an understanding: Valentina Fürst was too good for him. To think there was a time when he would have scoffed at such a thought. After all, he was a prince, and she was but a farm girl and a human, at that. However, after months spent together, he'd come to regard her as a holy treasure guarded by the gods. As Crispian had stated, she was the Reinheit, and her calling was to protect dwarves and humans.

"You are a woman of quality, Valentina Fürst, and my family is better for having you." He bowed at the waist. "Good day."

"Thank you, my lord," she said.

He left her standing there and went inside to change. His mind drifted back to the day at the market when he'd come to see for himself the incompetent human his vater believed was the next Reinheit. He hadn't expected to behold such beauty. She had made rags and hunger look inviting, and like the woman he'd met in the forest all those years ago who had left him naked and humiliated, Valentina had enchanted him. His thoughts hadn't been pure. The hatred in his heart for her kind kindled the desire to break her.

Obligated to follow his king's orders, he took on the mission to become Earl of Chateau Winslow, protector of the Reinheit. He'd watched her from the window that first day as she stumbled under armloads of wood and shovelfuls of manure. He'd caught his breath when she arrived at the evening meal bathed and dressed in a gown stored within the wardrobe in her chamber. He'd felt wonderment and then anger at the temptation his vater had placed before him. He'd waited for the opportunity to judge her unqualified to hold an endowment awarded to dwarves, but each time she'd proven him wrong.

When the Seelenfresser had broken through the barriers of the realm and Valentina risked her life to save Princess Zuna, it forced him to honestly look at her. Where greed and lack of empathy for the living swelled within her brother, the very essence of Valentina's soul gleamed with amity and benevolence. And he'd come to know in his heart that she was a woman of exemplary goodness, and for this reason, the Zwilling power had chosen the Fürst siblings as hosts.

CHAPTER 34

Kingdom of Himmelart—Tower

THE TRÄGER PEERED THROUGH THE TOWER window at the valley, a mere speck in the distance. She felt a vast ache to hold her children. When the loneliness and anguish became crippling, she forgot the reason she couldn't leave. And days like today, she stood at the window and dreamed of a life that was her own, but that would never be. A single tear rolled down her pale cheek. In her hand, she clutched the scroll with the answers King Jörg and she'd spent the last decade searching for, but never could she have conceived the answer would come at so high a cost. She shut her eyes and laid her cheek against the cold stone wall of the place that had been both sanctuary and prison. The realization of what she had to do daunted her. There was no other way, and time had run out.

Deemed possessed from birth, people inferred she'd sucked the life from her mother, as she'd never risen from the birthing bed. She had barely started walking when she showed the first signs of magic and sent the servants into a panic. Whisperings of a witch child cast fear over her hamlet. And her papa, wanting to protect her and give her a chance at a normal life, sold everything and moved her to northern Italy, to a little village by the sea, where no one knew of Piera Francesco, the girl rumored to be possessed. And it was there that she had been the happiest.

In her twentieth year, she met Timo Fürst, a handsome traveler who had wooed her and her papa into considering him worthy of marriage. Timo moved her to his home in Switzerland. By the time she'd become pregnant with her first child, a son, she was trapped in a loveless marriage, but foolishly, she'd hoped the child would change her husband's fits of rage and infidelity. After they lost their home in Schläfrigz, they moved to the homestead in the foothills of the Alps.

One day as she sat milking the cow in the barn, a weary traveler wearing a hooded, green calico cloak paid her a visit. Startled, she'd leaped to her feet, knocking over the pail of milk. She grabbed a pitchfork to defend herself. The cloaked figure lowered their hood and revealed their identity. Before her had stood a woman dressed in simple clothing with kind eyes and a gentle smile. Loneliness for the companionship of another woman prompted her to invite the traveler in for tea. They'd spent the next hour visiting, and as the traveler got up to leave, she reached out and embraced Piera, and it was then the woman revealed her true intent. A jolt had charged Piera's body and energy more powerful than the magic she'd known enveloped her. Her knees buckled, and she fell to the floor.

"What have you done to me?" Piera had gasped, gawking at the traveler in astonishment. But the woman never uttered another word. Like a spirit of the dead come to visit the living, she vanished before Piera's eyes.

After that day, Piera felt changes as the fetus continued to develop. Her hair fell out in clumps, and bruises spread over her flesh. Cuts turned into gaping wounds that would not heal. Her weight dropped, and her bones became like fragile china, yet the doctor said the babe thrived. Timo, repulsed by her appearance, found every excuse to stay in the village. Abandoned and scared, she believed the traveler had cursed her and her child. The magic that had existed within her since birth battled against the power of the newcomer.

Death had surely met her the day she gave birth on a bed of pine branches in the forest. She'd been at the river washing clothing when the first knee-bending labor pain hit. When it subsided, she'd gathered her basket and started for home. Then the next contraction hit, followed by another. Frightened and knowing she'd never make it, she prepared to give birth in the forest.

As her birthing screams rose between agonizing contractions, she'd seen the face of the healer. She bent over Piera and brushed the sweat-drenched hair from her face while offering words of comfort. The healer stayed by her side for ten long hours until her son, Orell Fürst, came into the world—red, fists swinging, and mouth open in shrill screams that blinded her with pain. She'd fallen back against the forest floor and closed her eyes, only to open them days later in a strange little hut. The healer knelt by her bed and offered her spoonfuls of warm broth.

In a basket nearby, her son slept peacefully, and seeing the perfect pinkness of his flesh, she knew he thrived. The instinct that she'd often noticed in other mothers rose in her, but the look in the healer's eyes gave her pause. When questioned, the healer told Piera of the mark that marred the child's flesh. She brought the babe to Piera to see, pulling back the blanket and pointing at the mark on the curve of his hip. The child's birthmark resembled two snakes conjoined. She asked the healer if she knew the meaning of the symbol, and the woman said it was the mark of the Zwilling.

The healer explained what she understood of the twin power—a dwarf power composed of both dark and pure energies, which manifested in two vessels—hosts possessing magical aptitudes. She said hundreds of years ago, a dwarf king, fearing the capabilities of the power, had it entombed in a lava catacomb guarded by fire spirits, and all talk of its existence was forbidden. The king tasked a dwarf with compiling all information relating to the Zwilling in a set of scrolls, including instructions for defeating the power if it was ever liberated from its confinement. Over the years, the healer told her, there had been whisperings that the Zwilling power had escaped the catacombs, but its manifestation had never been seen—and, to her knowledge, the power had never manifested itself in one host.

When Piera told her of the traveler's visit, and the magic she herself possessed, the healer's eyes had widened with surprise before her brow knitted. It was because Piera possessed magic of her own that she still drew breath, the healer warned her. The Zwilling had chosen Piera, assumed a human form, played on her loneliness, and when it found the chance, it had melded with her.

As she had done with her magical abilities, Piera kept her awareness of the power that she and her son carried a secret, fearing what would become of them if people found out. Soon her body returned to its former vigor, but she was plagued with excruciating headaches each time her son cried or threw a tantrum. She sought relief from the healer, but she didn't have the answers Piera sought to the mysterious power.

When she became pregnant with her daughter the headaches seemed to calm, but she worried, as she did with her son, that the babe would bring damnation upon the earth. Although Orell had been a beautiful golden-haired boy, he pushed away all her attempts at affection, and when she looked into her son's emotionless black eyes, it reminded her of the mark he bore.

However, her second pregnancy was not the same as the first. Instead, she developed the glow of most pregnant women, and hope sprang within her. She sang and spoke to the unborn babe, and the connection she felt with the fetus brought her peace.

The day the contractions came, she'd grabbed her son and hurried to the healer's hut in the forest. Her daughter had come out silent and lifeless, and as the healer fought to save the child, Piera looked helplessly on. When the child let out one loud wail and then was silent, the healer said, "She lives." While wrapping the babe in a blanket, the healer had paused, and turned troubled eyes on Piera.

"What is it?" Piera asked, but before the healer spoke, she knew what she would reveal.

"She too bears the mark." The healer placed the child on Piera's breasts. Peering down at her daughter, love had swelled in her chest.

The healer said the Zwilling had cursed Piera by making her the carrier of its offspring. She believed all children born of her womb would possess the power. After a day had passed, she told the healer to fix her so she could no longer conceive children.

Valentina was a few months old when Piera found Orell hovering over the bassinet, attempting to smother her. She'd yelled and pushed him aside and gathered Valentina in her arms, and tears flooded her eyes when the babe let out a wail. Then a shrill cry from Orell buckled her knees and hailed agonizing screams from the baby. She remembered her five-year-old son's words: "*I hate her.*"

Piera loved her children, but as they flourished her worry intensified. Orell lacked empathy and was prone to violent outbursts, and his hatred for her and Valentina oozed from him, while his infatuation with his vater was magnified. Piera found serenity and contentment in Valentina, a delightful child who found joy in the smallest things. She yearned to nurture and help, often accompanying Piera to neighboring farms and to the village to care for the ill and the poor.

Piera realized the headaches she and her daughter suffered came on when Orell showed signs of ecstasy or displeasure. As the pain worsened she'd sought help from the healer, but Orell had informed his vater of their friendship and he forbade Piera seeing her. Left with no choice, Piera contemplated sending Valentina away for her protection, but Timo had come up with the fool idea to enter the mountains to find his fortune in the dwarf mines. Afraid of King Gian unleashing his wrath on the village, she'd gone after Timo to stop him.

Her last memory of the real world was her blood staining the snow-covered mountain paths after Timo had beaten her in a blinding fit of rage and left her for dead. King Jörg said a peasant had found her in an alleyway and brought word of the human who'd broken through their barriers. The dwarf healer formulated potions to save her, and when she returned to the land of the living, King Jörg had come to visit her. Piera saw virtue in him, and desperate to understand the Zwilling power and free her children and herself of it, she shared her story. However, upon her revelation, the king's eyes had hooded with concern. He said an exorcism could mean death for her and her children, and because of the lack of knowledge surrounding the power, he wasn't sure if it was even possible.

Questions arose: How had the power been released from its confinement, and by whom? The king told her he suspected something more significant was at work, and the tales filtering through the valley of her disappearance may work to their benefit. If Piera was believed dead and her children remained ignorant of the abilities that lay dormant within them, they might remain safe until King Jörg and his men could uncover who had freed the power.

Uncomfortable with the plan for her to stay hidden while something or someone lay waiting to use her children for their own means, she begged the king to send someone to watch over them.

The door to the tower creaked open, and King Jörg entered. Piera moved away from the window and sat down in the chair at the small desk in the corner. "I don't know if I can do this," she said to the man who'd been her confidant.

He strode to her side, and with thick fingers, he lifted her chin and peered into her tear-filled eyes. "The love of a parent is a punishment of its own. The sacrifice that must be made is great, but if we do not do what is required, King Gian will raise an army of beasts that will wreak havoc. You're the Träger, and together with the pull of the Reinheit, we may be able to stop the Seelenfresser and the rise of the Vormacht. I wish there was another way…" His voice broke, and he turned away.

"I will hold my children one last time," she said, looking down at her hands clasped in her lap. "My life in return for theirs is a sacrifice I'd make ten times over, but I never thought I would have to kill my own child."

"He is evil."

"But he is my son." Her voice sounded brittle and broken, like tiny shards of shattered glass.

King Jörg returned to her side and clasped her hands in his. "I know, my friend. I wish I could wield my magic to save you from this pain, but I can't. You and Valentina are our only hope."

CHAPTER 35

Kingdom of Himmelart

Back at the palace, Sixtus paced the floor of his chamber. A mighty battle twisted in his heart, and he knew but one thing that would take his mind off the torment. What was becoming of him? Damn his vater for sending him to the village to mingle with humans. As his annoyance stewed within him, he thought about life before he'd met Valentina, and what it would have been like if he had not. Was he a better man for it?

There was a rap on the door. "Your Highness, it is I, Noelia, responding to your summons."

Lady Noelia's seductive voice drew him to the door, and he threw it open and pulled her into his chamber.

"Oh, Your Highness, such fire!"

Usually her excitement overwhelmed all miseries and

thoughts, but when it didn't, he cursed. Determined to drive Valentina from his mind, he pulled at the laces of Lady Noelia's bodice as he led her toward the bed. She giggled with anticipation, her eyes wild with lust. Her gown dropped to the floor, and he grabbed a handful of her breasts, pressing his mouth on hers. He tried to ignite feelings of old, but when they wouldn't come he stepped back and lifted her dress from the floor and threw it at her. "Leave me," he said.

She gaped at him. "But, Your Highness, do I not please you?" Tears welled in her blue eyes.

"It's me, not you," he said, running a hand through his dark locks. "Please, cover yourself and leave me to my misery."

She held her gown against her breasts. "Has your time in the village stolen your passion, or is it another woman?"

He dropped his hand and gawked at her.

"That's it, isn't it?" Her face grew taut, and her tears faded. "You have ruined me. No decent man will want me. I thought you would marry—"

"Marry? I will never marry," he said, hopelessness expanding within him.

"You will. Your vater will see to it. And you will continue to have your whores and ladies to fill your desire." She fumbled to dress, then marched to the door, where she paused and looked back at him, her eyes seething. "I see the elixir she has hypnotized you with, and I hope she crushes your heart as you have done so many."

"I said, leave me. Now go." He marched toward her and she fell back in fear, grabbed the doorknob, and dashed from the room. He slammed the door after her and leaned back against it and ran his hands over his face. *May the gods help me, what have I done?*

CHAPTER 36

Valentina

DRESSED IN A WHITE NIGHT-ROBE, I SAT ON THE window seat in my chamber, tracing the rain droplets pelting the windowpane. Visions of the Seelenfresser governed my mind before my thoughts turned to Mutter. What would she think of what had become of my brother? How was such a thing possible? A human turned beast. Unrest had plagued me since my discovery in the meadow, and the force of something more captivated my days. The ache to see Flicker and Nisse was like a blade to my chest. They would know what to do. I rested my head back against the wall framing the window, overcome with the loneliness that had chased me all my life.

Don't lose hope, my child, a soothing voice said. My eyes flew open, and I released my knees to glance about the room for the speaker. The voice had come to me the day the woman had shoved me out of the sewers. In the light of the lantern, I saw a mouse scurry across the floor and disappear into a small hole in the wall. I strained to hear the lull of the voice again, but it never came. I was alone.

A flash of light drew my eye to the pavilion that sat in the middle of the gardens. An aura of white and purple shone brightly before dimming to a glint. Pulling myself up on my knees, I stretched to see what caused the light, but the cascading sheets of rain made it impossible. I rose and threw a shawl around my shoulders before hurrying down the corridor and the back stairs. I wove through the corridors on the main floor until I reached the front door.

Outside, my bare feet slapped against the slippery marble stairs as I rushed down them. Shrubs tugged at my night-robe like fingers trying to pull me back, but I pushed forward with the need to know what magic was at work. Inside the pavilion, the light had faded to a flicker but provided enough light for me to discern the slender figure of a woman. She sat on the bench with her back to me. The thumping in my chest intensified.

"Who are you?" I shouted above the cracking thunder of the storm.

She sat unmoving.

"State your business here." I blinked away the rain-drops teetering on my lashes.

"I come in peace," the woman said. Her voice didn't have the calming effect of the one I'd heard earlier. She turned to face me as lightning lit the horizon and thunder cracked again. In the brief flash, I saw the woman clearly. Waist-length blonde hair cascaded over her slender shoulders, and her piercing, glowing gaze held me. "Step inside before the storm soaks you."

Drawn by curiosity, I stepped out of the rain, and as I did, an uncanny feeling gripped me. "Are you a witch?" I dared to breathe.

"I mean you no harm, dear one." She patted the seat beside her. "Come, sit."

I shook my head and remained where I stood. "Why are you here?"

"I've come to warn you."

"Warn me of what?" I asked.

"Your brother."

My brother? "What is it you speak of?" Did she know what had become of him? How did she find me?

"King Jörg has nurtured the Seelenfresser within your brother because he desires to resurrect the Vormact power," she said.

King Jörg? People had hailed the goodness of the dwarf king. Then I recalled the creature's words the day at the river: the dwarves are the enemy. You can't trust them.

"But why tell me?" I asked. Did this woman, or witch, have the answers I sought?

"Because you are the Reinheit."

"The what?" My heart drummed in my chest.

"You do not know?" She sounded incredulous. "Of

course, they didn't tell you. They set out to protect you by keeping you in the dark."

"I beg you, speak clearly." I stepped closer.

"Of course. You should know everything." The woman then spoke of a Zwilling power and her belief that Mutter was its carrier and her children its offspring. By the time she'd finished, I had sat down beside her, paralyzed by astonishment and building fear.

Could it all be true? Did magic lay dormant within me? I'd never felt it. But the transformation of Orell was undeniable. Had I not seen it for myself, I may have remained in denial. Even the woman who sat before me demonstrated that magic breathed. Tales of magic outside our borders were frequent, but like the villagers, it was hard for me to acknowledge something I had never seen.

"They've used all of this to keep you hidden." She swept out a hand, and before me the mansion and grounds faded and a dilapidated estate stood in their place. The white paint of the pavilion flaked and peeled, weathering with age. Beneath me, the bench rocked and creaked unsteadily under my weight.

"What have you done? The children and Lord Winslow—"

"It was all an illusion orchestrated by the mountain dwarves," she said. "There are no children or Lord Winslow."

I rose cautiously and stared at the woman. "What trickery is this? I've spent months serving his lordship's household." The cold encompassing the pavilion transformed my breath into a trail of rising white billows. I glanced around at the forest to find the trees naked and the grass brown with signs of winter. But that day it had been summer; I'd picked flowers in the gardens to place in vases in each room of the mansion. "I-I don't understand." I turned back to the woman, but she wasn't looking at me.

Alarm swept over her face as she leaped to her feet. The mirage faded, and before me stood a dwarf with a mangled face and glassy eyes. "It can't be! The Träger. She's alive," he said.

I stumbled back at the sight of him and lifted a hand to my mouth to stifle a cry. Fear like I'd never felt before surged through me as his gaze settled on me.

"We must leave. Take the girl," he said.

Before I could react, hands grabbed me from behind. "Let go of me." I clawed and fought to free myself, but when I caught sight of my captors, I cringed in horror and fear, all fight forgotten.

You are not alone. Fight, my daughter. The voice I'd heard in my chamber was with me again. *I'm coming for you.*

Mutter? It was the last thought that entered my mind before my world went dark.

CHAPTER 37

As I regained consciousness, my throat and lungs burned with the scent of sulfur so strong it twisted my stomach. The intense heat stung my flesh. I became aware of the squelching and bubbling of liquid and the flapping of wings. I opened my eyes and beheld fire-breathing creatures soaring in the black vault above me. *Where am I?* My heart beat faster and faster. I struggled to pull myself up, but the burn of restraints shaving into my wrists and ankles stilled me. Beneath me, the chill of marble bit through my thin night-robe. I turned my head, and the heat intensified as I looked upon the lava river churning around me.

There was a hiss, and something cast a shadow over me, and I stared into the citrine eyes of my captor. I recoiled and yanked at the bindings holding me, my eyes peeling away from those above me to another sentinel posted at my feet—a creature with brass armor strapped over the raven-like feathers of its chest, and a massive skull encased in a brass helmet. I froze, too afraid to breathe, as one captor leaned close. His forked tongue slithered out to scratch my cheek, and saliva dripped from his gray-tinged fangs onto my face. The beast nudged me with its nose before it straightened at the clap of multiple footsteps on the wet flagstone.

"I trust our prisoner is awake?" I recognized the voice of the dwarf from the pavilion before he came into view. The small legion of creatures attending him resembled the sentinels stationed by me.

One of my captors let out a rasping call, and the dwarf smiled. "Good." He lifted a hand, and a floating bridge expanded and granted him and two of his attendants passage. He stopped before me, garbed in black robes and furs, regarding me with glassy eyes sunken in blue-tinged sockets. Around his neck hung a golden eagle medallion with a dull amber gem embedded in its center. He tilted his head, ropes of his hair swinging, the wind of their movement fanning my face. "By the sound of your rapid breathing, I can assume you are scared."

"What do you want with me?" I asked, my voice hoarse.

He laughed. "Why, to bleed the power that courses through your veins."

He twisted as the beasts on the other side of the river parted to reveal a middle-aged dwarf dressed in rags. She edged forward, slowly at first, until a creature shoved her from behind. She regained her balance and moved more quickly. As she drew near, I saw the leather pouch she carried with trembling hands.

"Don't dally," the dwarf said.

Fear clogged my throat. "Please, don't do this. I'm not this Reinheit you speak of. I've never had magic of any sort."

"Don't fret, my little pet." I cringed as the dwarf stroked my hair as a parent would a child. "Soon your blood will spill, and when you've taken your last breath, your soul will be mine."

I don't want to die. My heart threatened to batter my ribcage. I wanted to scream for help, but I had no one to call on. Lord Winslow, the children, Mrs. Potts, Yara—none of them were tangible. The barrier between reality and fantasy had crashed around me, and I'd fallen into a world of necromancy.

"Why do you seek this power?" I asked, needing to understand the nightmare I couldn't wake from since the day in the meadow.

"Death will soon claim you. I suppose there is no threat in disclosing what will transpire when you are gone." He lifted the medallion and caressed it with admiration. "This holds the Vormact power, an energy that dates back to ancient Rome. It was fashioned by Roman senators. The Roman Empire unleashed brutality, terror, and tyranny, and its leaders were driven by greed and belief in their superiority. At his victory at the Battle of the Trebia, Hannibal, a Carthaginian military commander, acquired this supreme power during the pillaging. The

Vormact never returned to the Romans. Its last known whereabouts was somewhere in the Totholz forest. I've gone to great lengths to obtain the means to reawaken its ability, and you, my pet, are one facet of the plan."

The threads of my sanity frayed with this insight, stripping me of the normalcy and security I'd known in a world free of magic and creatures—a world I'd considered flawed but less complicated. I was forever changed because I couldn't unsee what I had seen. Tears blotted out the faces towering over me, and I jerked when cold hands touched my arm.

"I need room to work," the woman said.

The dwarf gripped her arm and placed his mouth to her ear. "Don't try anything, or your flesh and that of your kin will bubble and melt from your skeletons in the depths of what sprawls before you." As he breathed his threat, the elongated, shadowy heads of fire ghouls rose from the pool, their gaping mouths stretching wider as they groaned with desire.

The dwarf and his entourage stood back to observe as the woman unrolled the pouch, revealing various sizes of gleaming blades. Fern-green eyes brimming with pity and fear held mine. The straining muscles in my neck relaxed, and I lay my head back against the stone and watched her. "Forgive me," she whispered. "Take a deep breath, and it will be over before you know it."

I nodded, squeezed my eyes shut, and inhaled. Wincing as the blade parted my flesh, I kept my eyes closed, unwilling to look upon the world I'd been plunged into. Tears cascaded down my cheeks and dampened my neck. Warmth trailed along my arm as the blood left my body. Today I would die. The faces of Mutter, Nisse, and Flicker flashed before me, and a vast love surged. I would never feel the touch of Nisse's lips on mine and never again observe the glint of mischievousness in Flicker's eyes. A wail rose in my chest, and my lips parted. The walls of the cave heard my lament.

And energy erupted within me.

My eyes flew open as my body arched, and the marble trembled and fractured beneath me. The threads of the ropes confining me unraveled.

"Magnificent!" the dwarf's voice thundered. "The Reinheit is strong in her."

"Sire, the wound—it heals," a raspy voice said.

I twisted my head to look and found no blemish marring my arm.

"Impossible. She isn't trained. How can she hold such strength?" The dwarf lurched forward and clutched my arm. His long, grotesque fingernails crumbled into dust against my flesh. He snatched back his hand as if scorched, and his mouth hung open. "Bring chains and fetch the Seelenfresser, now!" He lifted a hand, and a purple aura burst from his fingertips and pinned me back, bleeding the tears from my eyes.

CHAPTER 38

Nisse

Ahead of me, Lord Winslow sat stiff and alert, scouring the terrain as we wove our mounts along the mountain path.

"Do you see anything familiar?" I asked.

"I need to get my bearings. The forest has grown since I was last here," he said over his shoulder.

Rocks skidded beneath my mount's hooves. "Steady boy." I stroked his neck. The horse had been my companion on many journeys and battlefields, but today he seemed skittish, his ears twitching with alertness. My hands were white-knuckled on the reins, and my eyes burned with weariness as we pushed deeper into the forbidden territory of the dwarf kingdoms.

Overhead, the bloated gray sky churned and seethed with the threat of more rain. "If we don't find the access soon, we will be forced to seek cover until this storm passes," I said.

After Lord Winslow had told me about what was happening, I'd spent the days leading up to our departure from Liverpool and then the voyage back worrying that Valentina and her family had fallen prey to King Gian. Each passing moment became grueling and unbearable. The return to Schläfrigz had been a crippling blow: ten more lives had been lost in my absence. It appeared the Seelenfresser's taste had evolved, and only the young would satisfy his cravings.

Lord Winslow and I had ridden to Chateau Winslow. The estate sat in abandoned decrepitude, as I remembered it. I felt confused and disheartened, but that had receded when his lordship pointed at the many sets of horse tracks leading from the forest to the pavilion. The grass had been uprooted under the treads of an army. Someone had come to the estate, but for what purpose, we did not know. We set out to find out.

Some hours ago, we'd lost their trail. We ventured farther into the mountains, relying merely on Lord Winslow's memory.

He lifted a hand, signaling me to stop. "Listen—do you hear that?"

"Sounds like a legion," I said.

"Do you suppose it's the ones from the estate?"

"Perhaps. Let's check it out." Heeling my mount, I guided him forward until I spotted the dwarf army through the trees. I urged my horse into the shelter of the forest and dismounted. Lord Winslow, light on his feet, dropped to the ground beside me. As the regiment drew closer, I observed the ginger-haired general riding next to a striking fellow who sat tall and proud upon his steed.

"That's Prince Sixtus from the mountain tribes," Lord Winslow said. "And that is General Crispian."

Behind them rode an older dwarf with a full beard and an ample stomach, who looked like he would teeter over with a shift in the wind. Beside him on a black stallion rode a woman cloaked in a red hooded cape with gleaming white tresses that cascaded over her chest and stopped at her waistline.

"It appears they are prepared for a battle," Lord Winslow said. "But against who?"

"And what is a human doing with them?"

"Your question is my own."

"Do you recognize her?" I asked.

"No."

"Well, I'm not about to stand around and waste more time. If what the villagers say is true, King Jörg is an honorable man, and I will take my chances with him." I swung onto the back of my horse. "Let's not repeat the mistakes of the past, and address him straightaway. Shall we?"

Lord Winslow shook his head. "And lose our heads in the process." But without hesitation, he mounted his mare. We guided our horses into the open.

Seeing us, the general held up a gloved hand. "Halt," he said, and the clang of armor and thudding of horses' hooves ceased. "Who goes there?"

"We come in peace," I said.

"Peace," Prince Sixtus said. "Humans are forbidden to enter these mountains."

"We need to speak to King Jörg about matters concerning King Gian and the disappearance of a woman from the village," I said.

The prince stiffened in his saddle. "What is the woman's name?"

"Valentina Fürst."

His eyes narrowed. "What do you want with the woman?"

"She is my ward of sorts," I said. "I've spent most of my life looking out for her."

"Nisse," a woman's voice said, and I looked to the human.

My brow furrowed. "Do I know you?"

She urged her mount forward, and the king grabbed her arm to stop her. "It will be all right," she said. He released his hold, and she closed the distance between us before reining her horse to a halt and lowering her hood. I beheld the majestic woman with pale, glimmering skin whose mauve eyes held mine in a tender gaze. "It has been a long time," she said.

"Do I know you?" I asked again.

"You used to," she said with a soft smile. "I am Piera Fürst."

I tensed. "I assure you, you're not. And I've had my fill of trickery." I looked at the king. "Your Majesty, we come seeking your help. It's urgent. And treaty or no treaty, what is at stake was worth the risk."

The king's knights parted to give him passage, and he joined the woman. "Speak freely."

Not looking to waste any more time, I reiterated what I knew, and Lord Winslow inserted his knowledge when needed.

"We too seek Valentina's whereabouts," Prince Sixtus said, sizing up Lord Winslow.

"We fear my daughter is in grave danger," the woman said.

"Enough!" I glared at her. "You aren't who you claim."

"I assure you, I am." To prove her claim, she spoke of the day Orell had scarred my face and the day I'd carried Valentina into the cottage after she'd fallen from the tree.

"How do you know these things?" I asked.

She went on to explain her past and the power embedded in her by the traveler. As she revealed the identity of the Seelenfresser, I seethed. Orell had murdered my vater, and with this newfound knowledge, I wanted to rip his throat out.

"If your son is the Seelenfresser, then that would make your daughter the Reinheit," Lord Winslow said.

The woman nodded. "And King Gian will stop at nothing to destroy my children to raise the Vormacht."

Could it all be true? Was Valentina the one they called the Reinheit? "I—"

I fell silent as the earth trembled beneath us, and a harrowing scream sent birds scattering.

"She bleeds," the Träger moaned in a tattered voice. She craned her neck in the direction of the bloodcurdling. "We must hurry."

CHAPTER 39

Valentina

THE DWARF'S FACE CONTORTED AS HE struggled to constrain the entity warring to breathe life within me. His bewilderment at the force's power was minuscule in comparison to my own. What was happening to me? His hold weakened, and my right hand burst from its bonds. Hope surged, but it receded as a sentry sprang forward to deter me.

No. Panic erupted, but as if some invisible force had filled the cave the creature's knees buckled and he went down.

"Stop her," the dwarf said as the ropes shredded on my other wrist.

I sat up and scoured the cave's shadows for the liberator of my bonds but found no one. Witchery had manifested itself. But from whom? Out of the corner of my eye, I saw two wardens skulking toward me. *Stay back*, I opened my mouth to say, but they too dropped to their knees. My heart pounded, and I gawked in astonishment. It wasn't possible, was it? I looked at the bonds imprisoning my legs. *Let go.* The ropes frayed before my eyes. I glanced at the dwarf woman, who had fallen back as everything unfolded. She stood quivering. My soul cried for her protection from the evil we had plummeted into. *Run. Don't look back.*

As if hearing my thoughts, she nodded, lowered her head, and bolted past the dwarf. I concentrated on her retreat. The beasts closed in to impede her. *No. Stop.* The creatures froze in mid-motion, hands outstretched.

A newfound awareness shook me—an invisible force thrived within me, manipulating my mind to fight against the dwarf's sorcery. The authority controlling my mind and body terrified me, but I lacked the mastery and knowledge to reject it. Unlike the dwarf's magic, the entity fusing with me silently presented itself without any demonstration of palpable energy.

Bouncing to my feet with foreign agility, I gulped back the nerves clenching my throat and inched toward the dwarf, seeking my escape before it was too late. *Please let this work.*

I'd walked a few steps when the earth shuddered, and a roar erupted. The pain that had racked my skull most of my life returned, and I clutched the sides of my head. "No." I fought against the incapacitating pain as the colossal form of the Seelenfresser plodded from the shadows of a tunnel on the far side of the lava river. Blazing amber eyes focused on me as he stomped and snorted like a bull ready to charge. As he'd done in the meadow, he arched back his massive head and raged at the cave's colossal dome. Again I had an epiphany: the witchery that had altered my brother had ignited in me.

The eerie dark aura encircling the dwarf intensified at the arrival of my brother. As it had withstood the dwarf, the entity governing me revolted against the Seelenfresser. But with every roar, my brother drained the energy of the force.

"She's weakening. Grab her now!" the dwarf said.

Claws snatched at my arm and broke the flesh. I heard the hiss of my captor's every breath as it yanked me backward onto the cold marble slab. Chains rattled, and I sobbed. Soon I lay stretched out like a sacrificial lamb, the chains cutting off the circulation in my limbs.

The dwarf approached and stood beside me. "I will bleed you myself." He held out a hand, and the blade lying on the cavern floor appeared within his fingers.

"Why are you doing this?" The bones in my body throbbed with the Seelenfresser's continuous howls.

Blade in hand, the dwarf said, "I can't allow you to nurture your power. You and your brother were connected from birth because of a fool king's desire to rid his tribesmen of the Zwilling. I bled this Earth of twins to extract the power. But the Zwilling had outwitted us all for hundreds of years, and I underestimated it. After I found the power and set it free, it denied me what was rightfully mine and hid in a human—your mutter. But its deception and brilliance weren't to be ignored, because not only did it make her a carrier, it jeopardized its rise by splitting and implanting itself in babes born years apart. It aimed to seed the earth with a human lineage of Zwilling. There is but one power known to suppress the Zwilling, and that is the Vormact. It has taken me decades to arrive at this day." A sinister grin twisted his scarred face as he placed the dagger on my wrist. "Rest, my pet."

The blade slashed my wrist. I screamed and blood gushed from the wound. A tendril of gleaming energy rose from my chest, moving through the air as if summoned by the medallion dangling around the dwarf's neck.

"Gian." A familiar voice ricocheted throughout the cave. "Stand down."

Lord Winslow? I twisted my head to locate the owner of the voice. Dwarves and humans emerged from a tunnel on the opposite bank from the Seelenfresser. Although fog shrouded my brain, I recognized the two dwarves who had watched over me. After them came a man. At first glance, he was the spitting image of Lord Winslow, but different in some way.

Behind him came a face that seized my heart. Nisse. He'd come. Fury and fear darkened his face as he scanned the cave.

My eyelids grew heavy. I glimpsed a beautiful woman with glowing purple eyes and white tresses, which glimmered as though woven from the stars. The dwarf beside me cried out, "The Träger." For the first time, I noted fear in his voice. Everything was becoming muffled. I closed my eyes. I wanted to sleep, just for a moment.

"Fight, Valentina. You must fight," a woman said. The passion in her voice pulled at me, but it was smothered in a growing commotion. *Open your eyes. You must wake.* I tried to call on the energy as I had earlier, but it had dimmed. It was dying.

Gentle hands touched my arm. "Don't you die on me," Nisse's husky voice said. The chains rattled as he attempted to release me. He hadn't abandoned me. Love swelled in my chest.

The weight of the chains holding my wrists fell away, and the entity flickered. I opened my eyes to find Nisse leaning over me. He moved to free my legs. The Seelenfresser's howls had faded. My blood pooled and stained the ground, but I stared at my wounded wrist as the flesh fused. I heard the clang of swords and harsh war cries as armored dwarves clashed with the sentries. In my peripheral vision, I saw the raven-haired dwarf who had been my guardian fighting with the dwarf who'd attempted to kill me.

Across the cave the woman stood with her hands raised, flashes of blue energy blazing from her fingertips to envelop my brother. He struggled to stay upright, legs trembling, his arms outstretched, straining to snatch her. She stood firm and unbending against his power as her own power imprisoned him in a transparent, energized dome that muffled his cries.

Arms scooped me up, and the scent of leather and the

musk of the forest wafted around me. I inhaled deeply and rested my head against Nisse's shoulder. "You will be all right, little one." The comfort of his words cloaked me in warmth.

"You came back."

"Always. Never fear," he said as he wove through the carnage of fallen creatures and dwarves.

A sentry lunged at us with his sword drawn, but the raven-haired dwarf stepped between Nisse and the creature. "Get her out of here. We will manage," he said, and hearing the voice, I started and pulled away from the safety of Nisse's neck.

Over his shoulder, I squinted at the dwarf. "Lord Winslow?" But preoccupied with his opponent, the dwarf had moved off.

I spotted the other guardian dwarf with ginger hair as he withdrew his sword from a sentry sprawled on the ground. Our eyes met, and he gave me an awkward grin— one which appeared forced, as if foreign to him. "Mrs. Potts?" I said.

He bowed at the waist. "Miss Wolf."

The last months unraveled, and everything became clear.

When the dank tunnels gave way to the crisp mountain air and the sun kissed my face, Nisse set me on my feet. I swayed, and he reached out to steady me. He removed his coat and wrapped it around my shoulders. Snowflakes drifted from the sky and I frowned. Snow in the summer?

"Nisse, what month is it?"

He looked up from inspecting my wrist and regarded me as though I were a delicate globe of dandelion seeds that would drift off with one released breath. "Almost Christmas."

"Imposs…" I started to say, but then I realized that everything I'd considered impossible was, in fact, possible. "I've been gone for almost a year?"

"Indeed. It appears the dwarves hid you inside an alternate realm to protect you."

"But I saw you in town that day. Didn't I?"

"You did. Why they allowed you to leave, I'm not sure," he said.

"Perhaps I can finally shed some light on the confusion."

That voice sang to my heart. "Flicker!" I bounded past Nisse and bent and embraced my friend.

His hand patted my back. "I'm sorry I couldn't protect you. It was my duty, and I failed." His voice faltered in my ear.

I pulled back to look at him, brushing tears away with the back of my hand. Over his shoulder I spotted horses and a small group of armored dwarves standing beside them, watching the tunnels. I followed their stares, and to my surprise, the entrance had faded into the backdrop of the mountains. Swerving back to regard Nisse and Flicker, I said, "Magic?"

"That would be my guess," Nisse said.

Flicker nodded. "King Jörg has had you watched since your parents disappeared."

"But why?"

Flicker nodded toward the invisible entrance to the tunnels. "If what happens in there turns out for the good, I will let someone else tell you. But for now, let me tell you what I can," he said. "When King Jörg came looking to recruit me to widen the boundaries of protection around you, I didn't want to take on the mission because with it came secrets. And we made a promise never to keep secrets. But who better to keep an eye on you than the one you trusted most?" He dipped his head. "All of that was before you entered the alternate realm. I wanted to tell you everything, but King Jörg forbade it. He sent his son, Prince Sixtus, and his general to ensure you received the advertisement for the position. He was never to go to your stall. However, in true Sixtus fashion, he disregarded his king's orders and took it upon himself to get a look at the woman he would spend the next several months with." He snorted. "I've never been particularly fond of the fellow. Couldn't understand why the king would choose him."

"But," I said, "when Lord Winslow—or this Prince Sixtus—purchased at my stall, you acted like you'd never seen him before."

"I was surprised to see him and nervous that he'd reveal my secret. Not to mention my poor conduct and the other misdeed." He winked before sobering again. "All punishable acts."

I recalled Flicker's offering of the ruby and his addressing the one he claimed was a prince as a "peasant" and a "pompous arse." My eyes widened with bewilderment at his unwise behavior.

He avoided my gaze and continued. "When we encountered Orell in the forest, I didn't know what to do. I'm not a warrior, and I wield no magic powers, so I reported back to King Jörg. Prince Sixtus and General Crispian were entrusted with keeping you safe inside the realm—the estate. The illusion of Mrs. Potts, Lord Winslow, his daughters, and the household staff were all put in place to give you a sense of security. Prince Sixtus thought it wise to allow you to leave the realm to journey into town—a decision that caused an argument between vater and son, but the prince believed it would provide you with some normalcy. He thought if you didn't have any doubts about the happenings in the village, you'd be content and not run off. When King Gian found out that Orell's sister also embodied the Zwilling he sent the Seelenfresser to capture you, but after two failed attempts I suppose he decided to take care of matters himself."

The clash of battle rose behind me. Nisse's hand went to his sword. I spun to find two dwarves carrying a man out of the melee—my brother in his human form. The lovely creature I'd seen containing him in the dome rushed along beside his bearers, holding his hand. All evidence of her fury had vanished, and she now wore a panicked expression.

Leery of my brother and his power over me, I walked cautiously toward them as the dwarves lowered his naked body to the ground.

"My son." The woman shook with silent sobs as she knelt beside him. Blood and body matter oozed from the gaping wound in his middle. His breathing was ragged and shallow, his chest rising and falling laboriously.

I gulped, and my limbs trembled as I stood over them, warily studying the pair before I dropped to my knees beside Orell, dismissing the cruelty he'd shown toward me.

His eyes fluttered open, and as he looked upon the woman, fear I'd never witnessed before shone in his eyes. "Who are you?"

She caressed his cheek. "It is I, Mutter."

I gasped. "Can't you see he's dying?" Although Orell didn't deserve my compassion, her deception angered me. "How can you be so cruel?"

At the sound of my voice, Orell swung his gaze to me, wincing in pain. He held out his hand. Taken off guard, I hesitated, but then I realized dying alone was a fate I didn't wish on him. His fingers closed around mine, and through quivering lips, he said, "I guess you ain't so weak after all." His eyes sliced through me, and with all the strength he had left he squeezed my hand until I thought the bones would crack. I bit my lip to keep from crying out. "Delicate like a bird, but too strong in mind," he growled. Collapsing, he shook off my hand as though burned by my touch.

The woman resumed her ministrations, stroking his hair with the devotion and love of a mutter. Runnels of tears glistened on her pallid cheeks before melting like snowflakes into the grass. My brother took a sharp breath, then his chest failed to rise again. Death had claimed him. I choked back the thickness in my throat, but shed no tears for the brother who had inflicted so much pain.

The woman threw herself across his chest and wept. All-consuming emotional pain radiated from every part of her. "I'm sorry. So very sorry. I was left with no choice."

I rose and stepped back. An arm wrapped around my shoulders, and I glanced up into Nisse's sorrow-filled eyes. He cradled me against his side and placed a kiss on my temple. I turned into his consoling warmth.

Several moments later, the woman rose. Blotting her tears, she peered down at my brother. "The guilt will be mine to carry." She waved a hand at a dwarf who stood by with a blanket.

As the dwarf covered Orell's corpse, I whispered, with rising numbness, "Who are you?"

The woman's tear-filled eyes met mine. "I am Piera Fürst…your mutter."

The absurdity of her words was overwhelmingly cruel, but then thinking of the form Orell had taken on as the Seelenfresser gave me pause. I cocked my head to study her, but no part of her resembled my mutter.

She gathered her composure and looked to Nisse and I, and her gaze settled on his hand cupping my shoulder. A tender smile parted her lips and struck my heart with its familiarity. "There was one thing I always told you. Make sure your prince—"

"Is truly a prince." I finished the words that I'd recited

in my head as a cherished lullaby. "Is it truly you?" Tears fractured my voice.

"Yes, my Valentina, it is I," she said. "I see you have found your prince." She smiled at Nisse.

His arm tightened on my shoulder. "If she will have me."

Dumbfounded, I swung my head to look at him, but the question on my lips was cut short as a victorious cheer erupted. A gateway to a tunnel opened, and armored dwarves marched out. Emaciated and half-naked humans and dwarves with bodies blackened with grime emerged behind them, lifting arms to shield their eyes from the bright daylight.

"Nisse." The duplicate Lord Winslow strode toward us. His gaze fell on me. "You must be the woman I've heard about until my ears bled." Prince Sixtus's illusion had mimicked Lord Winslow's dry demeanor and dashing good looks. However, the prince had failed to mirror the threads of gray hair and the face lined by life's burdens.

"How do you do, my lord." I curtsied. Becoming aware of my flimsy night-robe, I pulled Nisse's coat tighter around me.

"I want the cave sealed up," said a man who seemed important. "Let all of King Gian's corruption burn with his corpse."

"That is King Jörg," Nisse whispered in my ear.

I looked upon the humans and dwarves crowding the mountainside, and a familiar face gripped my attention. *Vater?* I pulled away from Nisse and pushed through the crowd until I reached the man. My hand flew to my mouth.

It was him. He stood wavering as though he'd collapse at any moment. His ribs pushed starkly against taut flesh and the mark of the lash scarred his body. My lips quivered, and I stifled a sob at his condition. Pity for the towering bogeyman of my past filled me. His piercing blue eyes had dulled, and the strong hands that had frightened me as a child hung trembling at his sides.

His eyes flitted around before focusing on me. "Piera, is that you?" He looked disoriented.

All words anchored in my throat.

"Valentina." The woman claiming to be my mutter came to stand next to me. "Be careful."

Vater glanced from her to me. No recognition dawned on his face when he turned his gaze to me. "We must get home, Piera. I have cows to feed." He looked anxious, and I realized that he lived in a confusing world somewhere between present and past.

Her tone gentle, the woman said, "There is nothing left, Timo. It is all gone." She looked upon him with compassion, and it became clear that she cared for him as she had my brother.

"Mutter?" I reached out and gripped the hand dangling at her side.

She turned and bobbed her head, silent tears staining her cheeks as they did mine. I rushed at her and threw my arms around her.

"My sweet, sweet girl," she whispered in my ear while smoothing my hair. "How I've missed you."

I crumbled into the safety of her embrace.

CHAPTER 40

THE CROWD DWINDLED WITH KING JÖRG'S instructions for his men to tend to the survivors found within King Gian's mines. Mutter, Flicker, and Nisse aided the last of them into a wagon. Underneath a spruce tree that extended to the heavens, I stood wrapped in blankets and wearing boots far too large, observing King Jörg and Lord Winslow.

"The Vormacht must be returned to the Totholz forest." The king held out the medallion to Lord Winslow. "It is a task we entrust to no other. The journey is long, but one you must make alone."

"I will ready myself and set out at first light, Your Grace."

"Very well." The king held out his hand. "We are indebted to you."

Lord Winslow shook it. "There is no debt to repay. I brought the power to this mountain, and it is my obligation to return it." He bowed.

Lord Winslow mounted his horse and turned it to descend the mountain. I stared after him, lost in thought.

"Quite a boring fellow, isn't he?"

I jumped and swung to find Prince Sixtus standing next to me, peering after his lordship. I hadn't heard him approach.

"A bit dry for my liking," I said with a smile.

He grinned but kept his gaze on Lord Winslow's retreating back. He sobered. "But he is an honorable man."

"You played him well, Your Highness," I said.

He turned to regard me. "You humans have a way of growing on people. When Vater sentenced me to the gallows, giving Crispian and I the task of being cooped up with you in that chateau, I thought I'd lose my mind."

"Gallows? That is a bit harsh, don't you think?"

He smiled. "I've never cared for your kind. The only good human was a dead one, in my opinion."

"And all that has changed after today?" I raised a brow.

"No, it's been changing for some time." He dropped his voice, and the tenderness I'd witnessed in him in the garden when he had been Lord Winslow surfaced. "You changed me. Days inside the realm equaled weeks outside. When Vater would send someone to summon me home, the journey and days away were long, and your face was the one I thought of. I shall miss our time together."

I glanced at Nisse as he walked toward us, leading his horse. The prince noticed. "The human will be a good match for you. When you return to your village, I hope that I may look in on you from time to time."

"I'd like that," I said. "I don't know where life will lead me from here, but with you a prince I'm unsure if us mingling would be appropriate."

"Utter nonsense," he scoffed. "A prince set to inherit the throne needs all the friends he can get, regardless of the fact one is but a mere human." Amusement played on his face.

I laughed.

"It's good to see you in good spirits," Nisse said as he joined us.

Prince Sixtus eyed Nisse with interest before offering his hand. "I hear they call you Nisse, and that your vater was the village's master watchmaker."

"That is correct, Your Highness." Nisse took his hand, returning the prince's examining gaze.

"We journey to the village to tell them what transpired in these mountains and attempt to repair the treaty. We could use your counsel in dealing with your people."

"I am at your service, sir." Nisse bowed.

"Good," Prince Sixtus said. "I will inform my vater."

Nightfall had descended, and fresh snow blanketed the ground by the time the dwarves and the village council departed the cathedral with the treaty restored. Mutter strode toward me, where I waited with the other villagers for the outcome.

"Come with me. I must speak with you." She took my

hand and guided me away from the crowd. "The council has agreed to the terms of the treaty, but with one condition."

"What?"

"No magic is to leave the mountains," she said. "Dwarves can come to trade as before, but I am not to return."

"But why? All you ever did was help them."

She glanced past me to the villagers. They huddled together, some whispering and looking our way. "I birthed the creature that butchered their families."

"No, I shan't live without you. I can't." I gripped her hands.

"You won't need to."

"But where will we go," I said.

"You will stay here."

In a low tone, I asked, "But what of the thing that lives inside me?"

"King Jörg thought it best if we kept that part our secret. As long as the Reinheit isn't nurtured, you will live your life as before. You can remain here."

"How will I see you?"

"King Jörg has agreed to allow you entrance into the mountains of your own accord." Her fingers pushed back a lock of my hair. "We have many years to catch up on." She smiled, and the gleam in her mauve eyes shone brighter. "Look." She nudged her chin, and I looked in the direction she indicated. Nisse stood a few feet away, alone, with his back to us. "He waits for you. Go to him."

I kissed her cheek and embraced her. "My heart is full."

"As is mine," she said. "Now go."

CHAPTER 41

The Valley—Prince Sixtus

IN THE SHADOWS OF THE BUILDING, PRINCE SIXTUS watched Valentina walk toward the watchmaker's son. A heavy loneliness filled him. He'd miss the lift in the atmosphere when she walked into a room, her soft laughter, and the way she looked affectionately at his sisters, Zuna and Farrah. The girls would not miss her; they didn't recall the woman who had played nursemaid to them. The princesses were only children, after all, and he couldn't risk them letting the truth slip. Their memories had been temporarily replaced with forged ones before entering the alternate realm, and restored after its dissolution.

"You love her, don't you?" Crispian said as he held out the reins of Sixtus's horse.

"It is a love that could never be. Her heart always belonged to him." Sixtus broke his trance, lowered his eyes, and turned to lead his horse through the village.

Crispian fell in beside him. "To love is the greatest of gifts; it is one of the true riches of life that one can savor for a lifetime."

Sixtus considered his words. "Perhaps she has taught me what love is. Because somehow life without someone to care for…now seems empty."

"Spoken by a different man, sir. You've proven to our king and your people that you will guide our people as a leader should. It will be an honor to serve at your side," Crispian said.

Sixtus mounted his horse. "Come, my friend. It's time I learn to adapt to the squabbling of old men if I'm to endure lengthy discussions between our tribesmen."

The general obeyed and swung up onto his steed. "The mission may have taught me a thing or two as well."

"Oh?" Sixtus looked at him. "What might that be?"

"To reevaluate our friendship."

Sixtus glowered at him. "That's what you learned?"

"You made me an old Irish woman," he said with a snort. "Since I gave up my rank to become a housekeeper, the least you could've done was make me a younger woman. Then I would have found comfort in admiring my beauty."

"You tire of your wife already?" Sixtus taunted.

A sheepish grin played on the general's face. "With all respect, sir, I may be married and not deemed a scoundrel like you, but my eyes aren't retired. I appreciate beauty as much as the next man."

Sixtus erupted in laughter and heeled his horse to catch up with the king and his men.

CHAPTER 42

Valentina

OONLIGHT POURED OVER THE VALLEY, AND
falling snowflakes blinked against the velvet sky.
I strode toward Nisse, my heart pounding with
uncertainty, but buoyed with hope. His tawny locks hung
loosely over his broad shoulders. At my approach he
turned, and a soft smile creased his face.

"Am I to believe your mutter informed you of the
outcome?"

"Yes. I'm happy peace will once again find Schläfrigz.
I don't know what will happen to Vater after what he did
to Mutter, and with his current state of mind, it leaves me
uneasy."

"The council is discussing it as we speak," Nisse said.

"What will we do now? Will normalcy ever return to
Schläfrigz?"

"In time it will." He peered down at me with the familiar tenderness that gripped my chest and sent my heart skipping. "Tell me, Valentina: what is in your heart?"

"A mess of confusion," I said honestly. "The day has been long, and my head is spinning from the aftermath. Mutter is alive. I've longed for this day, and the thought of spending another day without her is unbearable. I don't want to let her go, but now distance will again keep us apart."

He took my cold fingers in his, and his large hand swallowed up mine. I felt secure in his presence. "She is alive, and in that, you can take comfort," he said. "Do you recall what I told your mutter?"

The thumping in my chest quickened. "I do, but perhaps you can provide clarity," I said, needing to hear from him what I believed his eyes reflected.

He took my other hand, and his thumbs tenderly stroked my skin. "Our time has been limited since my return to Schläfrigz, but I've spent most of my life rescuing you from a certain fate." He smiled, and I lost myself in his eyes. "I can't imagine a life where I didn't slay the dragon to rescue the princess."

"I am no princess."

"Nor am I a prince." His voice thickened with emotion. "But I do love you. I want to spend each day roaming these forests with you at my side. If you will have me, Valentina Fürst, I would marry you right here, right now. And I promise the suffering you have endured from your vater and Orell will never come at my hands. I am a simple man without riches, but I'd spend the rest of our existence together cherishing your every breath."

My heart soared at his words and the love radiating in his eyes. "Truly," I said.

He nodded. "Truly. What do you say? Will you be my companion in this life and the next?"

Tears pooled in my eyes, and I squeezed his hands. "I-I want that more than anything."

His head lowered, and I rose on tippy toes. Our lips touched, and he released my hands to gather me into his embrace. Our bodies united as one, and his kiss was passionate but tender, as I'd always imagined it would be. Snow danced on my lashes as love ensnared my heart, and I curled my fingers in his hair, hungrily returning his kiss.

I had won my prince. Life had granted me the fairy tale that I'd spent a lifetime weaving in my head.

If you have enjoyed my work, please leave a review on the platform you purchased the books from or Goodreads. Your reviews are crucial to spreading the word about my books, and I am sincerely grateful for this support from readers.

Sign up for my newsletter and download
the epilogue to *House of Illusions*

www.subscribepage.com/pippanews

PIPPA J. FROST
UNTIL TIME
DO US
PART

About the Author

Pippa was born and raised in the Maritimes, and moved to Western Canada soon after graduating high school, where she has been an entrepreneur for over a decade.

She has always composed beautiful words and lyrical passages in her mind. When it comes to writing, her passion is to inspire and fill people with food for their souls. The loves of her life are her husband of twenty years, their teenage children, and her two dogs.